SHERLOCK HOLMES
and
The Circle of Blood

SHERLOCK HOLMES

and
The Circle of Blood

by
Steve Leadley

A Black Coat Press Book

Dedicated to Toni, Drew and Alex.

I would like to thank Kathy Pendlebury for her diligent proof reading and astute analysis. Her insight and opinions have been vital to the success of my writing endeavors.

It is unlikely that I would have written additional tales of the great detective were it not for the kind words of those who enjoyed *Sherlock Holmes in Cape May*. I would like to extend a sincere thank you to all those who urged me to further Holmes's adventures. I hope that you find *The Highland Intrigue* and *The Medium Problem* equally enjoyable.

S.L.

ISBN 978-1-934543-69-6. First Printing. March 2009. Published by Black Coat Press, an imprint of Hollywood Comics.com, LLC, P.O. Box 17270, Encino, CA 91416. All rights reserved.
Printed in the United States of America.

Table of Contents

Foreword

In 2006, I published a novella entitled *Sherlock Holmes in Cape May*. For those who do not know the city, Cape May is the oldest seaside resort in the United States and the entire town has been designated as a National Historic Landmark due to its preservation of Victorian architecture. Cape May even hosts a "Sherlock Holmes Weekend" twice a year. The city has been a vacation destination since the 1700s and is still a popular tourist spot. *Forbes Traveler* has listed Cape May as one of the twenty prettiest cities in America.

I wrote the story specifically marketed to the multitude of tourists who descend on the town each summer. The tale includes real historical figures present in Victorian era Cape May as well as descriptions of what life was like in the resort during the period. However, being an avid Holmes fan, I also endeavored to construct the story so that it would be consistent with Doyle's canon and true to his style. The book continues to sell well in Cape May and more than a few readers asked if I would write more Holmes tales. It is for these reasons that I decided to craft two more novellas and package the three stories together in one volume. *Sherlock Holmes in Cape May* appears in this edition as *The Circle of Blood*. Because the story was originally meant to appeal to those new to Doyle's work as well as established Sherlockians, some little time is spent introducing Holmes, his techniques, and other aspects that would not be necessary for those already intimately familiar with the canon.

I hope that the accounts of events and places associated with Victorian Cape May enlighten and entertain established Holmes fans and perhaps might even arouse a desire to visit this wonderful city.

The other two novellas have Holmes practicing his craft closer to home. *The Medium Problem* is set in the familiar streets of London while in *The Highland Intrigue*, the adventure takes place in Dundee, Scotland. These stories share a commonality with my original undertaking in that real historical events and personages play instrumental roles.

Of Doyle's four Sherlock Holmes novels, three are divided roughly in half. The first parts deal with Holmes's investigation, while the second half relates the considerably less interesting back story of the perpetrators and victims. Therefore, I felt a novella would be the perfect venue for a Holmes tale: it is considerably more developed than a short story, but does not climax in the middle and devolve into back story like the majority of the Sherlock Holmes novels. My goal was to offer the reader stories that would dovetail with Doyle's style and settings while presenting an authentic historical atmosphere. I truly hope you enjoy the three novellas contained in this volume.

Steve Leadley

The Circle of Blood

Chapter 1

There are several adventures shared by my friend and I that I was not at liberty to disclose at the time of their occurrence. One such escapade, indeed one of the most singular, I am now able to communicate to my readers. Those familiar with my writings will note that most of the cases undertaken by my colleague have been in England. Occasionally cases arose on the continent that were complicated enough to warrant my friend's attention. However, it must be surprising to discover that the case I am about to relate did not take place in the old world, but actually took us across the Atlantic to the shores of America.

My companion is no aficionado of travel, so as you might imagine, the issue that brought Mr. Holmes and myself to the United States was of utmost importance. In fact, I do not believe the trip would have been undertaken had the plea not come from the highest levels of the British government. On further thought, had it not been for the intervention of my friend's brother Mycroft on the behalf of a certain Minister, Holmes may well have dismissed the case out of hand.

Readers familiar with the adventure I chronicled as *The Bruce-Partington Plans* are already aware of the unique post Mycroft held within the government. His status was not official by any means; however his gift for memory and organization made him invaluable. The elder Holmes had the unique ability to cross-reference material stored in his mind's vast repository and thus provide a government official with fresh and unrecorded data. For example, if the Foreign Minister were about to enter negotiations with the Chilean ambassador regarding bank loans, trade deficits, and the impending naval limitations treaty, Mycroft could synthesize Chile's cultural characteristics, fiscal standing, tariff laws, and military levels into a coherent account useful to the Minister.

By Sherlock's own admission, Mycroft possessed abilities that eclipsed his own. However, while the younger Holmes became electrified when an opportunity to employ his gifts presented itself, his brother displayed no such vigor. It is true that my friend occasionally slipped into a state of indolence, but this was only out of stagnation brought about when he had no case to test his abilities. Sherlock's brother detested physical activity in all its forms, preferring to loiter about his beloved Diogenes Club.

Our mission to America is still classified as "secret" by her Majesty's officials, so I must describe the particulars of this very sensitive situation in the most general and vague terms. The case involved the forging of a British document that inflicted grave insult on the American President. Curiously, another letter, similar in many respects, though authentic, was a factor in the United States declaring war on Spain in the year 1898. Given the reaction to the Delome Letter, it is not inconceivable that Holmes' proving that a fraud had been committed might very well have saved our two nations from stumbling into an error of great severity.

As you have no doubt surmised, the case which brought us to America is not the one I am about to relate. Perhaps I will one day be permitted to describe the specifics of that adventure. However, while still in the States another problem presented itself. Though less significant in global terms it was much more bizarre and intriguing, which to my friend, marks it with far greater value.

Holmes and I were in our accommodations in Washington City, preparing for our return to England. I must admit, though I enjoyed the beautiful Greco-Roman architecture of the American capital, I was looking forward to removing myself from the oppressively muggy weather that had descended upon the city that August. Though my military service in India and Afghanistan had bolstered my endurance for heat, I found the humidity that coincided with the rising mercury more than I could bear. I was just fastening my last bag when hurried footsteps sounded in the corridor.

"I would be much surprised if we do not have an impending visitor." My friend remarked as he buckled his satchel.

Presently an impatient banging was heard on the door.

"Watson, would you be so kind as to let the hotel manager into the room?" Holmes directed.

Though long accustomed to my friend's apparent clairvoyance, his feats still gave me pause. I turned the knob and swung the portal open to reveal the very man Holmes had predicted.

"Dr. Watson..." he began between exhausted breaths.

The manager hastily attempted to reacquire his usually stiff composure by smoothing out his tousled suit. He twice tried to continue his message, but eventually gave up, waiting for his breathing to become more regular. Finally he straightened his disheveled attire and again opened his mouth to speak but my companion cut him off.

"You have a telegram, sir?" Holmes interjected.

The perplexed man shot a surprised expression in my friend's direction.

"Tut tut," Holmes smirked, "come now, give the doctor his cable."

The bewildered gentleman handed me the message, while still staring quizzically at Holmes. As I took the paper from the dazed manager, I empathized with the poor man.

"My dear Holmes, we are about to cross the vast ocean. Don't leave this man with no hope of explanation!" I laughed, sitting down to read the message.

My friend had long since wearied of describing the means to his conclusions, which to him were so elementary they did not merit any significant notice.

"Very well Watson, to humor you. Though I doubt we will be in England as quickly as you presume," he forecast.

"My dear sir, this is a very reputable establishment. I would hardly expect anyone to be running about the corridors unless it was urgent. When I heard the footfalls advancing up the hall, it was a reasonable assumption that you were coming to our room since we occupy the last chamber on this floor, the room across the hall is unoccupied, and the tenant in the preceding suite checked out hours ago. We are ourselves about to depart for home, thus another point in favor of the urgency being directed upon us. I deducted that you were hurrying to catch us before we left. We are strangers in not only this city, but this country, so it was rational to conclude that any urgent message would travel a great distance and thus be a telegram."

"But I heard you through the door. You asked Dr. Watson *to let the manager in*. How did you know it was me?" he asked, the puzzled look on his face but half removed.

"Well, there I had to deviate from merely the probable to the realm of specific fact. It would be sensible to assume that a bellhop or a porter would bring a telegram. However, as I stated, this is a very reputable establishment." Holmes swept his arm about in a grand gesture that the manager accepted with pride. "You are very considerate of your guests and do not wish them disturbed by the frequent comings and goings of the staff. To ensure this you have provided them with soft-soled shoes. *You*, however, my good man," Holmes said tapping the manager's foot with his walking stick, "wear much more formal attire. A footfall can be as distinctive as a voice," he concluded, pulling aside the drape to survey the sky.

"But, Mr. Holmes," he asked, his mystification receding with each round of explanation, "how did you know the cable was for Dr. Watson and not yourself?"

"Ah, I cheated a bit there my good man. When the door was opened, you addressed Watson directly, with the message extended in his direction," Holmes replied without turning around.

The manager's face was not yet vacant of bewilderment. "It all seems so simple now that you've explained," he said scratching his chin pensively.

"Alas, it is not magic. I have merely trained my senses to translate sights and sounds into useable information. Dr. Watson too has often found my conclusions to be quite apparent after I have described the machinations," my friend revealed, turning his hawkish features toward our visitor.

"Will you give us a moment of privacy please?" I broke in as I placed the communication on the table.

"But of course," the manager replied, bowing slightly and exiting the room somewhat embarrassed that he had ventured so far from his reserved, businesslike demeanor.

My friend took the seat across from me and rested his elbows on the arms of the chair, his long fingers gently tapping their opposite counterpart. This posture was a familiar one when my friend endeavored to listen intently.

"You were correct; it is to me, but only as a conduit to you," I stated.

"Do read it aloud, Watson."

"*Dear Dr. Watson,*" the missive began, "*My name is Emlen Physick. You do not know me, but I believe you are aware of my grandfather Philip Syng Physick. I hope that this association is sufficient to attest to my character, however if you require further reference, I was made aware of your present location by John W. Dawkins a friend of mine and countryman of yours, who is also a member of the Diogenes Club.*

"*I live in Cape May, New Jersey. It is a very comfortable and serene place yet... a most heinous crime has been committed against a peaceful and honorable citizen. I have sent a newspaper account of the incident to you posthaste. I would be most grateful if you could postpone your departure until it reaches you. After reading the article, please cable me at the enclosed telegraph office as to whether or not you and Mr. Holmes would be willing to investigate the matter. With all sincerity, Emlen Physick.*"

My friend sat motionless throughout this reading, and when I looked up his eyes were closed, his fingers still gently tapping one another.

"What say you, Watson?" he blurted stirring from his trance.

"He has provided us with very little..." I replied unsure of the response my companion desired.

"His grandfather was a distinguished doctor," Holmes said, though the tone of his voice made it difficult to determine if this were a statement or a question.

"You have heard of him?" I asked slightly astonished.

"No, not at all. But he addressed the letter to you and obviously assumed that you *had*. It is therefore likely that he was a physician of some note."

Though my friend displayed the most remarkable memory, it did not house facts that were not germane to his profession. If Philip Physick had been a pioneer in autopsy or forensic medicine, it is likely that Holmes would have known all about him.

"Yes," I replied, "he is indeed noteworthy. He is considered the father of American surgery. I studied many of his methods in medical school. He was an innovator in treating dislocations and fractures, was the first to practice capillary puncture of the head for hydrocephalus, and invented the tonsil guillotine, needle forceps and the stomach pump. He was also the first to use animal ligatures in surgery. He was so renowned that he treated many illustrious figures of the day including First Lady Dolly Madison. He also performed gall bladder surgery on Supreme Court Justice John Marshall."

"Our presence in this country is not well publicized. There is only one person at the Diogenes Club who knew we were here."

"Mycroft!" I blurted impulsively.

"Mycroft would never have told his compatriot Hawkins where we could be reached unless he thought the matter either important or interesting," Holmes surmised almost gleefully.

"I think we shall wait for the paper to arrive. What do you say to that, Watson? Would such a delay much distress you?"

"Not at all," I replied. Though anxious to escape the stifling atmosphere of Washington, I was concerned that the affair might be of extreme importance and thus warrant our help, though I'm sure my friend was more hopeful that it was the matter's complexity that required his attention.

"Capital! Be a good man and go down and wire a response that we shall indeed wait to see what the paper presents. Oh, and let that pesky manager know that we will need the room a bit longer. I will contact the steamship company and have it hold our tickets."

Holmes often chided me for "romanticizing" his exploits in my published accounts of our adventures. He had trained himself to be an engine of observation, calculation, and deduction reducing items, events, and even people, into data. However I have perhaps known Sherlock Holmes more intimately than anyone and can assure that beneath his cold scientific exterior exists a kind, empathetic, chivalrous core. Though my friend often appears brusque and indifferent to the plight of others, these characteristics are the result of his deliberate attempt to remain focused on his task. He often lectures that emotional involvement clouds judgment and reason. He feels that he is of far greater service to a client by not allowing himself to be drawn in by sentimentalities. Only with a clear head and keen eye could he hope to solve their problem and relieve their suffering.

It must be remembered that my friend could have employed his gifts in any of the fields of science or mathematics. Solving chemical equations or complex algebraic problems could have provided the cognitive tests he so craves. Yet, despite my friend's solitary nature and alleged disinterest in his fellows, he chose to pursue criminal investigation. I myself have often observed the humanitarian leak through Holmes's cold exterior, but those who know my companion less intimately need not look further than his elected profession for evidence of his benevolent nature. Innumerable times Holmes has used his unique talents to bring about justice in cases where the regular force had been stymied. Further, in his battles with the criminal element, Holmes had repeatedly put his life on the line. Though my friend believes that my accounts should be factual histories of his cases for the sole purpose of furthering his methods of deduction and analysis, I must defy him by including the more humanistic elements. I chronicle in this fashion not only for the benefit of my readers, but also to expose the suppressed but omnipresent benevolence of my dear friend.

Chapter 2

Next day, my friend and I were in our room awaiting the arrival of the promised paper. I was reading a recently published book that had garnered much attention. In *The Influence of Sea Power upon History 1660-1783*, the American Admiral Alfred Thayer Mahan argues that American economic growth was reliant upon a strong peacetime fleet with worldwide but strategically located naval bases and coaling stations. The Admiral's argument was exceedingly interesting since it demonstrated the exact policy the British Empire had been employing for two centuries. I found the premise ironic since the United States had rebelled against the system of empire. The ideal of self-government was the very foundation of their nation. Now that the American frontier was closed, would the lust for land turn the United States toward a more imperialistic policy? At the time, I was intrigued by the question, and at that moment, conducting a debate within my mind over the possibilities. Of course, many years have passed since our visit to America and the question has since been answered. With the American victory in the Spanish-American War came possession of Guam, Puerto Rico, and the Philippines.

While I was engaged in these contemplations, my companion was lounging languidly upon the couch. Blue rings drifted lazily above him, emanating from the long- stemmed pipe he was smoking.

"It is a good question," Holmes blurted between puffs.

"What?" I was jolted from my ruminations.

"Whether America will strive for an empire and forsake her founding principles," he idly replied.

"Holmes, you never cease to amaze me. I have been the victim of this mind reading trick before but I cannot possibly fathom how you have perceived my thoughts this time."

"Come now, Watson. You know it is no trick. Observation. Inference from observation. Deduction from inference. Deduction leads to a plausible explanation," Holmes replied without altering his reclined posture.

"Yes, Holmes, I know your methods, but I do not possess your gifts. I fail to see the thread which led you to your conclusion."

"Very well, then. I see that you are reading Mahan's treatise…"

"You have read it?" I broke in, amazed that such material would suit my friend's taste.

"No, certainly not. Though you are a former military man, I am not the least bit interested in navies or the economic ramifications of their size," he replied.

"But you seem to know the subject matter," I returned.

"Watson, you know that I read the daily papers in hope a singular case will catch my attention. That book has caused a stir, and thus been addressed in the papers. I grant you, I haven't read any article in its entirety, but the gist is hard to miss."

"Facial expressions mirror emotion," he continued. "Have you read my monograph on the subject? No? Well I assure you your countenance betrayed your feelings. First, your brow knitted in thought, and then, you pursed your lips and looked afar in the vacant manner of one who is pondering a subject…"

"But how did you know *what* I was pondering?" I interjected.

"I am only acquainted with the general premise of the book so I was in fact quite limited by way of data. However, I gained some aid by the decorations of this very room. Your gaze first gravitated toward that facsimile in the frame on the left." He pointed his thin index finger toward the document. "Ah, it is interesting that Americans take such pride in their Declaration of Independence that it adorns a hotel wall. I can't tell you the last time I've seen a copy of our *Magna Carta*!" he chuckled to himself.

"But I digress," he continued. "After considering that certificate for some time, you turned to the world map which decorates the opposite wall. Your gaze bounced back and forth no fewer than three times. It is apparent that you were juxtaposing the two. A moment later, your face assumed the unmistakable expression of one who is contemplating a question. By synthesizing the data, I was able to reach a plausible conclusion."

I was about to respond when my friend suddenly tilted his head to one side.

"I do believe our newspaper has arrived."

As always, once Holmes had made his methods known, they seemed quite simple. I now could easily discern the soft tread of a bellhop coming down the hall. A polite rapping was soon heard on the door. I was closer than my companion so I answered and received the newsprint. Holmes did not move but beckoned me to take the seat opposite to his own. I scanned the front page of *The Star of the Cape*.

The headline was far from subtle. *Vicious Murder!* the words leapt from the page. I turned the paper to face Holmes, showing him the bold type. He simply nodded seriously.

"Do read it aloud, Watson." He directed in a polite but grave voice.

"*Joseph Goodfellow, aged sixty-five years was found brutally murdered in his home on Hughes Street. Mr. Goodfellow, as local residents know, is the proprietor of Goodfellow's Dry Goods on Washington Street. An employee became suspicious when Mr. Goodfellow did not report to open his business on Monday. He proceeded to the home of his employer but received no answer. He tried the door, but it was locked. Mr. Goodfellow lived alone, and suspecting that he may have fallen ill, the employee inquired at the house next door. The neighbor was also alarmed by the news, knowing that Mr. Goodfellow had not missed a day of work in ten years. Together they forced their way in through the rear door. A horrible sight befell them when they entered the man's parlor.*

"*Mr. Goodfellow lay on the floor in a prostrate, face down position. A dagger had been driven through the back of his jaw where the jawbone meets the neck. This had been done with such force that it protruded out of his mouth, dislodging several of his teeth. On the floor next to the victim lay a small bust of Socrates, a circle drawn around it in the man's own blood. The police force is baffled not only by the vicious and bizarre nature of the crime but the motive. Nothing of value appears to have been taken from the home and Mr. Goodfellow was a kind and considerate resident who was not known to have an enemy in the world. He was a pacifist who did not promote violence or injury to anyone.*"

I lowered the paper to see Holmes still in his pensive state. He roused suddenly.

"What do you think Watson? Should we go to Cape May?"

"I do not think it would be a wasted trip."

"Splendid. Cable that we are en route. Insist that the crime scene and victim be disturbed as little as possible. I will question the manager as to our means of passage."

With that we hastily left the room and went our separate ways. At the telegraph office, I thought it fitting that I inquire about our destination.

"What can you tell me about Cape May, New Jersey? Do you know of it?" I asked the man behind the counter.

"Cape May? Are you going on holiday?"

"Oh, it's a resort then?" I queried, ignoring his question.

"Yes, the oldest in the country. I've never been there myself, though. People of my class head to Atlantic City. Cape May is mostly for rich Philadelphia folks. You ever heard of John Wanamaker?"

"The retailer?"

"…And Postmaster General," the man added proudly. "He's got a place there. He even set up a cottage for President Harrison."

"The President?" I asked with a bit of a smirk, recalling the service Holmes and I had just done him.

"Oh, yes, but he doesn't spend much time there; it's Wanamaker who keeps trying to coax him to stay. But former Presidents have stayed there as well. President Grant, President Pierce, and even Abe Lincoln, though before he became President."

I sent the message and returned to find Holmes waiting for me at the front of the hotel, our baggage already being loaded into a coach.

"Your mission is complete?" he asked with a sly grin.

"Yes, I did as you asked."

"Splendid," he snapped, as we climbed aboard the four-wheeler. "We must travel by rail to Baltimore and then on to New Castle, Delaware. The Philadelphia ferry stops in New Castle on its way to Cape May."

"Is there no rail service in Cape May?" I asked.

"There is, but we would have to travel all the way to Philadelphia to connect. The ferry is the most expeditious means of travel from here. Driver! To the railway station please," Holmes commanded, pointing ahead with his walking stick.

As we purchased one-way tickets for Baltimore, an eager porter grabbed our bags. "Oh, the Baltimore train? Right this way, sir. I'll steer you right. Follow me," he said, lugging our bags ahead of us. "Foreigners are you? Englishmen? I can tell by your bags. Stamped from the steamship journey."

"Ah, you see that Watson, deduction following on the heels of observation." Holmes joked.

"Have you seen the sights of our city? Oh, there's a lot to see. How did you like our monument to General Washington? It's somethin', ain't it? See this here platform, the one you're standing on, well, it was right here that President Garfield was shot. Now that's some history for you." The man prattled on. "He was on the way to meet his son and this touched lawyer thought the President had passed him over for a job. Guiteau was his name; he fired two shots into the President. Bang! Bang!" he momentarily dropped our bags to demonstrate, using his finger as a gun. "Here's the train right here, gentlemen.

Climb aboard the third car, that's the best one. I know this train, I do..."

Holmes leaned into my ear. "Watson, pray tip the man quickly and let's get aboard. If I have to listen to him a minute longer, I shall be forced to break my cane over his head."

I hurriedly followed my friend's direction, as I was not anxious to administer medical attention upon the poor soul. Aboard the train, I presented Holmes with what I had learned about our destination. However, the quaint history ricocheted off my companion.

"Sounds charming!" he responded with some degree of elation, though I knew my friend well enough to suspect that his excitement was the result of the impending play, not the stage upon which it was to be set.

I seated myself by the window excited to view the land-scape, particularly since this was my first trip to America. I turned to comment to my friend, only to find him slouched down in his seat, his bowler over his face. I should have ex-pected as much since the machine that was Sherlock Holmes cared little for the scenery, unless it contained some data use-ful to his peculiar occupation.

After a brief stop in Baltimore, the engine chugged to life again, moving us across the peninsula the locals call "Del-Mar-Va." At Newcastle, we disembarked and were quickly whisked to the ferry landing. It was not long before a side-wheeled steamer came into view. We boarded *The Republic* and were soon off again, headed across the Delaware Bay to the seaside city of Cape May.

The trip was a most pleasant one. The iron framed ship had three spacious decks, and even a band serenading the ea-ger vacationers. Seabirds trailed the boat, cackling vociferous-ly as they jousted for scraps thrown by children. While I soaked up the fine sea air in a stroll around the deck, my com-panion sat on a bench located on the ship's bow. He was in a meditative state, though on a few of my circuits I could see his mind at work dissecting the occupation or origin of other pas-sengers. To Holmes such activities were akin to an athlete exercising his body. Though our fellow travelers were not a party to any criminal malfeasance, they provided fodder for my friend to sharpen his skills.

While standing along the rail, a well-dressed elderly gentleman sidled alongside me. "Ah, quite a day!" he commented.

"Yes, it's lovely," I returned, taking in a refreshingly deep breath.

"An Englishman, huh? I'd know that accent anywhere!" he laughed. "Is this your first trip to Cape May?" he asked.

"Yes, it is," I replied, warming to the congenial white-haired character.

"I've been heading down since the forties!" he said with some degree of pride. "It's a lot different now! Did you know that when I first summered in Cape May, there were only three hotels and three boarding houses?"

The kindly old man assumed that I could contrast this against the city at present, but I refrained from reminding him that this was my first trip to the resort.

"'Course, by 1850 two dozen hotels had been built in the center of town. It was known as Cape Island back then. Bet you didn't know that!" the friendly codger added. "During the war, a rail line was extended from Millville, but you know I have always preferred the steamboat. Don't you?"

He was an endearing old fellow and I nodded along with his commentary to humor his recollections. In a moment, he continued his impromptu history of Cape May.

"'I used to stay at the New Atlantic Hotel in those days. 'Course, it burned down in the fire 'o sixty-nine." He trailed off staring vacantly into the horizon as if he were imagining the old hotel. "'Course, that fire destroyed everything from Ocean to Jackson Streets and from Washington Street to the beach."

Respectfully, I continued to pretend that I had some idea of the area the old man was describing.

"'Course, the fire 'o sixty-nine was nothing compared to the fire 'o seventy-eight! That fire burned for three days. Why, I remember that they even brought firefighters down from

Philadelphia! I got on the train with 'em. I just had to see it. Boy, that was a mess! The whole center of town went up! Let me tell you, I was with General Sherman when we burned Atlanta and Cape May looked worse!

"'Course, Congress Hall was the only one o' the burned up hotels to be rebuilt. Cottages replaced all the others. Oh well, that's progress! What can you do?" he laughed good-naturedly.

I enjoyed the old man's reminiscences, but thought I'd see how my friend was getting on. I bid the old chap good day, and meandered toward the front of the boat and seated myself next to my companion. "Have you any theories yet?" I asked to make conversation.

"Regarding the untimely demise of Mr. Goodfellow? Come now, Watson, you know my methods better than that. We haven't enough data yet. The newspaper account gave us only the most cursory information. However, there is a point of interest surrounding the motive. Let us see if you can expose it. What do you believe to be the motive for the crime?" my friend queried.

"Well, it could not have been robbery, since nothing was taken," I replied, thinking back to the report.

"Yet, the account also stated that the victim was well-liked and had no enemies," Holmes reminded me with a wag of his finger.

"Yes...that's true. Could it have been a random act?" I pondered.

"It is possible, but not likely. If this were the act of some madman, then it is probable that there would be similar murders in the vicinity. Also, there is the odd clue regarding the circle of blood. This appears to be a singular message of some type."

"If it was not a random act, then the newspaper account must be flawed..." I pondered aloud.

"Excellent, Watson!" Holmes said, slapping my knee, "There is hope for your analytical skills yet!" he laughed. "Either a robbery has been committed and the police are unaware of the missing item, or this man did indeed have an enemy unknown to the general public. We must examine the crime scene to see if we can determine which is the case. Until then, enjoy the trip." With that, my friend slouched into his seat and slid his hat over his eyes.

My comrade's sudden shift from activity to lethargy was not a unique phenomenon. He found it pointless to theorize further until he acquired more information. I took this as a signal to continue my stroll about the ship, allowing the salty vapors to sooth lungs accustomed to the labyrinth of London's streets.

Chapter 3

It was late afternoon when I spied the unmistakable strobe of a lighthouse beacon. Had it not been a cloudless day, I'm sure the light would have been visible from a much greater distance. The captain let loose the powerful steam whistle to signal our approach, and in a short time the ship chugged alongside the ferry dock known as "Higbee's Landing." The powerful engines caused the boat to shudder as the pilot skillfully maneuvered the large vessel as if it were a mere canoe. A team of sailors appeared out of nowhere and scurried about the deck busying themselves with their respective duties. The men were obviously seasoned in the mooring procedure as they buzzed around in perfect teamwork. The most complex knots slipped into place with effortless dexterity.

The gangplank materialized as the sailors worked in conjunction with their counterparts on the wharf. Baggage handlers, porters, and valets had joined in the orchestration and in a short time we were standing upon the dock. I was however surprised to find that this was not the city of Cape May, but that of Cape May Point. Cape May proper faced the Atlantic Ocean and this settlement offered a safer landing point by its position on the Delaware Bay.

We briskly walked down the long pier. Once on dry land, Holmes was anxious to replenish his supply of tobacco. He scurried across the dirt street to the "Delaware Bay House," an ample hotel with several stores occupying its first floor. While he was gone a dapper, mustachioed man in his mid-thirties approached me.

"Dr. Watson?" he asked, extending his hand. "The porter directed me to you. I am Emlen Physick."

"How do you do? Mr. Holmes will be back in a moment... Ah, here he is. Holmes, this is Emlen Physick, the man who cabled us."

"Charmed," Holmes replied, tipping his hat. "Obviously, you received our cable." Always direct, my friend delved straight into the matter. "I trust that the crime scene has not been further disturbed?"

"Of course, the police were there initially, but after receiving your telegram, they agreed to quarantine the house. However, the undertaker has been at them to remove the remains," he added, a bit flushed.

"Certainly. I should like to be brought to the site as quickly as possible."

"The most direct route would be for us to take the trolley into the city. My valet can take your bags to my estate," Physick replied, as his man grabbed our baggage and headed toward a parked coach.

"Good enough. Let's be off!" Holmes commanded without hesitation, leading the way to the trolley car. We boarded the thin-gauged rail line and before long the electric trolley was buzzing toward Cape May.

"Good Heavens, Holmes, look at this!" I blurted, pointing out the window.

The car was passing a sixty-foot high elephant made of wood and tin. It appeared to actually be some sort of a hotel!

Holmes glanced out the portal and chuckled. "A bit larger than those you saw when stationed in India, aye, Watson?"

"That's *The Light of Asia*, or as the locals call it 'Old Jumbo,' " Physick explained. "It is interesting no doubt, but has not been very successful. It was built as a tourist promotion, and is now being used as a real estate office. The advert, *Tourists Can Travel Light Because the Hotel Has Its Own Trunk*, failed to resonate with travelers!"

Continuing to look out the window, I noticed that the thin-gauged rails of the trolley ran parallel to a heavier set of tracks. Our host noted my examination and explained that the electric line had recently replaced a conventional coal-burning locomotive in ferrying travelers from the steamboat landing to Cape May.

Detecting my curiosity, Mr. Physick was kind enough to point out some of the sites as the tram whisked along the beachfront. A large "cottage" appeared on our left. Our host explained that Postmaster General Wanamaker owned this impressive building. He furthered that Wanamaker was the cofounder of Cape May Point (formerly known as Sea Grove). As we rounded a bend, a striking four-story hotel loomed on the left. Vacationers dotted the lawn engaged in games of croquet and tennis. Our guide explained that this structure was the Carlton Hotel, formerly known as Sea Grove House. Across the street adjacent from the hotel stood another "cottage." (I found it interesting that these large homes were referred to in this way since several London families could easily occupy such a structure. It turns out that the term derived from the fact that these were merely summer retreats for their wealthy owners.) This one was the home of Alexander Whilldin, Wanamaker's original partner in the Seagrove venture.

"And this one," said our host, indicating an attractive three story building, "is owned by President Harrison."

"Dr. Physick, did you examine the body yourself?" Holmes interrupted, completely disinterested in the surroundings.

"Doctor?" I blurted out, puzzled.

"Oh yes, Watson. Didn't you notice our host's ring? It indicates graduation from the University of Pennsylvania Medical School. Though like you, the doctor is not in practice."

Dr. Physick smiled in reply.

"Another similarity to yourself presents itself my dear Watson. I would be much surprised if Dr. Physick did not have some sort of military background, though the regular army is right out. He has been an important man in this community for too long to have spent significant time in the military. Real estate speculation is not *always* profitable, but obviously the good doctor has done quite well for himself." Holmes turned to our host. "It is a shame that this tragedy has interrupted your hunting. What kind of dogs do you breed anyway?"

Usually, a display of my friend's unique gifts effects an amazed reaction, but Dr. Physick merely chuckled silently. "True enough, true enough. My friend Mr. Dawkins warned me of your abilities, Mr. Holmes. I am indeed a doctor in theory, but not in practice. My father passed away when I was just four years old, but he stated in his will that he wished me to study medicine to 'learn the advantages of occupation.' He was kind enough to include that he did not expect me to practice if I did not desire to do so.

"I did not have the formal military service of Dr. Watson here," Physick continued, "but I did attend the Pennsylvania Military Academy from age seventeen to twenty."

"Yes, your bearing and posture betrayed you," Holmes replied.

"I do enjoy hunting and am indeed a dog breeder. I deduce that you came to your conclusion regarding my canine hobby by observation of the dog whistle upon my watch chain, but I am not sure how you concluded that I take pleasure in the hunt."

"The singed hair about your right wrist and eyebrows demonstrates that you often fire a blunderbuss or shotgun. This type of firearm is not employed in target shooting, so you must hunt," Holmes illuminated.

"And my real estate vocation?" he asked smiling.

"While purchasing tobacco, I inquired of the clerk about your occupation."

"Very good indeed," laughed Physick.

"But back to my original question," Holmes returned, "Did you examine the corpse?"

"I saw the body from the foyer, but after I received your telegram, I did not want to venture near the man for fear of disturbing some evidence."

"Ah, you see here, Watson, our host is a most intelligent and foresighted man. Well done, doctor," my friend nodded respectfully to Dr. Physick.

"Doctor, I assume that the employee who found Mr. Goodfellow has been absolved of suspicion?" Holmes asked.

"One of our constables, Officer Toland, knows him personally and has vouched for his character. However, added to this is the testimony of the next door neighbor who swears that the man was sincerely beside himself with grief upon the discovery of the body," the doctor replied.

"Did the constable question him about any possible enemies of the deceased? Did the man witness any recent confrontation between Goodfellow and a disgruntled patron perhaps?" Holmes followed up.

"That line was pursued. Not only was the employee questioned, but inquiries were also made around town. Mr. Goodfellow appears to have had no enemies."

"Quite right. The paper indicated as much, but I thought it prudent to ask. Who stands to inherit the man's estate?" my friend asked, probing another possible motive.

"Well it's not much of an estate..." Physick shook his head sadly. "He still owed on his house and the business was break-even at best. However, he has no heir anyway. Mrs. Goodfellow passed five years ago and the couple had no children. Attempts to locate any other relatives have been unsuccessful. In all likelihood the property will be auctioned off," Physick answered.

"Doctor, I would imagine that you are somewhat of an expert in local real estate. Is the deceased's dry goods store or home in a particularly opportune location? What I mean to say is, would anyone considerably benefit by purchasing either property at auction?" the detective investigated.

"I see where you're going Mr. Holmes. It is true that for fifty years, real estate developers have built large hotels in the city. Many blocks have been razed in their entirety for the construction of such places. However, this motive can also be dismissed. Both properties are in the middle of their respective blocks, and the surrounding structures are individually owned, so Mr. Goodfellow did not stand in the way of some grandiose development. The home is unimpressive and the dry goods store may offer a good businessman some opportunity for success, but only through laborious effort."

By the time this exchange had ended, our car had completed its path along the beachfront, and was pulling up to the station. I had been too engrossed in Holmes's examination of Dr. Physick to survey the scenery, but as we exited upon the boardwalk, I took note of our surroundings. A wide expanse of beach lay beyond the boardwalk, the blue gray Atlantic tumbling upon its shore. Though evening was approaching, a good number of people were still meandering about the sand. The boardwalk itself was beginning to draw a crowd as tourists emerged for their after-dinner stroll. South of us lay a number of tents and bathing houses across from which loomed several large hotels. The largest bore the name "The Lafayette Hotel." Across from the Lafayette, a long iron pier protruded from the boardwalk out into the sea.

"Come now, Watson, enough gawking!" Holmes joked as he pulled me from the seaside. We stepped down off of the boardwalk and in a matter of seconds were off to the murder scene.

Chapter 4

Rather than hailing a cab, we briskly walked the several blocks to the house of the late Mr. Goodfellow. It was a quaint, but plain structure. The building was by no means unattractive, but unassuming in comparison to some of the more elaborately decorated specimens we had passed on our way. The home was obviously not a summer cottage of a wealthy Philadelphian, but the fulltime residence of what in Britain we term "working class" folk. Two young men were seated on the front porch engaged in a casual conversation.

"Everything alright, Bill?" Dr. Physick queried one of the men.

"Yes, sir, nobody's been inside."

"Go and fetch Constable Gallachio, will you please?" the doctor asked.

"Right away, sir."

"We only have two policemen in the city," the doctor confided, "so we thought it best not to tie them up guarding the house. These two are trustworthy young men, and I'm sure they've done as instructed. Both Officers Gallachio and Toland have of course been involved in investigating this heinous act, but it was decided that Constable Gallachio would be put at your disposal while Toland handles the city's usual police business."

I assured the doctor that they had done the right thing as Holmes had already brushed past the men and was inspecting the door handle and lock with his magnifying lens. I have often described my companion's quiet calculating demeanor, but once he was on the scent his deportment was volcanic. At the moment he was a whirlwind of activity.

We silently observed my friend's machinations. After a minute of examination, he pushed open the door and leapt inside. The doctor and I followed, stepping into the foyer. The home was a simple one, commonly referred to as a "salt box." A short hallway ran from the door back to the kitchen. To the left, two steps led to a small landing and a narrow staircase that hugged the wall on its way up to the second floor. To the right of the entranceway was the parlor. It was in this room that the heinous crime had been committed.

Holmes quietly surveyed the setting. It was indeed a gruesome scene. About fifteen feet away lay the victim. His head was cocked back as the knife had protruded several inches from his mouth and imbedded the tip of its blade in the floor. A large amount of dried blood had pooled under the man's neck. Close to the man's head was a small bust of the famed Greek philosopher lying on its side. The statuette was circumferenced by a circle of blood.

Holmes threw himself on the floor and was crawling carefully across the rug. First, he used his lens to examine the carpet's fibers. These he studied in the minutest detail. He rose to his knees long enough to pull a candle from his pocket. He struck a match and again dove to the floor, using the light to reexamine the fibers. Next, he laid his ear to the floor to cast his view across the plane. A moment later, he crawled over to the body. He studied the position of his head. A tape measure appeared in my friend's hand and he collected several dimensions, which he then jotted down in his pocket book. Next, he scrutinized the knife itself. He seemed to notice something on the dead man's shoulder, and studied it with his lens. He carefully removed some microscopic item from Mr. Goodfellow's garment and dropped it inside a small envelope he had retrieved from his breast pocket. Finally, he inspected the bizarre scene of the bust and circle. He peered from several angles before descending to survey at close range. Again, he spied through the convex lens, first scrutinizing the bloody circle, and then the statue itself. Suddenly, he extinguished his candle and sprang to his feet.

"You may come in, gentlemen. Do examine the deceased's right hand," Holmes said as he turned his attention to the writing desk that sat against the wall just a few feet away.

"My Heavens," I stated in astonishment. "His first and second fingers are covered in blood. He himself inscribed the circle!"

"Indeed," my friend replied. "The bust sat here, upon this desk. See, you can make out the spot that is devoid of dust. As you can see, it is lying on its side, rather haphazardly. From the newspaper account, I had supposed that it was upright and that the killer had drawn the circle. Another lesson against theorizing ahead of the facts Watson!" he said in an aside. "Such a circumstance would have indicated that the murderer had left some sort of a message. This, however, demonstrates that it was the dying man who tried to give us a clue. Quite intriguing, I must say!"

"But what could the message be?" I asked, startled at this turn of events.

"Indeed..." Holmes' gazed afar, momentarily lost in thought. "We shall have to come back to that mystery."

"What say we let our friend have a crack at deduction?" Holmes asked with a small smile on his face. "Doctor, when do you suppose the dagger was driven through the man's head? Before or after he was on the ground?" my companion asked Dr. Physick.

Our new friend seemed to enjoy this little exercise despite the somber setting. "Hmm... Well, the knife is embedded in the floor, with several inches projecting beyond the poor man's mouth. Either he was knocked to the floor and was in the process of rising when he was stabbed, or he was attacked while erect, and then fell. I should suspect the latter," Physick said, pursing his lips. "Since the dagger is driven so stoutly into the floor, it appears as though the force of the fall implanted the blade not only through the carpet, but into the wood beneath."

"Precisely," Holmes remarked. "The man was standing here," my friend stationed himself in front of the desk, "was attacked from behind, and in his fall, knocked the bust upon the floor. Hallo! What's this?" Holmes continued, bending down to examine a pen lying under the desk. The next moment however, his attention was turned back to us.

"Doctors will you please examine the wound and tell me the exact extent of the injury?"

Dr. Physick and I did so and concurred that the blade had slashed the jugular vein, which resulted in the rapid loss of blood that led to the man's death.

"Ah. I had supposed as much, but it is gratifying to have not one, but two doctors corroborate my conclusion." Just then a uniformed officer stepped into the house.

Dr. Physick introduced the strapping young man. "This is Constable Gallachio."

We shook hands with the officer. "I hear that you are somewhat of an expert in these types of things, Mr. Holmes?" the constable asked. "I am glad to have you here. This is a pleasant little city and we have never had a murder here before. I feel we are ill-prepared for such an occurrence."

"That is to your credit," my friend graciously replied. "London is a much darker, dastardly place. Many would much prefer to live in such a peaceful and picturesque hamlet," he reassured with a sweep of his hand. "I have completed my examination; you may call the undertaker to remove poor Mr. Goodfellow."

"Do you see any hope of apprehension?" the constable asked. "I don't mind telling you that this crime has unsettled a great many people."

"Undoubtedly. It is early to anticipate such a climax, but yes there is hope. It is getting dark, and I would like to return tomorrow and examine the house by better light. Would that be alright?" Holmes asked the officer.

"Yes, certainly. Would nine o'clock be satisfactory?"

"Indeed, I shall see you then. Dr. Physick, can you tell my friend and I where we may obtain lodging for the night?"

"I have had your bags taken to my estate just a mile away. I have plenty of room and you would do me an honor if you permit me to act as your host."

"Wonderful. Do you suppose that Dr. Watson and I are too late for dinner, or should we find some nourishment in the city before coming to your home?"

"My valet indicates that supper is waiting for us."

"Capital! Let us be off then."

Holmes bounded past the officer and into the waiting four-wheeler. Dr. Physick and I followed, and after a short drive we were turning down the gravel path that led to the doctor's home.

Chapter 5

It was nearing twilight as we pulled up the Physick drive, yet even in that pale pink light the house was impressive. Its features were unique, unlike any I had ever seen. There was a distorted, oversized feel to its architectural aspects. The exterior walls were covered in a distinct grid-like pattern. The dormers were hooded, and explained to me as a "jerkin-head" design. The chimneys were corbelled, extending through the structure itself. These had an exceptional design, as they appeared inverted; the smokestacks were narrow at the bottom and got broader as they ascended. Huge stick-like brackets held the porch. The whole structure gave the appearance of being comprised of odd symmetrical pieces put together like blocks. Holmes was not normally interested in architectural aesthetics, but even he was taken with this unique house.

"What an interesting design!" I said to our host.

"Oh, thank you," he replied graciously, rousing from his thoughts. "It was designed by a Philadelphian by the name of Frank Furness, who coincidentally also has a cottage in town. He calls it *stick style architecture*. It is unlike any other home in Cape May," he added with some degree of pride.

We were left at the door as the driver continued on to the carriage house. "The butler will bring your bags to your room," our host declared, calling for the servant.

The interior of the house was no less impressive than the outside. Much of the moldings, fireplaces and furniture echoed the unique architectural design.

We supped in the dining room and enjoyed a delightfully prepared meal with the other inhabitants of the household. The doctor was unmarried, but his widowed mother, Mrs. Ralston (she had remarried after Dr. Physick's father had passed), and his maiden Aunt Emilie joined us. Our hosts were most charming. They regaled us with their family history, stating that Emlen's great-grandfather had fashioned the silver inkwell that was used to sign the Declaration of Independence. He was a friend of Benjamin Franklin, and along with Franklin and twenty others, had founded the University of Pennsylvania. The ladies were quite entertaining, but politely did not ask about the case. This was fortunate since Holmes was pensive, and mostly silent throughout the meal. I could clearly see that his mind was hard at work and he did not wish his calculations interrupted.

After dinner, the doctor invited us to his third floor library for brandy and cigars. We graciously accepted. Holmes sat silently smoking as the doctor and I discussed some of his grandfather's medical techniques. Physick did not take offense at my friend's silence. He seemed to astutely realize that my companion would discuss the case when he saw fit, and that disrupting his thoughts would not be constructive.

Suddenly, Holmes broke into our discussion. "You say this man had no enemies? Did *you* know him well?" he directed his question to our host. My friend was obviously gravitating toward this hypothesis, which led me to conclude that he had not seen any evidence of theft at the crime scene.

"He was a kind and benevolent man. He was a Quaker, and displayed the tolerant, peaceful ways of that religion. We did not really socialize, but I did know him. Year-round residents in this community are limited, and thus we are all acquainted with each other more intimately than might otherwise be imagined. Neither I, nor anyone that the police questioned seemed to be able discover any evidence of ill-will toward Mr. Goodfellow."

"In examining the lock on the front door, I saw no means of forcible entry. From the foyer, I could see through to the kitchen where the back door is located. It locked with a sliding latch, which Officer Gallachio told me was fastened, as the employee and neighbor had to kick the door in. He also stated that all of the windows had been secured as well. Thus, the means of exit was through the front door, whereby the perpetrator locked the door and closed it behind him," Holmes related.

"Did he enter as an intruder or was he invited inside?" Holmes continued, posing a hypothetical question. "I have already stated that the lock was not tampered with. Could the door have been left unlocked, allowing a prowler to slip inside? Most certainly, since the constable has already told us that this is a very safe city. However, the facts support a more friendly ingress. As I crawled about the floor examining the carpet for marks—a most futile effort I might add due to the traffic of those that discovered the body—I noticed that several of the floorboards were loose and squeaky. It does not seem likely that the murderer could enter the home and creep all the way to the desk area undetected before striking the victim from behind."

"Perhaps the assailant burst in and then attacked Mr. Goodfellow?" I speculated.

"No, Watson, that won't do. If he entered the house uninvited, Goodfellow would have certainly heard him, and investigated. This would have produced a wound to his front section, not from behind. Ah, I know what you are about to say, what if he went to investigate and finding the man armed, turned and fled? No, had he done so, he would have run for either the back door or a weapon, not a desk. Given these circumstances, we can safely assume that the murdered rang at the door and gained admittance on some false and friendly pretext.

"It is interesting that this felon should stab *through* the throat. Why did he not slice across the throat?" Holmes said mimicking the gruesome procedure. "That would have been a much more effective method of attack," he pondered aloud.

"Did you gentlemen notice anything telling about the wound?" he added.

"How do you mean?" I asked confused.

"Well, you and the good doctor made fine work of the cause of death. But the severed artery is not in the center of the throat, is it?" Holmes smirked.

"I should say not," Dr. Physick replied, "they run along the sides... Ah, I see! The dagger was driven through on an angle, from left to right."

"What does that suggest to you, Watson?" my friend quizzed.

"That the murderer was left-handed!" I exclaimed, banging the arm of the chair.

"Indeed."

"Doctor, did Mr. Goodfellow regularly associate with Negroes?" Holmes asked.

Our host was a bit thrown by the question, but quickly recovered. "Well, I wouldn't say regularly, but he did not shun them as some do. Although Cape May is in a northern state, we are actually below the Mason-Dixon Line and there are many in this town who are a bit bigoted. As is the Quaker tradition, Mr. Goodfellow treated Negroes with the same respect and courtesy with which he treated everyone else."

"Holmes, you have piqued my curiosity, why do you ask?" I questioned.

Standing, my companion drew the envelope from his pocket and passed it over to me. "Look inside, Watson. I know that you have read my monograph on the distinctions of human hair. It is sometimes difficult to differentiate the follicles of certain ethnicities, but ones belonging to those of sub-Saharan African descent are easily identifiable even without a microscope."

"Yes, I can easily see that it belongs to a Negro," I said, passing the envelope to Dr. Physick. "Do you suspect him as the assassin?"

"We mustn't discount it. I have already established that the murderer was admitted into the house voluntarily and the good doctor here says that Mr. Goodfellow was not adverse to the company of Negroes. However, this hair fiber is merely circumstantial and could mean nothing at all. It simply provides us with another fact to file away and possibly plug into a subsequent hypothesis if any corresponding data presents itself."

"Have you any ideas about the circle of blood?" I asked.

"A few ideas, but nothing of which to speak yet. However, it does say something about the murdered man's character," Holmes replied.

"How so?" I asked.

"This man was a Quaker, a pacifist, presumably an unassuming man unacquainted with conflict. However, our Mr. Goodfellow was a very cool customer. After being struck with a hideous and debilitating blow, and rapidly losing blood, he not only avoided going into shock, but also was able to think cogently enough to leave a message. I must say that this is quite remarkable."

"Yes," I replied, "during my time in the service, more than once I witnessed trained soldiers reduced to hysterics over wounds that were far less severe. What admirable fortitude this man must have possessed!"

"It's queer; he always seemed like such a soft, gentle soul. It is hard to imagine what possible experiences he could have had in life that could have produced such steel nerve beneath his benevolent exterior," Dr. Physick considered.

"Yes..." Holmes said with a distant stare. "I might suspect as much from a veteran of your Civil War, or even more so from one who served in the Indian campaigns on the western frontier. Yet, this man's religious tenets prevented him from such endeavors. Curious indeed," Holmes said to himself, puffing away on his pipe.

Dr. Physick and I left Holmes to his ruminations. My friend had slipped into that meditative state I had so often witnessed. I am sure that the ignorant observer would regard Holmes's inactivity as some sort of respite. However, I knew better. It was almost as if his body assumed a languid condition in order to divert its precious energy to his mind. Although he lounged almost motionlessly in his chair, my companion's brain was firing away like the pistons of a steam engine.

Our host invited me to a game of billiards. I was only mildly familiar with the sport, but soon came to admire it greatly. The doctor himself was an excellent shot and was courteous enough to tutor me in the art, rather than simply beat the britches off of me. Perhaps it is a byproduct of my army days, but I have a knack for following directions and quickly became proficient. I began to wish our rooms in Baker Street were large enough to allow for a table of our own.

After a few minutes of play, Dr. Physick expressed alarm that we were being discourteous to Holmes since the impact of the clay balls created such a clatter. This notion was certainly considerate, but the doctor failed to perceive the degree to which my companion could detach himself. Despite the clamor, Holmes sat just a few feet away, silently smoking his pipe.

After some time, the doctor and I were ready to retire. Holmes, however, asked our host if he might remain and make use of the contents of his library. The room was well stocked with books and Holmes was at a disadvantage being so far from the voluminous indexes he kept at Baker Street. Doctor Physick graciously acquiesced and we left Holmes digging through the shelves.

The one negative aspect of the Physick house was the heat. Mrs. Ralston insisted that the temperature remain at eighty degrees year round, so the boilers were stoked even in the summer. However, I was able to crank the radiator shut in our bedchamber, and opened wide the windows. Despite the somber chore that had brought us to Cape May, I enjoyed a wonderfully relaxing night's sleep. A gentle salty breeze billowed the curtains and a symphony of katydids and crickets reverberated through the evening air.

Chapter 6

Next morning, I awoke refreshed and full of vitality. The sun fell upon my face, the beams streaming through the gently fluttering sheer drapes. The rich musical "o-ka-leeee" of a red-winged blackbird echoed from a nearby marsh. A glance at Holmes's bed proved that it had not been slept in, yet this was by no means an ill omen. I knew from experience that my friend's energies were invigorated by the chase and that he must have found a clue amongst the doctor's books.

The household breakfasted together, and Holmes was cheerful and charismatic. The ladies assumed that his liveliness was the result of a refreshing night's sleep such as my own, and he humored their belief. Dr. Physick, however, was a bit more perceptive and had heard my companion scurrying about his library into the wee hours. As we finished our meal, Holmes withdrew his pocket watch.

"We are approaching the time of our appointment with Constable Gallachio. Will you join us, Dr. Physick?" my friend asked dabbing his face with a napkin.

"I am afraid that I have some business to attend to at one of my farms. However, I will have Robert—the coachman—take you into the city. I should not be long. I will try to meet up with you at the Goodfellow homestead, but pray do not wait around for me if you fall upon a clue."

"Very good, doctor. There is a distinct possibility that some evidence escaped me yesterday. The light was ebbing and really insufficient for a proper examination. However, I thought it expedient to scrutinize the deceased posthaste. Though you say Mr. Goodfellow had no enemies, I am sure the residents on Hughes Street would not appreciate him so much once he had started to ripen."

Such a comment seems indifferent and callous, but Holmes meant no disrespect to the fallen man. It was simply his explanation as to why he wanted to see the body right off. His use of terminology lacked warmth to be sure, but my friend had trained himself to reduce circumstances into data and present it as efficiently as possible without softening his language. Some found Holmes's manner distasteful, but our host showed no sign of offense. I am not sure if his friend Dawkins had apprized him of my companion's brusque nature beforehand or not. It is possible that as a learned man he understood that eccentricity is a trait that has infected many a genius. Perhaps his grandfather even possessed similar idiosyncrasies.

Holmes and I stepped onto the front porch and waited for the coach. As we stood there, I considered putting the time to some use. I left the porch and strode out onto the lawn to admire the house in more detail. The structure was even more impressive by daylight. The mansard roof draped over the exterior of the third floor and the effect reminded me of a handsome woman wearing a low fitting cap. In viewing the exposed timbers that ran both horizontally and vertically along the exterior walls, I could easily understand why the design was termed "stick structure." Holmes came alongside and, ever the scientist, commented on the function of this gable or that rainspout. I, however, was more interested in the aesthetics of this unique building.

Sliding around the side of the house, we were able to view several aspects of the property that had escaped observation the night before. Behind the dwelling lie several outbuildings including several large greenhouses. The grounds themselves were as impressive as the home. Roses, lilies, and other fragrant plants formed an opulent garden in the adjacent area. Several peacocks strutted about the ample lawn, adding an exotic flavor to the whole scene.

Robert arrived with a coach and we were soon crunching our way up the gravel drive, retracing our path to the murder scene. The previous evening, we had taken an enclosed four-wheeled carriage, which did not allow much of a view. However, the open two-wheeler in which we now rode afforded an unobstructed panorama. The homes that lined the streets were quaint and colorful. The elaborate, yet delicate gingerbread trim and fanciful pastel colors gave the town a storybook-like quality that differed greatly from the drab grays and browns of London.

"I can see that you are quite effervescent this morning, Holmes. Would you care to enlighten me as to the reason?"

"Not yet, Watson. I am sure you recall the case you entitled *The Yellow Face*, where I jumped to conclusions and misread the clues. You are correct in assuming that I stumbled upon something last night, but I must make further inquiries before I am confident enough to elaborate further."

Robert pulled up at the Goodfellow house at ten to nine, but the dutiful Officer Gallachio already awaited us on the front porch. Holmes did not approach him, though. He jumped from the coach and slowly scrutinized the exterior of the structure. He stood for a moment, contemplating the building as a whole. After this, he turned and looked across the street, then up and down it in either direction. A second later, he returned to the Goodfellow house and began to walk carefully around it. He examined the ground, the window frames, and even the foundation. In a moment, he disappeared around the rear of the house. I did not accompany my friend, but engaged the perplexed constable. I apologized for my companion's apparent rude behavior but assured him that Holmes meant no affront. I tried to explain the depth of focus that obscured Holmes's manners once the game was afoot.

The good-natured officer chuckled at my friend's unconventional behavior and took no offense. "Did you enjoy your stay at Mrs. Ralston's cottage?" he asked with a smile.

"Mrs. Ralston's cottage?" I echoed a bit confused.

"Yes, that's how everyone refers to the Physick house. The doctor had the home built, but his mother is in charge of the household."

"We met Mrs. Ralston and her sister. They were very courteous hosts."

"Oh, I didn't mean to imply otherwise, doctor. They are both very nice. I was merely commenting on the devotion Dr. Physick has to his mother. A great many people could stand to treat their mothers as well."

It had not been two minutes before Holmes had circumvented the house and bounded onto the porch. "Shall we enter, gentlemen?"

The policeman unlocked the door and we stepped inside. Holmes reminded me of a bloodhound before he has acquired the scent as he scurried about in great haste. He made a beeline for the kitchen and examined the rear door in detail. He scanned his magnifying lens over the latch that had been broken by those that had discovered the body. He examined the edge of the door and then the doorjamb itself. He disappeared outside for a moment, but was back in a flash, examining the action of the door's hinges. From here, he sped back to the foyer and bolted up the stairs. We followed, silently watching him work. He gracefully moved about the dead man's bedchamber. Holmes opened each drawer of the dresser and not only examined its contents, but stooped down and inspected the underside of each. A moment later, he disappeared under the bed, only to reappear on its far side. He knocked on the floor and walls, presumably in search of secret compartments. Finding nothing, he performed the same operations in the sparsely furnished second room on that story. Next, Holmes vanished into the hall closet and pushed aside a panel in the ceiling that led to the garret. The constable and I could hear him shuffling about above our heads. Less than a minute later, Holmes dropped back through the aperture and brushed past us without a word. He raced back downstairs to the entryway. In reading my friend's expression, he had apparently found nothing of value on either of the upper floors.

We silently trailed Holmes back down, where he again scanned the foyer. Still, nothing appeared to catch his eye. He finished his inspection in the room in which the murder had occurred.

The body was now gone, but the foul aroma of dried blood remained. My friend reexamined the desk, shifting through papers and inspecting the various items resting upon it. He slid it out and looked behind and under it. He pulled out the drawer and conducted an inspection similar to the one he had executed upon the dresser drawers in the room above. My friend moved quickly and I could see that he was not pleased by his inability to detect anything of use. After sliding the desk back into place, he directed his attention to the shelf above. It was a simple, single plank that held a dozen books, apparently inconsequential in content. However, as Holmes scanned past these, the bookends suddenly arrested his attention. On either side of the volumes was a lantern. These looked quite ordinary though the glass was somewhat tinged in appearance.

"Constable, would you mind getting down the left lantern? Yes, thank you. Place it on the desk there." Holmes commanded, as he reached for its companion.

"Watson, do you have matches? Good. Will you be so good as to light that lamp?" he said as he struck a match of his own and lit the other.

I followed Holmes's instructions and, much to my surprise, vivid amber light emanated through the tinted glass. I shifted my gaze to the one my friend held. The corresponding lantern emitted a dark blue glow.

"What could be the meaning of this? Are they purely ornamental?" I puzzled.

Holmes turned to the policeman. "Do you have any knowledge about this? We are, of course, not natives of this country and I am curious if these lanterns have some commonplace meaning that may be alien to us as Englishmen."

"I have an idea..." the officer began, "but I do not see how it could relate to this case. The only connection I can make is that railroad men use colored lanterns as signals. My uncle worked for the West Jersey line and we used to listen intently to his stories. A blue lamp meant 'men at work' or 'do not move.' An amber or yellow globe indicated 'proceed at reduced speed' or 'prepare to stop.' However, as far as I know, Mr. Goodfellow never worked for the railroad, so they may just be gifts or souvenirs," the constable theorized.

I noticed an almost unperceivable gleam in the eye of my companion. Something the constable said had resonated with him.

"Should I check with the railroad authorities to see if there is any record of Goodfellow working as a rail man?" the dutiful officer asked.

"Yes. Do that. It is a long shot, but we must discount it before investigating other possibilities..." Holmes said, almost to himself. "I feel that there is nothing more to see here at present." Holmes recovered and led the way out the door.

The constable was locking the premises when Dr. Physick arrived by carriage.

"Any news to speak of?" he asked, as Officer Gallachio sped down the steps on his way toward the Grant Street rail terminal.

"Nothing of note...yet," Holmes replied coyly.

"I think my friend is juggling a few clues, but he is reluctant to share," I jibed to Dr. Physick.

Holmes merely smirked.

"Doctor," he said addressing our host, "where might I find the largest concentration of Negroes in this community?"

The doctor chuckled at Holmes's idiosyncratic nature. "Well, the majority of help in this city's hotels are Negroes, but I doubt that they will be able to converse with you during working hours. However, West Cape May is where most live. There will certainly be some at home if you head there. Shall I accompany you? I am not unknown to the families of that community."

"That is very gracious of you, but I would like to poke around a bit myself. I move very quickly when I am on the hunt and I often end up in unexpected places. If you don't mind extending your hospitality to Watson and myself, I shall see you at your estate for dinner."

"Of course, you are welcome, Mr. Holmes."

Without conversing further, my friend bounded off of the porch and hailed a cab.

"Dr. Watson, I am afraid that I have some banking to do in town, should I have Robert take you back to the cottage?" Physick asked.

"No, I think I shall stroll about the city a bit and take in the sea air."

"Very good then. I know you have a military background, do you care for marching band music?"

"I do not find it offensive."

"At noon, there will be a concert at Congress Hall, featuring the compositions of John Philip Sousa. He spent some time in this city, you know. Would you care to attend?"

"Yes, that sounds delightful."

"I will meet you there at noon. Congress Hall is but a few blocks from here and if you ask directions, you will find it quite easily. Until then." With that, Dr. Physick tipped his cap and was off.

Chapter 7

I was pleased at the opportunity to see the sights of the city. There are few things more invigorating than a stroll through fresh salt air, and Cape May proved to be full of interesting sites. Bicyclists and horse-drawn vehicles jockeyed the dirt streets as pedestrians meandered the sidewalks. Everywhere the tourists were abuzz. Across the street, I could see the rear of a large house, which a resident said was "The George Allen House." I was impressed by its southern architectural style. It very much resembled photographs I had seen of plantation houses in the American south. I walked east up Hughes Street, taking note of a large square, simply shaped building called "The Baltimore Hotel." Soon, I made a right onto Franklin Street, and then another right onto Columbia. I had no prescribed path, but wandered where the sites drew me. The plentiful cottages were all ornately decorated with vibrant trim, and each possessed a unique flavor and distinction. Besides these individually owned homes, there were also rooming houses whose verandas and porches gave their occupants access to both vistas and fresh air.

I walked along Columbia until it met Howard Street. Here stood a beautiful white hotel known as "The Chalfonte." Like the Allen house, this hotel displayed a southern flair. Numerous guests were already rocking away their troubles on the two-tiered porch.

"You like the Chalfonte do you?" One of the vacationers shouted from the porch, noticing my scrutiny of the building.

"Yes, it is quite impressive," I returned to the elderly gentleman rocking on the porch.

"Do you know we have Abe Lincoln to thank for this hotel?" he replied cordially.

"Abraham Lincoln?" I asked.

"Sure, come on up and I'll tell you the whole story!"

I climbed the steps and pulled a rocker up alongside the old codger. After we exchanged introductions, the hospitable fellow was kind enough to order me a glass of lemonade.

"When the Rebs broke away from the Union, the President asked for volunteers to put down the rebellion. Henry Sawyer, a local carpenter, ran up to the county seat to enlist. In fact, he was the first county resident to sign up. He became a Captain in the First New Jersey Cavalry," the old chap began.

"In June of '63, he participated in the Battle of Brandy's Station where he was wounded. He took one bullet in the thigh and another through the cheek. His troubles didn't end there though! He was captured and taken to Libby Prison in Richmond. Now, Captain Sawyer was none too happy 'bout this, but he thought that he would be home before too long as it was the custom at the time to exchange prisoners. However, things kept goin' from bad to worse.

"Two Reb officers were caught recruiting behind Federal lines. General Burnside had them executed. Well, this caused uproar in the South and the Rebs vowed to retaliate by killing a couple of their Union prisoners. They held a lottery at Libby to see who the unfortunate men would be. Don't you know the first name pulled was Captain Sawyer?

"The Captain was allowed to write his wife a farewell letter, and she, of course, was beside herself with grief. Fortunately, she had prominent friends. These individuals hastened to Washington and met with both the Secretary of War and President Lincoln himself. Now, the Union took prisoners too, and we had a couple of goodies!" he said, slapping his thigh. "Do you know who we had? We had the son of Reb General Robert E. Lee, and also the son of the Reb Provost Marshal, General Winder. Well, Abe let it be known that as soon as word reached Washington that Captains Sawyer and Flinn— that was the name of the other condemned man—had been executed, he would have Lee and Winder's sons killed in retaliation!" he said, reveling in Lincoln's audacity.

"Well, that did the trick! None of the men were executed, and a prisoner exchange eventually took place. In '67, Sawyer took over the Ocean House and in '75, he built this here hotel. So, young man, you see, had it not been for President Lincoln, you and I would not be enjoyin' a lemonade on this here porch!" he concluded with satisfaction.

I was quite impressed. It was certainly an entertaining story. I spent another few minutes with the kindly old fellow, but I was anxious to continue my tour. I thanked the gentleman for his hospitality and bounded down the steps of the stately hotel.

"Not at all, young man. Enjoy life, you never know how long you have!" he cried as I left, attempting to add a moral footnote to his tale.

Gazing toward the beach, I could see the Atlantic sparking beyond the end of Howard Street. I continued my leisurely walk in that direction. Reaching the beachfront, I shaded my eyes as the sun dazzled off of the waves. Across the boardwalk, bathers were already wading into the ocean.

A huge structure loomed one block down. I decided this building bore further examination. I turned right and, in a minute, was admiring the large U-shaped hotel known as "The Stockton." Square posts climbed the full four stories to support the over-hanging roof. Matching cupolas sat atop either wing, their flags gently fluttering from a refreshing ocean breeze. Guests had begun to line up at the hotel's red roofed bathhouses to receive their freshly laundered swimwear.

The "Stockton Baths" was architecturally different than the hotel, its design being of the gothic revival style known as "Queen Anne." In actuality, it shared the exposed skeletal framing design of Dr. Physick's house. There were many bathhouses along the beachfront; however, the Stockton Baths was the most elaborate. The Baths were actually a series of buildings each serving a particular function: an office, photography studio, and of course private cubicles for changing.

I navigated between carriages and cyclists and crossed over to the boardwalk. Turning toward Cape May Point, I sauntered in the direction of the intriguing iron pier that bisected the beach. After a few blocks, I reached the Lafayette

Hotel and the iron pier. Various shops flanked the entrance to the pier. One sold candy, fudge, salt-water taffy and ice cream. Another was a photography studio. "Swartz's Novelty Bazaar" promised "Mexican Hand-Carved Leather Goods." Yet another sign read "Japanese Art Goods," boasting wares from the far off orient. I entered the archway at the entrance, and ambled down the thirty foot wide, one thousand foot long structure. The "Outer Pavilion" was the pier's most impressive feature. Here, an eight thousand square foot dance floor hosted dances, concerts, theater, and even light opera. The end of the pier acted as a wharf, and I was busy admiring a ship that had just pulled away when I was distracted by a "whiz...plop!" Peering over the rail, I was surprised to find that the pier had a lower level for fisherman. I was directly above an angler who had just made a well-placed cast into the Atlantic.

Back at the entrance to the pier, I enjoyed an ice cream, and asked directions to Congress Hall. Walking along the boardwalk, I made it to the hotel before my host. As I arrived, the attendants were still setting up the grandstand and seating. Beyond this commotion, I could spy some sort of athletic event in the background. I decided to investigate further. It turned out that it was a baseball game between a team of guests and the squad from the Cape May Athletic Club. All appeared to be having jolly good fun, though the vacationers did not stand a chance against the Club's crew. Wealthy community members had brought in top college athletes from Princeton and Columbia to ensure their club would succeed against rivals from Staten Island, New York, and Philadelphia. This was my first experience with this game, and it did not take long to comprehend the rules and enjoy the spectacle.

An hour sped by before I noticed the band warming up. I returned to the lawn in front of the L-shaped hotel and, despite the throngs of tourists, easily found Dr. Physick. Our cordial host offered me a seat, and we spent a delightful afternoon listening to the concert. The band regaled us with many timely favorites, including one that drew a particularly long and enthusiastic ovation. As might be imagined, "The Congress Hall

March" proved a fitting finale. Though a minor composition, it had been a local favorite since John Philip Sousa debuted it on this very spot in August of 1882, to honor the hotel's owners H.J. and G.R. Crump.

Following the concert, I joined Dr. Physick and some other noted locals for lunch, served upon the broad porch of Congress Hall. We followed the meal with several rounds of refreshments. The company and conversation were both quite good, and I thoroughly enjoyed the entire afternoon. It was not until five o'clock that the party broke up and the doctor and I drove back to his home.

Holmes arrived back at the estate just as dinner was being served. The vigor he had displayed earlier had left him. He was polite to the ladies, but pensive and quiet. After the meal, our host suggested that we take advantage of the cool evening air and adjourn to the screened porch. I much preferred this setting to the hot interior. We settled into three wooden rockers and partook of a smoke.

"I take it that your foray to West Cape May was less than successful?" I asked my meditative friend.

"I had hope of acquiring some information…but they are a tightlipped people," Holmes replied dejectedly.

"You must remember what they have been through," Dr. Physick interjected. "Many are émigrés and were once slaves. Thus, they are not only somewhat mistrustful of whites, but also wary about giving a 'wrong' answer. They have often found that it is best to provide the response you *want*, rather than one that is accurate. If they are unsure of the answer you desire, silence is safest. Even those who were not slaves often react this way. Cape May is a segregated city, and Negroes are second-class citizens. It is unjust. Hopefully, our culture will evolve and adopt an attitude more akin to that of the late Mr. Goodfellow."

Holmes lounged in the rocker his eyes half closed, his long fingertips tapping each other. Suddenly, he bolted from his seat.

"Dr. Physick, would your household be much disturbed if I played my violin in your conservatory?" my friend asked.

"Not at all," our host responded, chuckling over my companion's distinctive character.

"Very good then." With that, Holmes disappeared into the house. A moment later, the closing of a solid oak door could be heard and, a minute after that, the sonorous whining of his bow leaked from an open window.

The method by which Holmes thought through difficult problems was familiar to me, but I tried my best to explain his actions to the doctor. He was most understanding and actually quite amused by my friend's singular nature.

The sky had begun to cloud over, and the breeze began to heighten as the leaves rustled noisily, straining their stems. The wind carried that unmistakable scent of dampness that betrayed the coming rain.

"I was going to suggest that this evening I might show you Cape May's nighttime sights. The boardwalk and iron pier are always active during the summer season. Unfortunately, I fear we are about to get doused," Physick said, surveying the sky.

Just then a large drop of rain plopped upon the flagstone in front of the porch. Two more followed, and then a virtual downpour erupted.

"Perhaps you would enjoy some more billiards?" our host suggested with a smile.

"Certainly," I replied. "I believe I may be able to improve my skills a bit further."

The doctor and I ascended to the library and were enjoying a fine glass of brandy as we knocked the clay balls about. After an hour, Holmes abandoned his Stradivarius and removed himself to our bedroom below. He paced the floor like a tiger; his pendulum-like tread clearly audible between our billiard shots. Suddenly, the footsteps stopped. A moment later, Holmes came rushing up the stairs and burst into the room.

"Doctor, I assume there are a few gambling establish-ments in the city?" he asked Physick.

"Yes—" The doctor began to answer, but Holmes inter-rupted again, as his impatience got the better of him.

"Is there one with a southern flair? Architecturally, etce-tera?"

"As a matter of fact, there is. The Jackson Clubhouse on Columbia Avenue."

"Wonderful. You won't mind if I borrow the dogcart, will you?" the eager detective asked.

"Hold on and I shall have Robert drive you. Would you like Dr. Watson and me to accompany you?"

"No, no. I must do some acting and I'm afraid that your presence would be too conspicuous. However, I will take you up on the ride from your valet. I will find my own way back, however."

"What is it Holmes? Have you a good lead?" I curiously inquired.

"Actually, no, Watson, I do not. I wish that I did. This is more of a fishing expedition, but it is the best idea I could con-jure."

Luckily, the rain had all but subsided, because scarcely a moment later, Holmes was out the door like a whirlwind and stomping off toward the carriage house.

Chapter 8

Next morning, Holmes was his chipper self again. It was evident that he had had some degree of success. After breakfast, he asked us into the parlor, closing the doors behind.

"Is there still hope of solving this murder?" Dr. Physick asked my companion.

"I have solved it."

"What?!" I exclaimed in astonishment. "But you were at a complete standstill just yesterday!"

"Yes and no. I had theories and clues that may or may not have been substantive. What I lacked was a suspect, which, as you know, is quite an important facet," he joked. "My sojourn last night was purely a calculated speculation, but it paid off. However, I must obtain some corroborative data if we are to make an arrest. I must ask both of you for your help in this endeavor."

"Most certainly!" our host responded jubilantly.

"Dr. Physick, I trust you are acquainted with Postmaster General Wanamaker?" Holmes asked.

"Yes, we may be considered friends."

"I believe that he is at his home in Cape May Point. I need you and Watson to go there and convince him to meet me at the telegraph office. I am confident that he will listen to Dr. Physick, but if he is resistant, Watson, you must use the name of the man at the State Department we dealt with while in Washington. Do this only as a last resort, as our mission to that city remains clandestine. I sent an important cable to Philadelphia this morning and I must see if a reply has arrived. Therefore, I will be at the telegraph office when you get back."

The doctor and I climbed aboard the four-wheeler and were off to board the electric trolley, which would give us the quickest passage to Cape May Point. Holmes, meanwhile, drove himself in the trap toward the telegraph office.

A word from Dr. Physick was enough to get the trolley conductor to make an unscheduled stop close to the Wanamaker home. We banged on the door of the large cottage. It was but a moment before the door was answered by a butler. The servant invited us in, and disappeared. A few minutes later, The Postmaster General emerged to greet us. Luckily, I did not have to resort to divulging our operation on behalf of his friend President Harrison, as he took Dr. Physick's plea quite seriously. In fact, he responded: "Of course I will help. *Courtesy is the one coin you can never have too much of, or be stingy with.*" I later realized this quote was one of his often-used credos in his retail enterprises.

Mr. Wanamaker sent his coachman racing south toward the trolley station to inform the conductor to stop in front of his home on the return trip. While we waited, Dr. Physick and I sketched the detail as best we could for Mr. Wanamaker. A half an hour later, we were back at the telegraph office, and I was introducing the Postmaster General to Holmes. My friend gave a very hasty greeting before handing me a piece of paper.

"Watson, I need you and Dr. Physick to collect Constable Gallachio and go to the Baltimore Hotel. You need to detain this man." The note read:

Baltimore Hotel
642 Hughes Street
Samuel Legree,
Room 214.

"Should we have him arrested?" I asked. Noticing the address, I was startled to find that the hotel was but a stone's throw from the home of the murdered man.

"No, we do not have the proper evidence yet, but I am hopeful that the word I have just received from Philadelphia and the telegram I am going to ask Mr. Wanamaker to send will provide enough."

"Holmes, can you please tell us what this is all about?" I asked in frustration.

"We must make haste my good man, or all may be lost, but I will give you a thin clue: the photograph you hung on the wall in Baker Street next to that of General Gordon." He winked as he and the Postmaster General disappeared into the telegraph office.

It took a second for the clue to register, but I quickly told Dr. Physick that I had hung a picture of Henry Ward Beecher, the noted abolitionist, in that very spot. Holmes's hint caused only the slightest illumination as Dr. Physick and I negotiated the busy crowd and trotted off toward the center of town in hopes of finding the constable.

Dr. Physick and I scoured the streets for the officer. Physick made use of his clout and sent several citizens scurrying off in pursuit of the elusive constable. He astutely thrust Robert into his coach and sent him to the Baltimore Hotel to inquire if our quarry was even in.

"It might be beneficial to know how hasty we actually must be," Physick added as we searched the streets.

The doctor and I went up one street and down another. We poked our heads into businesses and asked if anyone had seen not only Gallachio, but also Officer Toland, the city's second policeman. Physick grabbed several local citizens and added them to our search party, sending them to the corners of the town. Unfortunately, we were luckless. Block after block turned up no sign of Cape May's constables.

Eventually, our circuit brought us back to the boardwalk. Just then, Robert pulled up announcing that Legree had checked out. Across the boardwalk, I could make out Holmes and Wanamaker through the crowd of pedestrians. They were beyond the trolley tracks, engaged in earnest conversation. We rushed to join them.

"Holmes, Legree has checked out of the hotel. We were unable to find Officer Gallachio..." I was, however, interrupted by the appearance of the policeman himself. The constable leaped from the trolley as it squeaked to a halt.

"I heard you were looking for me!" the officer smiled at Holmes.

"Indeed. Our man's name is Samuel Legree. I fear he may have smelled danger and be fleeing the city. We should..." my friend broke off as his eyes fell upon the departing trolley. "There he is!" he yelled pointing to the car.

"Which?" I asked, following Holmes who had taken off at a sprint.

"At the rear of the car, that one-armed man!"

Standing at the back of the vehicle was a short, thickly built man, approaching the age of sixty. He was missing his right arm below the elbow.

The constable and I chased after Holmes, but his thin frame and long legs gave him a distinct advantage. The trolley was accelerating out of his reach when he made an all-out leap of desperation. The fingers of his right hand barely closed around the steel post at the rear of the car. My friend was dragged for several dozen feet before he lifted his feet together and then bounced off of the boardwalk reminiscent of a rider leaping into the saddle of a moving horse.

As Holmes hauled himself into the car, his quarry sensed the noose about to close and struck at my friend with his walking stick. Holmes dodged the blow. Again Legree struck, and again Holmes avoided having his brains bashed. The third swipe struck the side of the car, and Holmes succeeded in grabbing the stick. Legree wrestled for his weapon and pulled violently to retrieve it. Suddenly, the head slid from the cane and a hidden sword emerged in the felon's hand. This, however, was distressing not to Holmes, but to Legree. The force of his yank had sent him reeling backward. For a moment, he teetered on the edge of the car and clutched for the rail with his phantom right hand. A second later, he tumbled backward out of the car and onto the dirt road called Ocean Drive. At first, he appeared dead or perhaps merely unconscious. However, a moment later, he sat up. Unfortunately, this recovery was short-lived, as was Mr. Legree himself. A four-wheeled wagon had been approaching from the opposite direction, and the driver could not stop in time. First, the horse, then both sets of wheels, crushed the ill-fated man. Sickening cracks could be heard as his bones snapped.

By the time the constable and I reached the victim, it was already apparent that he was dead. Holmes had succeeded in getting the trolley pilot to stop and hustled back to meet us.

"Ah, poetic justice," he quipped, straightening his tie.

"Holmes, are you finally prepared to clear the fog around this whole affair?" I asked in exasperation.

"Yes, Watson. I shall explain the whole business if our visitor has arrived at Dr. Physick's estate," Holmes replied gravely.

"Visitor?"

"Yes, I told you I had sent a telegram to Philadelphia early this morning, and luckily, a reply was waiting for me while you were off collecting Mr. Wanamaker. You see, I had read in yesterday's paper that a certain notable personage was visiting Philadelphia. I cabled, explaining the situation, and implored her to help us. She agreed to return to Cape May by the earliest train and..." Holmes looked at his watch, "I believe she should already be at the Physick estate."

"Return?" I asked puzzled.

"Yes. She had been an inhabitant previously. But enough dawdling. Let us all proceed to Dr. Physick's parlor and there you shall learn everything."

Officer Toland arrived on the scene and took control over the situation, calling for the undertaker to remove the remains. Holmes, Dr. Physick, and I climbed into the doctor's carriage while Officer Gallachio and Mr. Wanamaker boarded a cab. Soon, we were all trotting toward the Physick house, hopeful that my friend would remove the confusion that pervaded over us all.

Chapter 9

We entered the home and piled into the front parlor. There, seated in a comfortable chair, and flanked by two Negro men, was a somewhat elderly black woman. She stood as we entered and I was much taken by her appearance. She was plump and kindly looking, but beneath the cherubic façade, I sensed an air of dignity and strength.

"Gentlemen," Holmes said, "may I introduce Miss Harriet Tubman."

The woman bowed slightly and returned to her seat.

I had heard of Miss Tubman, as had obviously the Americans among our party.

"Please take seats, gentlemen, and I will synthesize the whole matter. Miss Tubman has agreed to help by filling in my gaps."

After his directions had been followed, Holmes moved to the center of the room and began his tale.

"First, let us begin with the evidence in the Goodfellow house. Dr. Physick was astute enough to guard the murder scene from further molestation until we arrived. This was fortunate as the body itself held an important clue. The dagger had been driven through the rear left side, between his jawbone and neck and exited through the mouth. This was suggestive. The doctors corroborated my finding that the weapon was driven through from left to right, demonstrating that the murderer was probably left-handed. Watson, if you recall, I wondered why the attacker had not merely slit the victim's throat. We obviously now know why. Legree had only a left arm and thus could not secure Goodfellow with his right arm to employ a slicing attack. Therefore, he had to resort to a stabbing type assault. It is likely that his attack had been aimed at Goodfellow's back, but the victim stooped to retrieve the pen that had fallen under the desk, thereby changing the point of impact. I am speculating of course, but it is unlikely that anyone would direct a thrust at the rear of the skull. Regardless, the objective was achieved since the injury was terminal.

"Goodfellow fell, knocking the bust to the floor. Legree fled, locking the front door behind him. Though the attack was a surprise, the murderer must have uttered some cry to identify his affiliation, which is why the victim was able to give us the clue of the circle around the bust. The statuette was of Socrates, a *Greek* philosopher, which he encircled. A thin clue, but the best the dying man could do. Watson, what is the Greek word for 'circle'?" Holmes queried.

"*Kuklos*," I replied.

"Yes. Do you remember our adventure you entitled *The Five Orange Pips*?"

"Of course," I burst out, "it dealt with the Ku Klux Klan!"

"Indeed. The name for that nefarious group was derived from the very word *kuklos*," Holmes expounded.

"Ingenious," Dr. Physick mumbled to himself.

"My dear doctor, I am not sure if you are referring to my decoding or the message itself, but I assure you that all credit goes to poor Mr. Goodfellow whose courage, clear thinking, and coolness in the face of death have given us such aid in solving this mystery," my friend admiringly stated.

"I must admit," Holmes continued, "Mr. Goodfellow's message eluded me for some time. I am embarrassed that I did not decipher it more quickly. It came to me in Dr. Physick's library after you and the good doctor had retired for the evening.

"Following this revelation, I scoured the shelves for volumes which might expand my knowledge about the Klan. I fell upon a book entitled *A History of Reconstructing the South: 1865-1877*. This work was most helpful. It not only illuminated me about the Ku Klux Klan, but also provided valuable information regarding The Freedman's Bureau, The Force Acts, and various other tidbits that proved useful.

"I still had no idea what specific grievance a Klansman might have against Mr. Goodfellow when Watson and I returned to the murder scene the following day. However, a clue presented itself in the victim's home. I am speaking of these peculiar blue and yellow lamps." Holmes stated, retrieving the lanterns from a nearby table. "Officer Gallachio was present when we discovered these. He offered that the only connection he could fathom was the colored lanterns used by railroad men. We use the same system in England, but I did not make a significant association until I heard the word 'railroad' from the constable's lips. It was then that I connected not only the lanterns, but also the Ku Klux Klan and the Negro hair I had recovered from the dead man's jacket. Each of these points was suggestive in and of themselves, but together they were nearly conclusive. I ran off to West Cape May to see if any of the city's Negro inhabitants could help solidify my theory. Unfortunately, they were less than communicative. Miss Tubman can you please explain the significance of the lamps?"

"As most of you are probably aware, before the war, I was a conductor on the Underground Railroad. I lived here in Cape May from '49 to '52 working as a cook in several hotels. I used the money I made to pay for my trips back and forth to Maryland, bringing my people to freedom. There were three Underground Railroad routes that went through New Jersey. One was called the 'Greenwich Line.' Escaping slaves were transported across the Delaware River at night from Dover, in boats marked with a yellow light hung below a blue one and met by a New Jersey boat showing the same lights. The second boat led the way back to Greenwich."

"Who was it that piloted the New Jersey boats?" Holmes asked the woman, for our own edification.

"The Greenwich station was run by a ring of Quakers."

The blood went cold in my veins as I broke into the dialog, "Mr. Goodfellow was one of those Quakers?"

"Yes. I made nineteen trips total, and Joseph Goodfellow himself helped me on five of them," Miss Tubman replied.

"But, Holmes," I interjected, "how does Legree fit into this, and how did you find him?"

"Once I had deduced that the murderer was a member of the Ku Klux Klan, and that Goodfellow had been involved in the Underground Railroad, the search could be greatly narrowed to a southerner who had been a member of the Klan and, of course, had some reason for personal animus against the victim. However, still I feared I had hit a wall. This city is teaming with people, most of which are not even permanent residents. I eventually struck upon the notion that I should piece together a likely character sketch of the murderer. In all probability, the man would prefer the company of other southerners, and if possible, a southern motif. Members of the Klan take a singular pride in their southern heritage. It would also be probable that the man in question would enjoy gambling, as so many rouges do.

"I asked Dr. Physick if such an establishment existed, and when he named the Jackson Clubhouse, off I went to seek my quarry. My plan had been to watch the players and gravitate toward those that proved to be left-handed. You can imagine the beeline I made when I noticed a one-armed man in southern attire at the faro table! I engaged the chap in conversation and struck up an acquaintance. He was quite receptive to my generosity with liquor. I tested his confederate patriotism by stating that I was staying at the Chalfonte Hotel, and gushed about its builder, Henry Sawyer, Cape May's own Civil War hero. It was quite fortunate that you related that story to me Watson!" Holmes jibed. "Legree's acidic and quite vociferous reaction was enough to prove the point.

"Whiskey loosened the man's lips, and though he did not reveal anything outright, through inference and deduction, I was able to conclude with some degree of certainty that Legree had fled the south due to some past misdeeds.

"At two o'clock in the morning, Legree left the club and I hurried to the telegraph office. Luckily, the operator was sleeping upon a cot inside and my vigorous banging was enough to rouse him. He agreed to send my message to Miss

Tubman, though he did not see the urgency as she would undoubtedly not receive it until six or seven a.m. Still, I was insistent and obviously it did reach her early enough for her to catch the first train," Holmes said, with a nod in the direction of Miss Tubman.

"I returned to the estate for a few hours of sleep, but was anxious to get back to the telegraph office to see if Miss Tubman had replied. In the meantime, doctors Watson and Physick were good enough to travel to Cape May Point to persuade Mr. Wanamaker to meet me at the telegraph office. I knew that it was likely that the Postmaster General of the United States would be able to ascertain confirmation of my suspicions about Legree. I had Mr. Wanamaker contact not only the War Department, but also retired Major General Oliver Otis Howard, who had been the head of the Freedman's Bureau. Howard confirmed that Legree had been a Confederate soldier who had lost his arm at the battle at Chickamauga. After the war, he became a notorious member of the Ku Klux Klan, and numerous complaints had been lodged against him with the Freedman's Bureau. Once Congress passed the Force Acts, giving the Army the power to arrest Klansmen, Legree fled. It is fortunate for us that he was brazen enough not to have adopted a pseudonym. I suppose he felt that being in the North, along with the passage of some fifteen years, provided him sufficient safety."

"But, Holmes," I interrupted again, "what was Legree's grievance against Mr. Goodfellow?"

"I have discussed Legree's career during and after the war, but not before. Prior to the war, he had been a slave hunter. He was a typical member of that wicked class of uncouth ruffians who chased down runaway slaves. Legree's livelihood was predicated upon not only capturing runaways, but upon a successful reputation in that field. Our Mr. Goodfellow bested Legree no fewer than twenty times. Legree had built up an intense hatred for the man, though he had never met him face-to-face. The former Confederate had not come to Cape May on a mission of murder, but when he found that his former nemesis lived less than a block from his very hotel, he jumped at the opportunity."

Silence fell over the room as Holmes finished his tale.

"And the Negro hair you found upon the deceased?" I asked at length.

"Ah. That amounted to nothing. Well, perhaps I should not go quite that far. It helped direct me along the proper line."

Holmes gave the audience a cursory explanation as to the reason for our presence in the States. He emphasized the need for absolute secrecy about our adventure in Cape May as the governments of both Britain and the United States had no desire for any links to be made that might reveal our mission. Each agreed to swear an oath of silence regarding our role in solving the strange case of the murdered Quaker.

"But you shall get no credit!" Mr. Wanamaker complained.

"My good friend Dr. Watson will tell you that I play the game for the game's sake. Several Scotland Yard inspectors have added to their reputations as a result of my incognito and I see no reason why the same should not occur for Constable Gallachio. In fact, unlike many of his London counterparts, Officer Gallachio actually aided in solving the case. He facilitated my deduction by providing the 'railroad man' link." Holmes smiled, slapping the officer on the shoulder.

Next day, as we prepared to catch the train for the steamer depot at Philadelphia, Dr. Physick presented Holmes with a generous check for his services.

"Ah, thank you doctor," Holmes said, folding the paper and depositing it in his breast pocket. "The accommodations shared by Watson and myself back in London are quite humble, but our landlady Mrs. Hudson still must be paid."

Soon after, we sailed for home; our American expedition complete. I spent the trip organizing my notes in preparation for the day when I might be at liberty to relate our adventure in Cape May. My friend, however, remained in the cabin, slipping into that pitiable lethargy which consumed him whenever his mind was left without a challenge.

The Republic docked at Cape May Point

The "Light of Asia"

The trolley to Cape May

President Harrison's cottage

The Stockton Hotel

The Stockton baths

The George Allen House
(a.k.a. The Southern Mansion)

The Chalfonte

Postmaster General Wanamaker

Wanamaker Cottage

Dr. Emlen Physick

The Physick Estate

The Boardwalk and Trolley Shop

The Baltimore Hotel

The Highland Intrigue

Chapter 1

My wife and I made it a custom to recline by the fire-place each evening and read, although Mrs. Watson occasionally forewent a book for needlepoint. Prior to settling into a novel or occasional medical journal, it was my habit to sift through the correspondence if any had arrived that day. It had been a full afternoon and I was exhausted. In addition to my usual rounds, I was hastily called upon to administer emergency medical treatment when an omnibus overturned not far from our residence.

Wearily, I shuffled through the envelopes, and was about to sacrifice my novel and retire when I came to a letter that restored my vigor.

"Ah, it is Hamish Graham!" I erupted in a smile, and quickly tore open the envelope.

My wife knew the name, and the story associated with it, but for the edification of the reader I shall briefly relate the origin and nature of our friendship.

Those familiar with my chronicles are aware that I was wounded while serving as an assistant surgeon in Afghanistan where a Jezail bullet had knocked me down during the disastrous battle at Maiwand. Had it not been for the gallantry of Murray, my orderly, I might not have made it back behind the walls of Kandahar. It was not long however before the city was under siege and indeed it looked as if those of us spared at Maiwand had merely delayed the inevitable.

Although we did not know of it at that time, General Roberts had been dispatched from Kabul to relieve us. His ten thousand soldiers trekked over three hundred miles to not only save us, but help us claim victory in the ensuing Battle of Kandahar.

Among Roberts's force were two-dozen Gordon Highlanders. One of those brave Scots was Hamish Graham. Like me, he had fallen by being at the wrong end of a tribesman's rifle. We convalesced together for several months at Peshawar, where we became fast friends.

Hamish had been born of noble Scot blood, so one would have thought it unlikely that he would end up serving in the wilds of Afghanistan. However, he was an adventurous sort and, while attending university at Aberdeen, he had impetuously thrown aside his education and enlisted in the Gordon Highlanders. Unlike me, after he had healed sufficiently, he did not return to Britannia. Rather, he sought further excitement in India, eventually prospering in plantation agriculture. I had not seen the man since Peshawar, but we had maintained a vigorous correspondence over the years.

My friend's letter shocked me. Perhaps it is better if I display its contents verbatim. It read:

My Dearest Watson,

As you know, my uncle was laird of the manor and, although he spent a number of the past months in South Africa, he had recently returned home to dear old Scotland. He was not in the Highlands two weeks, however, when he was found dead. His passing now leaves me in possession of the estate, which is why this letter comes to you not from Bombay, but Dundee. Over the years, you have thrilled me with tales both in letters and print of your adventures with Mr. Sherlock Holmes. I was hoping you and your colleague might journey north and help with the problem of my uncle's death. You see, the circumstances are both bizarre and baffling. I dare not go into detail in this missive, as the particulars are...indelicate. I have been able to keep the affair out of the papers for now, though I fear I will not be able to do so for much longer. If at all possible, kindly come to my aid. Please cable me at the enclosed address as soon as you decide whether you can come.

I had wished that we would meet again one day, although under much different circumstances.

Your faithful comrade,
Hamish Graham

The next morning, I hurried to my old abode in Baker Street. Even though Holmes and I had ceased to lodge together, we remained intimates. I still enjoyed the company of that eccentric fellow and I frequently called upon my friend, either to enjoy the society of his company or to surreptitiously monitor his health. Of course, I could never fool Holmes, and on the occasions when I tried to perform my clandestine examinations, he would break in with comments such as: "My dear doctor, I assure you I have not been at the cocaine since our last meeting!"

My old companion was no stranger to my home either. I believe I remained his only friend, and his trust in both my loyalty and tenacity had led him to enlist my services on many instances since I had separated from Baker Street.

Holmes was not in, but Mrs. Hudson stated that he had asked her to hold breakfast for him, so he should be back soon if I cared to wait. Ever the attentive landlady, she offered me a spot of tea while I waited in my old lodgings.

I could not help but smile as I sunk into a familiar chair. The fabric was scented heavily with Holmes' shag tobacco. The room was in less disarray than normal, but the pile of papers on the floor and the careless manner in which his violin had been cast onto the sofa, suggested that my friend was indeed engaged in one of his "little problems."

I was roused from nostalgic reminiscences by the quick tread upon the stairs, which I easily identified as belonging to my friend.

"Ah, Watson, it is good to see you," he let fly before he was fully through the door.

"Was I expected?" I chuckled at his lack of surprise.

"Not at all," he returned, unceremoniously flinging his hat into the corner.

"Well then, you encountered Mrs. Hudson upon the stair."

"Hardly."

"Would you care to explain your clairvoyance then?" I smirked back.

"Watson, since your marriage, you have clearly left some of your old army habits behind. Where your morning toilet used to be accomplished in an unfanciful manner, since your union, you have taken to shaving with scented water. My nose marked your presence halfway up the stairs."

"Simplicity," I laughed. "You have often told me that I see, but do not observe. I suppose I also inhale but do not smell."

"Ha! Indeed Watson!" he chuckled, as he tumbled into the opposite seat. "Now what troubling event has brought you to Baker Street?"

"How do you know this isn't a social call? I've paid you many." My eyes narrowed in scrutiny.

"That is undeniably so, but if this were one of those occasions, you would have come before breakfast or well afterward. You would not have been rude enough to catch dear Mrs. Hudson mid meal. No, I take it you have come on behalf of a Scotch associate, recently arrived from India."

Holmes read the quizzical expression on my face and answered before I could ask. "The letter protruding from your pocket, Watson. I can clearly see the seal of Scotland upon the postmark and the envelope is unmistakably made of the cotton fibered paper manufactured in India," he replied offhandedly, his look urging me to get on with the business.

"Yes, well, you are of course correct. It is from a friend in Dundee requesting assistance."

"From the thinness of the envelope I gather that it is not a long missive. Perhaps it would be best if you read me the contents directly." He leaned back, half closing his eyes, as was his habit when focusing his hearing upon a subject. I read him the letter, but his reaction was hardly what I had hoped.

"Impossible, Watson," he said, as he began to dig through the pile of papers on the floor. "I am presently engaged, and cannot get away."

I will admit I was a bit perturbed by his dismissal. Many times I had put aside my own practice when he came asking for assistance. "Holmes, surely, you will at least consider it. He is a friend in need!"

"Watson, I cannot possibly throw over my current client simply because you received the vaguest of letters from the Highlands." He continued to rummage through his pile.

I had, of course, been a bit presumptuous, I then realized. "Well," I began again in a softer tone, "can you make any suggestions, then?"

He replied without looking up, "Your friend uses several intriguing words: 'bizarre, baffling, and indelicate.' Yet, these terms are subjective. What strikes him as bizarre might appear commonplace to you and I given the cases we have seen. Baffling to him might actually be simplicity personified."

I leapt at the opening. "All the more reason why we should come to his aid. We may be able to dispose of the problem in an instant."

"Watson, you have spent more than a few years observing my methods. If the case is indeed transparent, I feel fully confident that you can see it through without me. If, however, you find yourself stymied, I will decline any new cases and make the long trek to Dundee after I have concluded my current problem."

At that moment, Mrs. Hudson pushed her way into the room bearing an abundant breakfast tray.

"I take it you'll be joining Mr. Holmes for breakfast then?" Mrs. Hudson asked.

"No, I am afraid that I must be on my way." I turned to Holmes "I will cable you from Dundee once I have news."

He merely grunted a reply as he read through one of his documents.

"Mr. Holmes, your breakfast," Mrs. Hudson tried unsuccessfully to roust her tenant from his reading.

"Yes, yes, put it on the table. Thank you," he blurted out dismissively.

The poor woman gave a sigh before exiting, knowing her culinary efforts had been largely wasted.

My wife understood the allegiance between friends and did not object to my journeying to Scotland. I made arrangements for my neighbor to carry out my practice in my absence, a courtesy he had done for me during previous excursions with Holmes. I had, of course, repaid the favor when he was away and his patients were without their physician.

I did not forget to telegraph Hamish Graham that I was on my way, though I made no mention of whether or not Holmes would be accompanying me. I intended to ease his mind, at least temporarily. I hastily threw my clothes, toiletries, and traveling medical kit into a valise. However, I hesitated before closing the satchel. Of a sudden, I made the decision, and retrieved the small wooden box from the shelf inside the closet. I opened the lid to reveal my old service revolver. I removed the weapon and emptied the cartridges from the cylinder, sliding the bullets into an inside pocket. I tossed the pistol atop the clothing and fastened the clasp.

At King's Cross, I was able to purchase a ticket aboard a departing train for Edinburgh. I will not bore you with the details of the 330 mile trip, aside from the fact that it eroded nearly nine hours from my life. Upon arriving at Waverly Station, I booked passage for the remaining 60 miles to Dundee. However, an incident occurred at Waverly that I should mention.

My friend Holmes has often chastised me for "romanticizing" our adventures. In his opinion, my accounts should be confined to technical recitations of the application of his methods. Holmes does not seem to comprehend that no publisher would print my writings if they were merely academic texts on the science of deduction. My companion will therefore approve of my inclusion in this tale of an incident that has no bearing on the case at hand, yet does demonstrate the applicability of his methods.

As I approached the locomotive bound for Dundee, several porters scurried about the platform hawking their services to travelers. As I had but one small bag, I was in no need of assistance. However, a well-dressed couple next to me was happy to unburden themselves when a young man in uniform offered to carry their bags aboard.

The gentleman had checked his watch before the porter arrived, and I could easily make out the intricate etchings in the gold case and the high quality enamel of its face. Judging by the quality of their dress and the jewelry they wore, the man and woman were apparently wealthy. The porter had made a beeline for the pair, passing several other passengers in need of service. This in itself was not unordinary. A man whose livelihood is largely determined by gratuities will often focus his attention upon the well-to-do.

There was something that did not ring true, however. The porter was clean and well groomed; his buttons were polished, and the rest of his uniform was in order (if a bit rumpled). Yet, my instincts told me that something was amiss. It took me a moment to mark it, and by the time I did, the couple had boarded and the porter was just climbing the steps of the baggage car with the couple's two cases. I will tell you what troubled me: it was his shoes. Despite the appropriateness of his outfit, the shoes he wore were worn, scuffed boots rather than the polished shoes of his profession.

I suppose I had assumed some of my friend's habits of observation, after all, and I picked my way through the crowd toward the baggage car. Although I had a difficult time snaking through the oncoming throng, when I made it to the steps, I was in time to see that the porter did not turn left into the car itself, but rather traveled directly across the compartment to the corresponding doorway on the other side. He exited to the other side of the tracks.

I scurried up the steps and down the others. A quick survey showed me that the scoundrel was heading around the corner of a shack. I dared not yell out, as he was far enough away that I would never catch him if he chose to run. If I ducked back aboard the train for assistance, he might be long gone before I returned. No, I judged it best if I continued to follow.

I tread as carefully as I could, afraid that I might slide on the loose stones and give myself away. Upon reaching the shack, I braced my back against the wall and inched my way to the corner. I could hear the man rustling through the bags. I placed my case on the ground and stealthily unclipped the latch. Slowly and silently, I withdrew my revolver. It was not loaded, but I hoped the fellow would be surprised enough not to notice. At least I could use it as a club if need be.

With a leap, I exposed myself. "Hands up, you!" I shouted to the crouched figure.

The rascal was so startled that he fell over backward. His stunned expression quickly turned to one of rage. He did not even attempt to fabricate a story, knowing he was done in. I bade him to stand up, and face the wall of the shack before he could notice the empty cylinders in my gun. As he stood silently, inches from the wall, I tossed the articles back into the bags. I moved behind the villain and ordered him to pick up the satchels and march back toward the station, warning that I was no more than five feet behind, and that I could easily deposit lead in his buttocks should he attempt to flee.

I retrieved my own bag as we went. As one might imagine, back at the station our presence immediately produced an outburst of attention. At first glance, it appeared that *I* was the rogue, accosting a poor railroad man. However, it took but a few moments to explain the situation to the true railway authorities.

"You—you ain't a bleedin' railway peeler?" The impersonator reacted in rage to the revelation that I was not an officer of the law, as the true constables dragged him away.

The sergeant remained to take my statement. It turned out that he happened to have read many of my accounts, and although he was disappointed that Holmes was not with me, he listened with great interest as I pridefully explained my execution of his methods. He assured me that since the couple's names were embossed upon the bags, it would be easy enough to reunite them with their property.

Sometime later, I recounted the event to Holmes.

"Watson, I do believe that you are coming along nicely!" he praised. "I only hope that if you choose to include it in your annals, you will confine yourself to the scientific aspects and spare the dramatization."

Chapter 2

The train ride to Dundee was uneventful, although I must admit to some apprehension in crossing the Firth of Tay. It had been almost fifteen years since the Tay Bridge railway disaster, but that catastrophe still loomed in the back of my mind. All seventy-five lives aboard had been lost when the bridge collapsed and, although the new bridge had been in flawless operation for nearly seven years, William McGonagall's poem *The Tay Bridge Disaster* had become so renowned, the event would not erode from the collective memory.

I breathed a quiet sigh of relief when the estuary was left behind. Twilight was settling behind the city, and the smoke stacks from the dozens of jute mills painted a jagged silhouette against the pink sky. It was but a matter of moments before the train chugged into the Tay Bridge Station. The lamplighters were at work on the platform, but had not yet torched those on the street. In the thinning light, I searched for a cab to carry me to my friend's abode.

"Would ye be Dr. Watson?" The voice from behind gave me a start.

"I am," I replied, turning to the tall, gaunt, white-whiskered man.

"I am Liam. Master Graham sent me to collect ye," he replied, in a thick Scottish brogue.

"Out of curiosity, how did you identify me?"

"Before ye pulled in, I inquired at the station which carriage ye were in. I saw ye exit, but couldn't catch up to ye 'til now. Shall we be off then?"

Liam confided that he had been the butler for Hamish's uncle and he and the others who had staffed the household had been delighted that my friend asked them to stay on under his ownership.

We rode to the north side of the city. Enough light remained that I could see the outline of the home, even at some distance. "Is that where we are going?" I asked, trying to mask my astonishment.

"Aye, have ye never seen Fintry Castle?"

"No, I have not." In all of my correspondence with Hamish Graham, he had never mentioned the castle.

It was an impressive reminder of the middle ages. The castle's most prominent feature was a six story square tower, but several other buildings were also visible, as they joined a wall forming the perimeter around an interior courtyard.

"It was built in 1562 by Sir David Graham. Have ye not read William McGonagall's poem *The Castle of Mains*?" Liam inquired.

"I have," I replied, though that poet's tale of the Tay Bridge calamity had had a far greater effect upon me. "The poem was about this castle then?"

"Aye, and a bonnie poem it is. *Ancient Castle of the Mains, with your romantic scenery and surrounding plains, which seem most beautiful to the eye, and the little rivulet running by, which the weary traveler can drink of when he feels dry...*" By the time he had recited the whole poem, we had arrived.

Liam had swung the carriage around to the northern side of the structure, which obviously housed the main living quarters.

"Watson! It is so good of ye to come!" Hamish greeted me warmly, as though my visit were a purely social one.

"It is good to see you again, Lieutenant Graham. The last time I laid eyes upon you, you were considerably younger, but in less fitful health."

"Aye, and the same could be said of you!" His tall frame shook as he laughed. His auburn hair now held flecks of grey, but his abundant sideburns remained of a pure ginger hue. He glanced past me, and I preemptively answered the question forming on his lips.

"Mr. Holmes was detained by a prior commitment. He sent me along in his stead, but promised he would follow if need be, as soon as his current obligation is concluded."

"Aye, I should have figured that a man like Mr. Holmes would hardly be sitting idly by," he mused. "But I'm glad to have ye here. Where are my manners? Ye must be famished!"

I had to admit I was.

"Kyata, set the table and have Mary prepare us some dinner," he addressed the exotic looking maidservant. The caramel skinned lass averted her pale blue eyes and curtsied before scurrying from view.

On the way to the dining room, I curiously surveyed the castle. It was oddly bare of adornments and much of the furniture was covered. The only real decorations I perceived were the stained glass windows that lined the eastern wall of the dining room. Most of the dozen panes depicted the usual motifs of the middle ages: saints, knights, and coats of arms. One, though, was unique. It was comprised of odd, irregular patterns of glass, the leaden dividers snaking across the multicolored field. Along the bottom, the dividers alternated in a haphazard series of vertical and horizontal lines.

"You see, Watson, the castle has been shut up for almost a year. My uncle had been in South Africa doing some business with the diamond mines. The staff was still on here at Fintry, but the tapestries and paintings had been stored and the furniture sheltered. They will be replaced now that I have assumed residence," he explained between bites of mutton.

"You wrote that your uncle was not back a fortnight before he died?"

"Aye."

"And you believe his death to have been susp—"

"How do you fancy the chops? I have missed the taste of Highland sheep these many years." He cut me off as one of the servants entered to refill our glasses. He shot me a furtive look as a footnote, and I immediately caught the hint and held my tongue.

86

"Ye know, Watson, one of your cases helped me solve a murder in India," he smirked.

"Really? How so?"

"On the plantation, I had a Sikh lad as a foreman. He was a bonnie foreman, he was. He got an honest day's labor out of the workers. Well, one morning, he didn't show up in the fields. I went to his room, and when he didn't answer, I entered. Don't ye know, the laddie was stone dead upon the floor. When I reached down to turn him over, I heard a faint sound; a sound all living in India learn to dread, even though it's no more than a whisper. I jumped back just as the cobra lunged at me. Lucky I was. I shut the door and came back with a shotgun and made short work of the snake. Though I couldn't think how it got in," he drained his glass of whiskey and continued, "we searched the room and found a hole in the mud wall."

"That explains it," I added.

"Aye, but there was something strange about that hole. I thought on it for a day before it came to me. The opening was roughly square, and about fifteen centimeters wide. About as wide as a spade."

"Ah," I paused before my glass could reach my lips.

"I recalled one of your stories, Watson. I believe you called it *The Speckled Band.*"

"Indeed," I responded, retrieving the events of that case from my memory.

"Mr. Holmes figured that a poisonous snake had been used as an instrument of murder," Hamish continued. "I considered that this might be a similar instance."

"Did you find that it was?" I asked.

"To be sure. A week earlier, my Sikh foreman had been considerably hard on one of the workers he found loafing about. He gave him a good thrashing, although it wasn't the beating that injured him as much as the shame of being punished in front of his peers. I searched that man's bunk and found a spade that fit the hole in the wall. I deduced that he created the opening and then fed the viper through while my foreman slept. He would not admit to the deed outright, at least not to me, but the magistrate got a confession out of him."

I longed to tell Holmes this story. Romanticized or not, my publication of the events had proved instrumental in helping to solve a serious crime.

After dinner, we adjourned to the library for cigars and brandy. It was in that secure environment that Hamish Graham explained why he had appealed to Holmes and me for help.

"Watson," he began, "when I heard that my uncle was found dead in his bed, I was shocked. He was near sixty years of age, but he was vigorous and fit. At first, the doctor considered that his heart had attacked him, but when he examined the body in more detail, he discovered something...curious."

Hamish took a long sip of brandy before continuing. "How shall I put this?" He stared into his glass. "His member was pitch black."

I nearly choked as I tried to force the swallow of brandy down my throat. "Do you mean to say, his...organ...was...?" I had as hard a time expressing the idea as he did, even though I was a man of medicine not unaccustomed to discussing human anatomy.

"Aye." He knitted his brow for a moment. "The doctor shared this information with no one but me. He thought it might have been the consequence of a disease acquired from an encounter with an unwholesome woman. But, despite extensive study of his medical books, he could not find any such affliction."

"Did he determine if this discoloration was instrumental in your uncle's death?"

"Nay, he couldn't say one way or the other. Do ye have any medical opinions on the point, Watson?"

I thought for a moment, and swirled the brandy in my glass. "I cannot say that I do. I would have liked to have examined the body, though."

"That can be arranged, if ye don't mind a bit of stealth."

"How do you mean?"

"Well, my uncle was placed in the family mausoleum. But I do not want to arouse suspicions. If murdered he was, I'd rather the killer not know we are on the trail. So, if ye have no objections, we'll conduct your inspection late tonight."

"No, that seems prudent." I would be lying, however if I did not admit feeling a slight chill at the prospect of poking around a crypt in the middle of the night.

I shook off the thought. "Graham, this discoloration is certainly unusual, but I can't see how it would lead you to suspect murder."

"There is more to it, Watson. When I unlocked this drawer," he said, sliding open the compartment in the large oak desk before me, "I found this message."

The page he handed me read:

GIVE MORE GOLD TO DUNCAN. KEEP IT NO LONGER. SAVE IN THE HIDDEN. FOR US ITS PUT BACK IN WRITING. TO REMAIN VERY SAFE WE WILL KILL ALL. THE CLAN MUST SUFFER BUT IF I USE THE GLASS THEN IT LIVES. HIS NOT YOURS WILL SUFFER AND THEN OURS SURVIVES. LAND WILL BE GRANTED IN CLOTH, THIS IS WHAT IS IMPORTANT. SOON ENOUGH WE WILL GAIN SILVER, THE WORTH IT WILL BE GREAT. MARK THE MACGRIOGHAIR'S DEATH, MUCH WILL IT BRING YOU. SPOT IT MONTROSE FOR MORE GOLD AND TITLE.

The message was indeed both intriguing and suspicious; however there was another aspect to it that shocked me.

"Graham," I tried to master my unease. "I have received many letters from you over the years…"

"Indeed ye have."

"This message you found… I recognize that it is written in your own hand!" I feared my tone was accusatory, but my time with Holmes had taught me to observe such things as handwriting.

His response disarmed me entirely. It was that thick hearty laugh I had heard so often back when we shared a hospital room.

"Watson, I found that *message* in the drawer, not *that paper*. The original was in Gaelic, so I translated it for ye."

I joined him in his laugh now, realizing what a stone head I had been; despite thinking I was displaying my analytical talents.

"Do you have any ideas about what this message could mean?" I asked.

"Nay, not especially. The ending addresses my uncle, for he was the Duke of Montrose. The rest perplexes me, though I find it full of suspicious elements."

"Yes," I scratched my chin, reading over the text again. "Holmes would definitely call this 'suggestive,' especially considering the markings found upon your uncle's body. With your permission, I will outline the case, as well as copy this message, and send it to Holmes by post first thing in the morning. I don't think these details should be carried over such a public forum as the telegraph wire."

"By all means," he enthusiastically replied.

It was after midnight. The servants had all retreated to the southern wing of the building to retire a good hour before, but the extra time was given to ensure that they were fast asleep.

Like any good stronghold, the castle sat atop the high ground. Not a light shone in the Dichty valley below as we crept away from the ominous stone walls. The night was an especially dark one. There was no moon and thick clouds curtained off the stars. Even though Hamish knew his way about the estate, he often had to lift the cover on the shaded lamp. Occasionally however, heat-lightning pulsed in the distance, giving the horizon an ominous glow. I have always found the phenomena a bit unsettling. I suppose it is the uncharacteristic silence that accompanies the flash. It seems unnatural, or if you will forgive my reference to the pagan, supernatural.

"Careful here, Watson," he whispered as he paused. "We have to cross Gelly Burn and the rocks may be slippery."

I could now hear the gurgle of this tributary of the Dichty River. "Is there not a bridge?" I asked.

"Aye, but I don't trust it, man. Sometimes fishermen are there at night trying to catch their eels."

The crossing was less treacherous than I expected, and a few moments later, the sky glowed long enough for me to make out the irregular outcroppings of the headstones of the old Mains graveyard. I followed closely as Hamish snaked through the ancient monuments. He paused before a large stone structure, with a wrought iron gate baring the entrance-way. I could hear keys rattle as Graham dug through his pock-et. An owl cried out and fluttered off of the roof, startling both of us. Though not a superstitious man, that night, I wondered whether that gate was meant to keep the living out or the dead in.

"Hold the lamp, will ye, Watson? Lift the cover so I can see the lock."

He produced an antique key, and the mechanism clanked. The hinges groaned loudly as the barrier swung in-ward.

Once inside, Hamish uncovered the lamp. The flame flickered over the names embossed on the stone drawers that lined the walls. A sense of melancholy fell over me as I thought how one day my friend would join this company of lairds of Montrose.

"Give me a hand, will ye, Watson?"

He had produced an iron bar, and we pried back the stone square. Together, we slid out the slab. I had pulled my handkerchief out, expecting the corpse to reek. To my sur-prise, the smell was negligible.

"Has he been embalmed?" I asked.

"Aye, to a degree. Dr. Dunbarton and I took the under-taker into our confidence, and he agreed to do the job here to avoid anyone else finding out about the markings. He was without the full extent of his instruments and chemicals, but he did a bonnie job, I'd say."

I gave the Duke a general going over before unfastening his trousers. Carefully I slid the garment down, exposing the man's private considerations. Despite as thorough an examination as possible under the circumstances, I could discern nothing unusual—excepting that the organ was as black as the night itself.

Chapter 3

For two days, Hamish and I pondered the message and the condition of his uncle. By day, we walked the grounds, away from the servants' ears, and each evening we sequestered ourselves in the privacy of the library.

GIVE MORE GOLD TO DUNCAN. KEEP IT NO LONGER. SAVE IN THE HIDDEN. FOR US ITS PUT BACK IN WRITING. TO REMAIN VERY SAFE WE WILL KILL ALL. THE CLAN MUST SUFFER BUT IF I USE THE GLASS THEN IT LIVES. HIS NOT YOURS WILL SUFFER AND THEN OURS SURVIVES. LAND WILL BE GRANTED IN CLOTH, THIS IS WHAT IS IMPORTANT. SOON ENOUGH WE WILL GAIN SILVER, THE WORTH IT WILL BE GREAT. MARK THE MACGRIOGHAIR'S DEATH, MUCH WILL IT BRING YOU. SPOT IT MONTROSE FOR MORE GOLD AND TITLE.

"*Give more gold to Duncan.* Do you know of a Duncan hereabouts?" I asked.

"Aye, many. It's a common name. I don't ken of any dealings my uncle had with any one Duncan, however."

"Hmm. Well, I suspect that that is something we should inquire about," I mused.

"*We will kill all,*" I read aloud. "All of whom? Was your uncle meant to do some killing or is his death part *of* this killing?"

"*We will kill all* certainly could be a threat, and I think this was sent *to* my uncle, given the last line. Could the sender be ordering my uncle to kill this MacGrioghair? It says that he will gain by the man's death."

"Ah, perhaps that is the case, and this MacGrioghair found out about the plot and did in your uncle first," I speculated.

"And this bit about the clan; is it your clan or another that is meant to suffer? Have you had any other recent deaths amongst the Grahams?" I furthered.

"Not that I know of, but I've only been back in Scotland a wee time. There are no shortages of Grahams in the highlands, ye know."

As these discussions went on, I longed to hear from Holmes. I did my best to model his methods, but frankly, the message and circumstances were so mysterious, the best I could muster were speculative stabs in the dark.

On the third day, we lunched on the patio. Earlier that morning, we had diverted ourselves from the mystery with a bit of sport, and between us, we had bagged two pheasants and three grouse. Our mid-day meal thus featured fresh game bird, which Hamish's cook Mary had grilled to perfection.

"Kyata," Hamish called forward the exotic-looking girl. "Would ye please fetch us another bottle of wine?" The young woman curtsied, and disappeared through the stone archway.

"Graham, I have never heard that one speak. Is she mute?"

"Nay," he laughed. "My uncle brought her back from South Africa with him. She understands everything, but hasn't mastered the language in speech yet."

"Oh," I brought the glass up to my lips, but put it back down before drinking. "South Africa. At first, I thought she might be Welsh. Her complexion is far too dark for her to be Irish like the other housemaids."

"Aye, that is true, but she's about as much Taffy as she is Erin. I suspect that her father was either English or Dutch but it's obvious her mother was a native of the tribal savannah."

"Yes…" I thought of her odd combination of bronze flesh and azure eyes.

"Master Graham," Liam approached through the archway. "A messenger just brought this for Dr. Watson."

I took the envelope, and began to open it when Kyata returned with the wine. I patiently waited until Hamish dismissed her.

"It seems we are in luck; Holmes is on his way." I informed my host.

"Does he have any ideas?"

"I am not sure." I read him the curt telegram: *WATSON RECEIVED YOUR LETTER [STOP] MOST INTRIGUING [STOP] AM ON MY WAY [STOP] HOLMES.*

"Holmes, it is good to see you," I bellowed, approaching my friend, who had just entered the castle.

"Aye, a pleasure indeed Mr. Holmes, welcome to Fintry," Graham echoed, giving Holmes's hand a firm shake.

"Liam, take Mr. Holmes's bag to his room, please."

"Holmes, may I present Hamish Graham, the new Duke of Montrose?" I made the formalities, despite Graham's previous welcome.

"So I gathered," Holmes laughed, handing his hat to Liam. "I am glad that you have just begun dinner. I hope, however, you have enough for a third party. I am famished."

Hamish looked at me dumfounded, before he recovered enough to turn back to Holmes. "Aye, 'tis true, Watson and I had just sat down when Liam announced your arrival. But how did you know of it?"

Holmes laughed. "Your trousers are creased in the rear, mid-thigh. You have recently been sitting on a rigid wooden chair; the kind I doubt occupies any other room in this house save the dining room. And of course, there is the napkin in your hand." He pointed to the linen Graham was holding. "It is wrinkled at one corner, indicating that it was recently tucked into your collar. Had you finished your meal, you would have removed it and set it upon the table, rather than merely tugging it loose on your way to greet me. Additionally, it is absent of any stains, showing that you had yet to touch your food. Although Watson's whiskers betray the fact that he has sampled the bread."

"Astounding!" Hamish applauded. "Although I have read enough of Watson's accounts not to be surprised."

"Ah yes, my trusty chronicler." He clapped a hand on my back. "Fortunately, he has proven to be of equal value as a partner. Many of those problems you have read about would have been more difficult to solve were it not for my brave companion." I blushed under this rare praise from Holmes.

"Well, let us not prolong Mr. Holmes's hunger. Liam, have Mary prepare another bowl of stew, and another cutlet," Graham called after the retreating servant.

In the dining room, the banter was kept light. No discussion was made of the case at hand. Although I had blundered ahead with questions upon my own arrival, Holmes was far too seasoned to make the same error. He gave no indication that his call was anything but a visit to the United Kingdom's northern dominion.

After dinner, we made our usual sojourn to the library. Holmes flopped carelessly onto a divan. As Hamish poured the brandy, he cast an anxious look in my direction, silently imploring me to address my friend.

"So Holmes, you believe that there may have been villainy involved in the Duke's death?" I asked, handing him the drink.

Holmes did not answer immediately. He got up and walked to the window. "I cannot say, Watson."

"But certainly you found the circumstances bizarre enough to make the trip?"

"Bizarre." He repeated the word and stared through the window into the blackness of the night. "No Watson, I would choose another word: 'intriguing.' You see, Mr. Graham," he addressed my old comrade, "two other appeals came in for my aid when I received Watson's letter, but your case was by far the most curious. This discoloration on your uncle's person is certainly singular, but that message…" he stared out the window again. "Together, they paint a dark picture."

"You have an idea of how they fit together then?" Hamish asked.

"No, and that is what brought me here. Watson will tell you that the more complex a problem, the more it inspires me to action. I have but one idea so far and if I am even correct about it, it is but a small piece to a much larger puzzle."

"Watson, I am sure that you and the Duke have been hard at work in my absence. Kindly inform me of your doings." With that, Holmes set his brandy upon the table and returned to the sofa. He reclined fully and closed his eyes.

"Well, honestly, Holmes, there is not much more to tell. As I indicated in my letter, I made an examination of the body but I could not perceive any indication of foul play."

"Could you deduce *any* reason for the man's death, or the darkening of his appendage?" he asked, without lifting his eyelids.

"I could not. As for the cause of death, Graham assures me that his doctor is both competent and honest, so I am prepared to accept his diagnosis of a coronary. However, he was as perplexed as I was over the discoloration."

"What about the message? Can you offer any insight, Mr. Graham?" Holmes asked.

"Nay, Mr. Holmes. I have just returned to Scotland and don't ken what that message might mean."

"I asked Graham if his uncle had any dealings with a 'Duncan.' He does not know of any, but I thought perhaps we should inquire in Dundee if there was any such connection."

"Excellent, Watson. What did the inquiry yield?" Holmes opened his eyes.

"Well, nothing, Holmes, we were waiting for you before we acted. I did not know if you would approve of such a course."

He settled on the couch again, a wry grin on his face. "Did you make any other deductions about that message?"

"We both seem to feel that the letter was written to Graham's uncle, considering the closing. We also discussed that the clan mentioned may be a threat to that of Graham, or of course another clan. We also felt that it seems possible that the writer wanted Hamish's uncle to kill this MacGrioghair, and that possibly the aforementioned preemptively murdered the Duke."

"Splendid deduction." Holmes sat upright and dug his pipe from his pocket.

"Do you think that is what happened?" I asked.

"That, I cannot say," he stated, as he lit his pipe. "Only that it is a fair presumption at the moment. This message bears further scrutiny, but only after we follow the threads you and your friend have already pulled from this tangle."

"How do ye mean?" Hamish stepped forward, eager for action.

"This message is complex business. There are simply too many possibilities at present. Watson has often heard me espouse the precept that once you have eliminated the impossible, whatever remains, however improbable, must be the solution. We must narrow the field of the possible by eliminating the impossible."

"Tomorrow," he continued, turning to me, "you and Mr. Graham will head into Dundee and see if you can shed any light on this Duncan business. Your instincts there were correct. If you find a connection, we will follow it. If not, we will point our compass in another direction. I will head into the Highlands and follow the clan thread. I will try to ascertain if there is any bad blood against the Grahams that could have led to the Duke's murder."

The following morning, Graham and I headed into the city while Holmes left to pursue his inquires in the countryside. Graham offered to drive us himself so that Holmes could benefit from Liam's knowledge of the area, but Holmes would not hear of it. He contended that he could find his way and that, in fact, he thought the presence of the Duke's driver might compromise him if he chose to assume a fictitious identity. So, Holmes was granted use of a trap and Liam drove Hamish and me into Dundee.

As with most signs in Scotland, the one at the entrance of the city was written in two languages. Below the word "Dundee" appeared "Dun Deagh." Graham laughed as I tried to pronounce the Gaelic version of the city's name.

"*Dun* actually means 'fort.' It probably refers to the old battlements that stood on Dundee Law. Ye can make out the *law* from here, see?" He pointed to a knoll within the city.

"Do you mean the hill?" I asked.

"Aye, *law* means 'hill.' Dundee Law is what remains of an ancient volcanic plug. It is one hundred and seventy-five meters in height."

"Liam, didn't you tell me that the city was once walled?" I asked of the driver, recalling a comment he made when transporting me from the station to the castle.

"Aye," came his curt reply.

Hamish furthered the answer. "It was walled in the mid 1500s but the name predates that period. Most of the city was actually destroyed in 1547 when the Royal Navy bombarded it. A hundred years after that, the Marquess of Montrose led the royalists in a siege of Dundee."

"This English favoring fiend was a relative, I presume?" I joked to my friend.

"Aye, that he was."

"And yet, you are still welcome in the city?" I continued my jest.

He smiled. "There are just as many who favored union with your country as those opposed to it. But later, John Graham, Viscount of Dundee, climbed the *law* and raised the flag of our James II after the English had deposed him. So ye see, Grahams have fought on both sides of the issue."

"How politically advantageous," I laughed.

"Where would ye like to begin our query?" Hamish asked, shifting the conversation to the job at hand.

I lowered my voice to afford us some privacy from Liam. "Holmes suggested that we first see your uncle's lawyer. He stated that most rich men disclose matters to their attorney, given the protection of confidentiality. Perhaps he knows something of this Duncan character."

Graham whispered back, "I met with him to formalize the transfer of the estate, but of course, I did not discuss the mysterious nature of my uncle's death. He seemed a bonnie fellow though, this Mr. McCloud." Hamish raised his voice and called to the driver, "Liam, drive us down to Mr. McCloud's office. Ye remember, over by Murrygate and Commercial streets."

"Aye, sir."

Mr. McCloud was a jolly gregarious sort. He welcomed us into his office and did not seem to mind suspending the dictation he was giving to his secretary. Nor did he show the least bit of suspicion about our questions.

"Hmm…Duncan, Duncan, I do believe that the late Duke mentioned some business he planned to conduct with a Duncan Dunnahue."

I had assumed that Duncan was the surname and not the man's Christian name. After years of Holmes tutelage, I should have known better than to make such a presumption.

"Who might this Duncan Dunnahue be then?" Graham asked.

"I really cannot say except I recall some mention of whale oil. Your uncle was partner in several of the jute factories and may have been procuring oil for jute production. That is just a guess, however."

The lawyer read the disappointed expression on our faces. "Ye might want to try the Clayton Club. The Duke spent a lot of time there after his return from Africa. Perhaps one of the members can give more information."

"Well, Watson, what is our next move? The Clayton Club then?" Hamish asked outside on the sidewalk.

"I think you should head to the Clayton Club," I rubbed my chin in thought. "Act as if you mean to take over your uncle's membership and act as sociable as possible. When appropriate, pretend that you are trying to tie up some of your uncle's unfinished business dealings, which were but vaguely outlined in his ledgers. See if you can get any of them to speak of this Duncan Dunnahue or any other Duncan for that matter.

"I will go down to the wharf and see if I can find this Duncan Dunnahue amongst the whaling operations. I suggest that in three hours, we meet for a bit of lunch and compare notes. Do you have a suggested rendezvous point?"

"Liam," he called to his man minding the horses, "where can Dr. Watson and I get a wee spot of lunch this afternoon?"

"There's a bonnie café on High Street called The Round Tree," he called back, without hesitation.

"Until then," Graham said, shaking my hand.

Chapter 4

It was decided that Graham would take the coach to the Clayton Club. It would be wholly appropriate for the new Duke to arrive in such a fashion, while the conspicuous vehicle would hamper my own investigation. Even though I did not know my way around Dundee, and thus could have benefited from a guide such as Liam, I thought it not unlikely that I could find my way through use of Dundee's ample public transportation.

I climbed aboard a southbound horse-drawn tram, which in London we called an omnibus. I ascended the curved stairway toward the second level in order to possess an unobstructed view of the environs. The placard that adorned the front of the top level advertised "Keiller's Cocoa Chocolate." This surprised me. It was common knowledge that Dundee considered itself the birthplace of marmalade. Legend has it that Janet Keiller invented the jam at the turn of the 18th century, and in fact, Keiller's marmalade was one of the city's worldwide exports. However, I was not aware that that company had branched out into cocoa production.

The stops were frequent so it took some time before the tram turned onto Dock Street, along the waterfront of the Firth of Tay. The ship building industry was booming along the estuary. It was well known that The *RRS Discovery*, which had carried out Robert Falcon Scott's Antarctic expedition, had been built here, but that historic ship was but one of the thousands churned out of the Dundee shipyards.

I left the tram at Victoria Dock and plied my way through the chaos of activity found in any prosperous port. It was not hard to locate the section of waterfront that housed the whaling vessels. The whalers are a breed apart and their battles with the leviathans instilled a certain pride and swagger unique to their occupation. Whaling was a dying trade, but the needs of the jute spinners of Dundee kept the practice alive for the time being.

I attempted to inquire if anyone could help me find Mr. Duncan Dunnahue, but seafarers did not think a landsman such as myself worthy of their time and rudely brushed me aside. I was growing irritated and stopped for a moment to consider how Holmes might handle such an inquiry, when an alarm bell startled me back to consciousness.

Men began to scurry in one direction, calling loudly to one another in language so thick with Scottish brogue that I could not decipher their words. My eyes followed the men, and I at once saw the trouble. Thick black smoke was piling from the portholes of one of the ships further down the wharf.

I ran toward the fire, which had already attracted the aid of dozens. The wind shifted in my direction, causing the cloud of smoke to curtain my view. The dark fog was accompanied by the unpleasant odor of unprocessed whale oil.

By the time I negotiated my way to the edge of the wharf, a bucket brigade was already at work and the clanging of a bell grew increasingly louder, announcing that the city's fire brigade had almost reached the scene.

Within minutes, the firemen had arrived and their engine's steam pump was coursing water through the hoses. All who participated in the effort performed exemplarily, and inside of fifteen minutes the conflagration was under control.

"I am a doctor!" I bellowed, pushing my way forward. "Is anyone hurt? Does anyone require medical assistance?"

There were several men who had suffered scrapes or bruises, but although many still coughed to dispel the black fumes from their lungs, no one I attended to had sustained severe damage. I was just patching up the last lad in line when several firemen emerged from the ship's hold, carrying another victim. The man was black as coal from his emersion in the smoke filled hold, and smelt heavily of the ignited whale oil.

"Over here!" I called. "Over here, I am a doctor!"

"I'm afeared ye are too late for this lad," one of the firemen said, as they laid him on the planking in front of me.

Unfortunately, they were correct. The man had died of smoke inhalation and try as I might, he could not be revived. The victim was not dressed as a typical sailor or dockworker. His clothing, though blackened and oily, consisted of a fine tweed suit.

"Ah, poor Mr. Dunnahue," one of the longshoremen muttered removing his hat.

"Mr. who?" I gasped.

"Mr. Dunnahue. He had come aboard to do the barrel count. I guess he got trapped below when the fire started."

"Mr. Duncan Dunnahue?" I asked, still unsure I had heard correctly.

"Aye, that be him." The man lowered his head out of respect for the dead.

"So, captain, you say you do not know the cause of the fire, only that it began in the hold?"

"Aye, doctor, that's what I'm telling ye. We'll be sure to investigate, but these matters are usually the result of some bugger carelessly casting his match after lighting his tobacco. They usually get filed away as 'unsolved' and that's how they stay."

"I take it then that there is nothing noteworthy about this incident?"

"Nay...except," he paused.

"What is it, man?" I goaded him to continue.

"I wonder how the latch on the hold door locked." He rubbed his whiskers.

"What's that you say?"

"Oh, it's probably nothing, but the latch on the hatchway to the hold was fastened. I guess maybe it fell into the slot," he mused. "It is unusual, since most hatches are kept open when the unloading is about to commence."

"So, this Mr. Dunnahue was locked in the hold during the fire?"

"Aye, that he was. Though, I will go on record that he was nowhere near the doorway when he was found, so I doubt he even knew it was locked. I doubt it played a part in his death," he followed up, sensing the suspicion in my voice.

"Did anyone hear any banging? Perhaps he tried to draw attention, and when he could not, he searched for another means of exit," I continued.

"I will go on record," he repeated the phrase, "as saying that I doubt it. Given where the hatchway is situated, I believe that someone would have heard him banging."

I was unsure how to negotiate the trams to get me to The Round Tree where I was to meet Graham, so I hailed a cab instead. The driver knew the establishment and spurred the horse to get underway. As the waterfront receded behind me, I pondered the seemingly mysterious circumstances surrounding the demise of Mr. Dunnahue and his possible link to the dead Duke.

Graham was already seated when I arrived. He appeared to be on his second whiskey. Using Holmes's techniques, I recalled his pace of consumption from our nights in the library, and thus surmised that he had been waiting between twenty and thirty minutes.

"Ah, Watson, take a seat," he boomed. "Bring the gentleman...what would you like, man? An ale? Bring the good doctor an ale, lad!" he ordered the waiter.

Graham launched into his report. "Good news, Watson. I did as you said; I let on like I was trying to clear up some of my uncle's business concerns and the act bore fruit! Several of the gentlemen said that they heard my uncle discussing this Mr. Dunnahue. It was as the lawyer suspected, he was trying to negotiate a good deal for whale oil to be used in the jute mills," he beamed. "Why so glum, man? Do ye not hear what I'm telling ye, we're making progress!"

"Can I get ye gentlemen anything else?" the waiter asked.

"Aye. Gie a couple of peh's and tatties. Would that suit ye, Watson?"

It took me a moment to decipher his Scottish slang, but a meat pie and potatoes seemed fine to me. After the boy disappeared, I told Hamish what had occurred at the wharf.

"'Tis dark business," Graham said, his elation leaving him.

"Perhaps..." I rubbed my chin in thought. "Holmes would call it suggestive, but hardly conclusive."

We finished our meal, which I must admit, was quite good. "I didn't see Liam outside when I arrived..."

"He ran off to do some errands; he should be back by now." Hamish answered. "Ah, here he is."

We boarded the coach and rode back to Fintry Castle anxious to hear what Holmes had discovered on his sojourn into the Highlands and equally eager to get his views on the unfortunate Mr. Dunnahue.

Holmes assumed his comfortable position reclining on the couch. He closed his eyes and rubbed the base of his nose with his forefinger and thumb. "So, you found a Duncan with whom the Duke had recent contact, but he turned up dead."

"Do you suspect a connection?" I asked.

"Impossible to say. It is certainly curious, though." Holmes did not stir.

"But Mr. Holmes," Graham furthered, "the message said *give more gold to Duncan* and here we find my uncle negotiating a business transaction with this Duncan Dunnahue, who then met a sudden death."

"Indeed. The message may allude to the business association between the late Duke and the late whale oil agent. You and Watson also speculated that the writer might have been collaborating with your uncle to murder this MacGrioghair, who, in turn, killed your uncle in a preemptive strike. If that assumption is correct, the same individual may have killed this Duncan, as he is also mentioned in the letter." He grew silent for a moment. "But it is all speculative!" Holmes banged his fist on the wall, in an unusual display of frustration. "Data, we need concrete data!"

My friend caught himself, and smiled a self-deprecating smirk. He stood, lit his pipe, and began to pace the room. "If this Duncan was murdered, the felon is a crafty devil," he said, pointing at me with the stem of his pipe.

"What of your efforts, Holmes? Did you learn anything in the countryside?" I shifted the conversation.

"I learned to be more prudent in my investigations!" he smiled. "Here is another example of my fallibility, Watson. I hope you will include it in your chronicles. I did find out more about MacGrioghair. MacGrioghair is the Gaelic version of MacGregor, and MacGregors litter the region to our west, an area called 'the Trossachs,' around Loch Katrine. I could not uncover any evidence that any member of that clan bore ill will toward the late Duke; however, I did find tell of a Duncan who sought to confiscate land owned by the MacGregors. I was excited by this news and scampered off in search of this fellow they called 'Black Duncan!' "

"Did you find him?" I asked earnestly.

Graham broke out into a hearty laugh, and was joined by Holmes.

"Did I say something amusing?" I asked, confused.

"No, Watson, my haste is what is amusing, and I hope it provides a lesson against action before planning," Holmes spat out between chuckles.

"Black Duncan of the Cowl, did try to confiscate Mac-Gregor lands. He even tried to have the clan branded as out-laws. But it was in the 1500s!" Hamish explained the source of their merriment.

"Mr. Graham, Watson mentioned that your uncle recent-ly returned from South Africa?" Holmes asked, after his gaiety had subsided.

"Aye, that he did."

"What was his business there?"

"Diamonds, Mr. Holmes. He came to fancy the romance of the diamond and began to invest some capital in the mining operations. He originally planned a short stay in Cape Town, to check up on some of his investments. He ended up staying for nearly a year."

"Diamonds..." Holmes echoed the word. "A girl's best friend. Watson, and sometimes a man's worst enemy!"

"Do you suspect this business has to do with the diamond trade?" I ventured.

"There is no data to suggest it, but it bears further investigation. Those dazzling pieces of quartz have been the motivation for more than one murder."

That evening, like several before it, we discussed the case in detail. To be more precise, Graham and I discussed the case, while Holmes smoked, paced, or reclined. Occasionally, he would interrupt us to correct a detail or disprove an idea.

At breakfast the next morning, Graham attempted to revive our humor. "Watson, do ye recall my mentioning Jean Grenet in my letters?"

"I believe so...did he not own a neighboring plantation in India?"

"Aye, rubber was his game. His father had a plantation in Indo-China and he took the bold step of expanding their enterprise in India."

"If I remember the chap correctly, he served in the French colonial army in North Africa. I believe you said that you got on well considering that you were both former army men."

"Aye, he was not a bad sort. I have known Frenchies who were not worth their weight in truffles, but Grenet...well, I'll give Grenet credit for audacity! A Frenchy setting up shop in British territory? It is hard to imagine the nerve! Still, I have a small soft spot for the French. They did after all protect our Bonny Prince Charlie and lend support to the Jacobites.

"Well, you are right that I got on well with him," Graham continued, "except for one matter. In his outhouse, he hung a painting of the Duke of Wellington. Granted, we Scots have had our troubles with the English, but I was an officer in the British Army and I didn't take kindly to this insult. When I broached the matter, Grenet laughed and said that there was no more appropriate place for the Duke's image.

"The next time I hosted Grenet at my home, he was in for a surprise. I hung a painting in my own outhouse."

"Let me guess," I interjected, "it was of Bonaparte!"

"Nay, I hung my own portrait of Wellington."

"Wellington? Why on Earth would you do that?" I was flabbergasted.

"Grenet found it hysterical, complimenting me on the selection. I responded that I finally figured out why he had hung the picture in his own privy and thought I would be courteous enough to help him at my house as well."

"Grenet then gave me a confused look and questioned what I meant by 'helping him out.' "

"Well," I returned, "you obviously suffer from severe constipation and realized that the best method for making a Frenchman shit himself was to see the Duke of Wellington!"

Even the brooding Holmes laughed heartily at the amusing story.

Chapter 5

"Sir," Liam interrupted. "Donald says Bruce is dead."

Holmes suspended his coffee before it reached his lips.

I quickly explained, "Holmes, Donald is the gamekeeper and Bruce is one of the dogs, an English Pointer I think, used to flush fowl."

Holmes smiled and shrugged his shoulders, continuing his cup to his mouth.

"Alright, Liam, thank ye." Graham replied in a dismissive tone.

"Sir," Liam had not retreated. "He says there's something odd about it. The dog was young and should've lived a long time..."

"Aye, well these things happen, Liam. He was a good dog and will be missed."

"There's more, sir." He came closer. "His snout turned black as pitch."

The three of us tramped out to the kennel. There, Donald stood behind a wheelbarrow. Across the handles rested a shovel and inside the bed lie the dead dog. The hound's fur was white, but it had begun to fall out in patches around and behind his nose. It was easy to see the sharp blackness on the skin.

"Hold it there, Donald!" Graham commanded.

Graham questioned the gamekeeper as I examined the corpse, with Holmes peering over my shoulder.

"So you found him this way this morning?" Graham asked.

"Aye, sir," Donald replied. "Just like that." He gestured with a nod of his head.

"Is it similar, Watson?" Holmes whispered.

"Yes, it is the same affliction, without a doubt."

"Some dogs have black skin. Are you certain that this is the same markings as the other?" Holmes breathed into my ear.

"We hunted with this dog the other day. I'm certain that his snout did not have black skin. Further, look at this fur. It is falling away in clumps. No, something is afoul here and in my professional opinion, it shares an unpleasant resemblance to the appendage of the dead Duke."

"Alright, my good man, we won't delay you further," Holmes said, abruptly turning to the gamekeeper. "However, I would like to know a few things first. Do any of the other dogs seem ill?"

"Nay, sir."

"Have any of them begun to act oddly?"

"Nay."

"Was this dog, what was his name? Bruce?"

"Aye, named after Robert the Bruce, he was," Donald explained.

"Indeed. Was Bruce out of his pen recently?" Holmes finished his question.

"Aye, last night, when I let him out to do his business."

"Was he out of your sight at all during that interlude?"

"Nay. He ran around a bit. He scampered off that way a few hundred yards, near them shrubs, and ducked into that thicket to do his business. He always was a shy one about that." He mused over the dog's odd desire for privacy.

"What time would you say that was?"

"Oh, between seven and seven-thirty."

"When he came back to the pen, was he his normal self?" Holmes queried.

"Aye, he was the same old scampish mutt," Donald recalled in a somber tone.

"Very good then. I hope he has a frolicking time in Heaven, if such a place exists for canines," Holmes stated, in an awkward attempt at easing the gamekeeper's mind.

After Donald had wheeled his cargo around the corner of the castle, Holmes made a beeline for the thicket without uttering a word. Graham and I hurried to keep up.

"What is it Holmes?" I panted.

"Come now Watson, surely you must see that either someone crept into the dog pen last night and singled out that hound, which is highly improbable, or the dog met his doom as a result of an encounter in that thicket."

When we reached the bushes Holmes dove in, leaving us unsure whether to follow him into the shrubbery or simply wait for his reemergence. I instructed we do the latter, knowing Holmes's ire at the disruption of a crime scene. Many times I listened to him blast a policeman for treading over footprints or disturbing evidence.

It was but a few minutes wait however before Holmes beckoned us from inside the thicket.

"Watson, Graham, come here!" the disembodied voice called from the brush.

We ducked and twisted our way through the tangle of branches until we came to a very small clearing, perhaps two meters in diameter.

"Look here." Holmes pointed with his walking stick.

On the ground, there was a hole approximately fifteen centimeters wide.

"You can clearly see that the dog dug this out. See his nail prints here at the edge?"

"Aye, I see them clearly now that you've pointed them out," Graham stated.

"However, he is not the first to dig here, nor was he the last one in this clearing. You see the bits of grass clinging to these clumps of dirt? The grass is dead. It was not merely dug out last night."

"You mean someone buried something here, and the dog found it?" I asked.

"Precisely."

"What was it, and who buried it?" I asked.

"Ah, those are the real questions! What it was, I cannot say because whoever buried it returned to remove it after the dog left."

"What? How do ye know that?" Graham asked.

Holmes stood and tapped several broken branches with his cane. "This was done recently, see the sap? It is still wet. Unfortunately, this ground is too hard to hold any footmarks. I had hoped the perpetrator would have stepped on the pile of soil, but no such luck."

"Let us walk a bit," Holmes stated, abruptly diving through the brush. We followed, and after Graham and I emerged back into the field, we three strolled along the grounds.

After a good minute of silence, Holmes spoke. "Mr. Graham, if I recall Watson's letter properly, your uncle's routine was no different the night before he died than any other night. Is that correct?"

"Aye, Mr. Holmes. He gave some instructions to a few of the staff, and then retired about quarter past eleven, which was his habit. A few of the servants preceded him to bed, but Liam helped him prepare for the night, and checked to make sure he had no other needs. Having assured himself that the Duke did not require any victuals, Liam informed Mary, the cook that she would not be needed, and could retire. The night passed quietly, seemingly without incident. Liam found my uncle's body the next morning."

"You said that he gave a few of the staff instructions. Which ones? What did he tell them?" Holmes asked.

"According to Liam, he told Donald to clean his fowling piece in the morning, as he would like to scare up some game after breakfast. He also told Erin, one of the maids, to continue removing the tapestries from storage, and replace them on the walls. He also said something to Kyata, but it was difficult to ascertain exactly what, since her English is almost nonexistent. Liam believed that he told her to help Erin with the tapestries."

113

"Kyata. Yes. That is the African lass, if I'm not mistaken?"

"Aye, Mr. Holmes."

"If indeed the dog ingested some undetectable toxin back in that thicket," I mused, "he showed no ill effects until sometime later."

"Precisely, Watson. The same might well be said of the Duke. Whatever overcame that dog led to a silent death some time later. We can estimate that his life ended somewhere during the following eight hours."

"I must correct you, Holmes, the interval was closer to eleven hours between the time the dog returned to the pen and when Donald found him the following morning."

"Ah, Watson, you forget the Duke. His death occurred between the hours of eleven-thirty and seven-thirty a.m. If anything, I would suggest that the dog succumbed in less time than the Duke, rather than more, given his inferior weight."

"So ye believe it was poison, Mr. Holmes?" Graham interjected.

"It seems likely. You said that Mary the cook held no ill feeling against the Duke?"

"Certainly not. She wept terribly at his passing. She had known him since his boyhood. Also, she and Liam ate the remains of my uncle's dinner the night he passed, yet they did not fall ill."

"They said they ate the leftovers," Holmes stated, with a wry grin. His point reminded us that the alleged innocuous behavior of the staff was based solely on their own statements, taken after the fact.

Holmes stopped abruptly. "I am going to Edinburgh. I need to consult with a couple of professors at the university, and send a cable to Antwerp. Watson, I need you and the Duke to do a bit of grave robbing."

Graham and I froze in our tracks. "What's that?" I gasped.

"Oh, don't be so dramatic, Watson. Dig up that dog and perform an autopsy. Do so on the sly, however. I have suspicions about the staff."

"Holmes, I am hardly a coroner," I objected.

"I know, Watson, but you will have to do. In my bag, you will find a small chemistry kit. You have participated in enough of my chemical analysis over the years that you can test the beast for toxins, of that I am sure."

I had indeed learned to perform that task, but poisons can be a complex business and I was not sure that I, or even Holmes for that matter, could uncover this venom if poison was even the true culprit.

"Mr. Holmes," Graham gently grabbed his arm before he could leave us. "Ye suspect one of the staff in this business?" he asked, the concern evident in his voice.

"Do not worry yourself. I have only the faintest notion, but it will do no harm to be cautious. If what I suspect is true, neither you nor Watson are in harm's way."

That afternoon, Graham nonchalantly coaxed the burial place from Donald, and late that night we prepared for our ghoulish enterprise.

The moon was the thinnest sliver of crescent, and the clouds were sparse. The stars were bright, but since the moon emitted so little light, the night was a dark one.

I carried the spade and sack in one hand and my medical bag in the other. Hamish led the way, holding Holmes's case of chemical equipment and the shaded lantern. The spot was easy to find since the overturned earth formed a small mound devoid of grass. The shovel bit into the soft pile and in a matter of minutes the deceased pup was in the bag and we were creeping to a shed where the gardening equipment was housed.

Hamish took a discarded sack and covered the lone window to prevent our lamplight from escaping. We cleared the workbench and placed the departed upon the planking. Using my medical tools, I opened up the dog and took tissue samples from his vital organs and drew a vial of blood. I reexamined the snout, but as I had found earlier, I could not discern anything beyond the conditions already described.

This seemed odd business indeed. In my wildest imaginations, I would never have guessed that I would be conducting a postmortem on a dog under the cover of night. Yet, the peculiar nature of my mission should not have caused me such bewilderment since it was always the irregular, the bizarre, indeed the complex cases, that Holmes relished and have enthralled my readers the most.

I set up the test tubes, beakers, and other equipment from Holmes's kit and began performing experiments upon the samples. I endeavored to be as methodical and precise as Holmes would have been himself. Yet, despite the thoroughness of my analysis, I did not detect any evidence of toxin or even of any malfeasance.

I was dejected by the results. I wiped off my scalpel and other instruments and replaced them in my bag. I began to disassemble the chemical equipment when Hamish grabbed my arm.

"What is it?" I asked, startled.

"Hush! Listen!" he hissed.

I heard nothing, but I trusted my companion's judgment. Although we had both served in the army, I had only served in the medical corps while Graham had been a member of an elite regiment. I have known soldiers to possess an uncanny instinct attuned to danger.

I remained still as a statue, but I still did not hear anything above the normal symphony of nighttime insects.

Suddenly, the door burst open. The action was so startling that I jumped backward and fell over a crate, bringing down the shelves that lined the wall. An avalanche of burlap, boxes, and other implements crashed down, burying me completely.

I struggled to free myself, but the mass of cloth and equipment was daunting. Voices filtered through the pile as I clamored fruitlessly to extricate myself. I dreaded that Graham was left to face the intruder alone. Frantically, I worked to throw off the heap. Suddenly, hands pierced the debris, gripping each of my wrists. I was yanked forward, finally emerging from the mess. It took a moment for my eyes to adjust, but I was ready for action, prepared to help defend my friend.

"As graceful as ever, eh Watson?"

"Holmes? What are you doing here?" I stammered, perplexed to see my friend.

"Oh, I thought of something that could not wait, so I had to return. I am sorry that I put a fright into you," he chuckled. "The Duke nearly crowned me with a piece of firewood, and I expect I would have deserved it for bursting in here in such a way."

"What is it?" I asked, brushing the dust from my clothing.

"First, let me ask, have you tested the specimen?"

I explained the tissue samples I took and the experimentations I made.

"I would have conducted the very same tests, Watson."

His confirmation of this fact put my mind at ease. I was fretful that I had fouled up the endeavor.

"Did you come back suspecting that I would neglect one of the experiments?" I asked, still after the reason for Holmes's abrupt return.

"No. I had complete confidence in you, Watson. I merely wanted to examine the corpse myself. I did not think it wise to dig up the fellow a second time and tempt discovery."

Holmes moved over to the workbench and slid the lantern near the dead dog's face. He pulled his magnifying lens from an inside pocket of his coat, and bent close to the hound's snout. Graham and I stayed a short distance away, for fear of disturbing the light or disrupting Holmes's concentration. Yet, from our vantage point we could see that Holmes played his lens completely over the dog's muzzle, examining its entirety in great detail.

The examination took a long five minutes. Although we stood several feet behind Holmes, and the light from the lamp was dull, I thought I detected the faintest hint of a smile flash in the corner of my friend's mouth.

"All right, gentlemen," Homes abruptly addressed us, returning his lens to his pocket. "You may re-inter dear old Bruce."

"Did you find something?" I asked.

"Perhaps. There is a glimmer Watson, nothing more. I should have a better grip on it after my trip to Edinburgh. If you gentlemen do not mind replacing the body, I would like to retire. It would be helpful to grab a few hours rest before returning to Dundee to catch the earliest train to Edinburgh."

As we returned the body to the sack, I peered as intently as possible at the snout. If Holmes had indeed discovered something new, it escaped my faculties.

Chapter 6

I hope you do not think me a brute, remaining away from my wife for such an interval. I thought of her often and wrote her practically every other night. Our bond was a strong one, and she offered me full support. She was sympathetic of the duty I felt to help a man who had been instrumental in my own rescue in Afghanistan, but she also intimately understood the value of the cases undertaken by Holmes and myself, since my introduction to her came from her own entreaties for help. Solving her case was reward for Holmes, but she was my prize in the problem you have doubtlessly read, entitled *The Sign of Four*.

"Watson, when do you think Holmes will return?" Hamish asked.

"I cannot say. As precise as Holmes appears, his schedule is hardly regular. Once he is on a scent, he follows where it leads. He may be back tonight, or perhaps not for several days."

"Surely if he were to be absent for any length of time, he would cable us, would he not?" Graham asked.

I thought for a moment. "I expect we would only receive word if he had instructions for us. The idea of keeping us informed of his progress, or that we might be concerned for his safety, would not occur to him."

"Ye and he have been comrades for some time now; certainly, he would consider your distress in not knowing if harm befell him."

I chuckled. "That is not how his mind works. He is analysis personified, and thus, not overly preoccupied with the feelings of others. That is not to say that he is inhuman. He would put his life on the line for a friend, for a stranger in fact, but sentimentalities are foreign to his nature."

"Given that Mr. Holmes has left us for an undetermined amount of time, and that he has left us without any task of our own to perform, I wonder if ye would consider a pleasant sideline to take our minds off of this business for a short spell?"

"What do you have in mind?" I asked, curious.

"This is the last weekend in August, which marks the beginning of the Cowal Highland Gathering. I have been away from Scotland for a long time..." A pang of regret crossed his features. "I thought it might be a nice distraction to attend the games."

"The Cowal Gathering? That is the site of the Highland Games is it not?"

"Aye. Ye are a fan of athletic contest, are ye not, Watson?"

"Indeed. The Gathering is in Dunoon, if I am not mistaken?" I asked, intrigued at the possibility, though concerned about traveling away from the site of our mystery.

He sensed both my enthusiasm and apprehension. "Aye, but we could make it in under four hours. The Caledonian Railway runs a line from Dundee to Glasgow. It is but a short trip down the Clyde to Dunoon from there."

I pondered for a moment. "Alright," I stated, decidedly. "However, Liam must be instructed to leave word at the telegraph office if Holmes returns, or has sent instructions for us. We will wire the office regularly to see if we are needed."

In a short time, we were in the Tay Bridge Station booking passage to Glasgow. The train rumbled westward toward the central lowlands and the "Second City of the Empire."

Graham and I gave our minds some respite from the mysterious events at Fintry Castle. On the journey, we spoke of events big and small, literature, and even football. Our compartment echoed with peals of laughter and boisterous camaraderie. On later reflection, I hoped our conduct did not greatly disturb the other passengers.

The red and blond sandstone buildings of Glasgow rose in the distance, and a short time later, we were in Buchanan Street Station. I would have preferred our train terminate in either the St. Enoch or Queen Street Stations, given their much greater architectural grandeur. Graham informed me that those outlets were for the North British Railway, and we would have had to first travel to Edinburgh, rather than straight from Dundee to debark at either of those sites. Before leaving the station, we cabled back to the prearranged telegraph office in Dundee, but no message from or about Holmes had arrived.

Hamish's long sojourn from his homeland had not eroded his familiarity, and he effortlessly led the way to the proper wharf and booked us passage upon one of the many paddle steamers heading down the River Clyde to Dunoon.

Glasgow was the second most populated city in the British Isles, and the fourth largest in Western Europe. Yet, those en route to the Highland Games had swelled that number even further. We jostled our way through an odd assortment of conservatively dressed professionals and proud folk adorned in the traditional kilts and tartans of a time gone by.

The climate in this area of Scotland was markedly different from that of Dundee and Edinburgh. The Gulf Stream kissed the west coast and even penetrated the estuary of the Firth of Clyde. The result was a warmer, milder atmosphere.

The ride "down the water," as the locals called it, was a pleasant one. We chugged past Cloch Light House in Gourock, and slipped past Holy Loch on the Cowal Peninsula. Above the town, the ancient remains of Dunoon Castle came into view. Little remained of the structure, but Graham explained that it had been built in the 1300s by the Lamonts. Mary Queen of Scots had resided there in the 1560s, but the Earls of Argyll assumed control, demonstrating their loyalty to the English crown with a titular rent payment of a single red rose each year. The castle had been reduced to rubble as a result of the 1685 rebellion.

We bounced down the gangplank and joined the other passengers in the journey up the pier. At the end of the structure, a sign announced that we had arrived in Dunoon, or "Dunomhainn" to those who preferred the Gaelic.

The town teemed with people, and the number wearing traditional Scottish garb had multiplied twenty-fold. If somewhat subdued elsewhere, here, it was evident that the Scottish flaunted the fact that they are a separate people from the English. I did not find this offensive in the least. In fact, a measure of Scot blood runs through my own veins, as evidenced by my middle name, which is the same as Graham's first.

We walked up Ferry Brae, in search of a telegraph office where we might check back with Dundee. As we strolled, Graham told me the origin of the Highland Games. It seems that in the 1200s, King Malcolm II was in search of a royal messenger. He sought the fastest man in Scotland for the job, so he held a footrace to the top of Craig Choinnich and determined that the winner would be his man. These were the first Highland Games. During the Jacobite rebellions, the Games became a surreptitious means for Scots to train as warriors. The English had forbidden clansmen to bear arms or practice martial skills. The Games allowed the clans to gather and practice under the auspices of athletic competition.

"Any word from Holmes?" I asked, as Hamish stepped from the telegraph office.

"Nay, nothing yet."

After a bite of lunch, we continued on to the festival. Vendors hawked their wares, and the wail of the bagpipes filled the air. I know many, even in England, who consider the song of the pipes inspirational, but for some reason, I have always found the tones sad. Perhaps it is simply the moaning pitches that stir a melancholy mood, or perchance the music draws subconscious recollections of the poor Highlanders trying to eke out an existence from the cold deep lochs and pilfered cattle.

Graham was correct in asserting that I enjoy sport, and thus, the competitions that formed the basis for the games were of interest to me. The first event I had the pleasure of witnessing was the Braemar Stone Put where the men hurled stones of approximately twenty-five pounds in weight. I have watched similar contests elsewhere, but in those cases the thrower was allowed to run up to the line before releasing his projectile. Not so with the Braemar Stone. The bulky tartan-clad Scotsmen had to throw their load from a standing position. The average toss was between five and seven meters. I was amazed at these distances, but even more so when I edged up to a discarded stone and hefted it myself. I doubt I could have tossed it a single meter, and even at that paltry distance risked injury to my spine and musculature.

The next competition was the Scottish Hammer Throw. In this event, a round metal ball approximately twenty pounds in weight is affixed to a wooden shaft approximately one and one quarter meters in length. The thrower stands in a stationary position and spins the hammer over his head before releasing it over his shoulder. Again the distances were astounding. Most throws were greater than fifteen meters.

Another contest not dissimilar to the hammer throw is the "weight for height" contest. Here a fifty-six pound weight is attached to a handle. Contestants attempt to toss the weight over a lateral bar. They must use only one hand, and if successful, they advance to a subsequent round where the height of the bar is increased. The chap who won cleared over four meters.

Similar to the weight for height event was a rural adaptation called the "sheaf toss." Here a bundle of straw weighing nine kilograms is thrown over a bar, like in the weight for height competition. However, rather than being thrown by hand, the contestant must use a pitchfork!

There were other events not terribly unlike the aforementioned. However, the most unique had to be the caber toss. In this contest, the athlete tries to "turn the caber." What this entails is amusing, bizarre, and difficult all at the same time. A long tapered pine pole is stood on end and lifted, with the larger end in the air. The fellow holds the tapered end, balancing the shaft in this upright position. Next, he runs forward and hurls the log. The objective is not distance, however. The goal is for the throw to cause the pole to spin in such a way that the larger end hits the ground first, and then the tapered one follows, striking the ground in a twelve o'clock position (perpendicular to the ground). Judges score the contest based on how closely the throws duplicate the perfect twelve o'clock toss.

"What do ye think of the games?" Hamish asked, when the caber toss had concluded.

"Very entertaining. In India, I believe I once saw a makeshift version. I was some distance away, confined to a ship waiting to sail. A few soldiers on the shore found a rusted cannon ball. They proceeded to perform throws in a fashion similar to that of the stone put we saw earlier. At first, I thought the fellows had invented a contest to pass the time, and their odd stances a mere lark. I could offer no other explanation as to why they would not run before throwing, to achieve the greatest distance possible. Now, I understand that they must have been Scots imitating games they had played at home. In fact, now that I consider it," I recollected, "they also procured a discarded telegraph pole and tossed it in a fashion similar to the caber toss we just witnessed!"

Hamish laughed. "That's the wonderful thing about Scottish sports, they are not very complicated. It seems like they all revolve around throwing heavy objects."

After the athletics had concluded for the day, the crowd moved in the direction of a large platform.

"What is going on over there?" I asked, indicating the direction with my cane.

"The dance competitions are nearing the finals."

All day long I had heard music and the familiar stomping of the Highland dances echoing across the fields. There had always been a crowd near the pavilion, but obviously spectators were massing to watch the best dancers compete for the crown.

"Let us have a gander. They are about to begin the Gillie Calum," Graham announced.

"Gillie Calum?"

"Aye, the Sword Dance."

As the musicians readied, contestants loosened their muscles. The men were dressed in the familiar kilt and tartans hose, but wore black shoes that laced up the calf. Tucked into one stocking was a "sgian dhubh," a type of ceremonial dagger. Their torsos were covered with a small jacket and a bonnet sat atop their heads. Hanging around their waist was a sporran, or small leather pouch adorned with silver.

Looking around at the competitors, I asked, "I don't see any women preparing for the contest. Are all of the dancers men?"

"Aye, do ye recall how I told ye that the games were used to secretly train warriors?"

"Yes."

"Well the same is true of the dances. They are artistic, without doubt, but the endurance, dexterity, and strength of the men is tested as well. The dances allowed for training and also for chieftains to judge the abilities of the men."

"I do believe I once saw the soldiers of a Highland regiment dancing before an officer. I thought it queer at the time. Do you suppose they were training?"

"Aye. The Highlanders still use the dances to train."

The musicians began playing the tune of "Gillie Challum" which I am told dates back to the King Malcolm of whom Shakespeare wrote in *MacBeth*.

"Is the dance a victory dance, or a pre-battle ritual?" I asked as a lad with a huge claymore sword passed in front of me.

"Some claim the former, some the latter. One story tells of King Malcolm dancing over his bloody sword and the severed head of his enemy. Another states that the clansmen danced over the swords before battle, and if they kicked them, it was an ill omen boding a difficult fight ahead."

The contest finally began, as the men took turns dancing over their crossed claymores. The determination read on their faces and their skill and agility was evident as they pranced over the swords. When a champion was eventually named, I must admit that I did not see any difference from the other contestants. They all seemed exceptionally skilled to me, but then again, I am sure I missed the nuances visible to an expert.

We stayed for two other dance competitions. The first was the Highland Fling. Hamish informed me that this was the oldest of the dances and originated as a celebration after a victory in battle. It was not hard to determine that the dance had martial origins, as the men pranced over a "targe," a small round shield with an iron spike protruding from its center. One bit was confusing though.

"What are they doing with their hands?" I asked, confused as to why they appeared to be clutching at the sky.

"That aspect imitates a stag on a hillside. The clawing represents his antlers."

"Oh," I replied, unsure how a stag on a hill related to victory in battle.

The final contest was the "Seann Triubhas" which translated to "old trousers." This dance told a historical story. In 1745 Bonnie Prince Charlie lost to the English on the field at Culloden. As a result, Highlanders were forbidden from wearing the kilt. The dance commemorated the Proscription Repeal, which restored the right to wear traditional Scottish garb. The movements clearly pantomimed legs shaking off the trousers in favor of their beloved kilt.

It had been a long day and we returned to the streets of Dunoon for our supper. Together, we traveled to the telegraph office to ascertain if we could remain in town for the night, or if we needed to travel back to Fintry immediately.

"Ah, there is a message from Mr. Holmes!" Graham announced as the device clicked away and the operator busily scribbled.

The clerk handed the note across the counter. Graham paid him as I read the message.

"Well, what does it say, man?" Hamish demanded.

"He will be back tomorrow morning. He says that he has gathered another piece of the puzzle."

Chapter 7

We chose to stay the night in Dunoon and catch the earliest paddle steamer to Glasgow in the morning, and then the
next available train to Dundee. Due to the games, most of the
hotels in town were filled. There were a few vacancies at the
more expensive establishments, and luckily Graham's wealth
and title enabled us to procure lodging along the firth at the
spacious Hunters Quay Hotel.

We ate a late supper in the dining room, and adjourned to
the lounge for a bit of brandy and tobacco before retiring. In
guarded tones, we discussed the case and speculated upon
Holmes's discovery. Although our deductions and opinions
were dubious, the discussion served to focus our attention
back upon the mystery after our day of diversion.

We awoke to a bright, sunny August day and crowded
onto the ship for the trip back up the River Clyde. In Glasgow,
we retraced our path to the Buchanan Street Station and
boarded an eastbound train for Dundee.

We shared a compartment with a gentleman and his wife
as we steamed across Scotland, so we avoided any discussion
of the case. The trip seemed a speedy one, despite my mind's
preoccupation with hypothesizing upon our puzzle.

We left the train at the now familiar Tay Bridge Station.
Since we had only planned to be away for the day, we had
traveled lightly and did not require waiting for any luggage.
As we moved away from the train, I noticed a peculiar fellow
who appeared to be eyeing us. He carried a small carpetbag
and wore a black coat and slouch hat, as well as small dark
spectacles. Stringy gray hair peaked from beneath his hat. He
wore a bushy mustache that was the same tint as his hair. His
nose was bulbous, and appeared rather too large for his face.

As we walked toward the station house, I noticed that he
followed our movements. I stopped and bent down, feigning to

tie my shoestring. I threw a sideways glance in his direction, and noticed that he had halted as well. He surveyed the cloudless sky and then pulled out a pocket pad and pretended to sift through the pages. I have partnered with Holmes long enough to observe when a fellow is disingenuous in his activities.

I stood and walked on, unable to alert Graham that we had attracted a shadow. Fifty feet further, I stopped again and offered Hamish a cigarette. He declined, but I pulled the silver case from my breast pocket to obtain one myself, using the case as a mirror. The man had stopped as well.

"I have to use the water closet before we acquire a cab," I informed Graham as I closed the case.

Hamish followed, and I pulled him aside as soon as we entered. The room was busy, as one might expect in a crowded station, but I hazarded that if overheard, it would do no harm.

"There is a man following us," I whispered.

The expression on my friend's face betrayed both his surprise and alarm. "What do ye propose we do?" He looked around.

"I do not suspect him to enter, he will undoubtedly be waiting outside and continue his pursuit when we exit. It is no secret where we are going…yet I would like to know the purpose of this chap." I collected my thoughts for a moment and concocted a stratagem. "When we leave here, we will separate. He will have to choose one of us to follow, and when he does, we may know more about his intentions. Whichever one of us is not being tailed should double back and follow in turn. But be very careful, as not to be seen."

"If he chooses me, where should I lead him?" Graham asked.

"Hmm. Whichever one of us is being followed should lead him through the busy districts so that it will be easier for the other to trail. If he stays with you for ten minutes, turn the next corner and duck into the first doorway. I will run up and we will confront him together in an ambush. If he is following me, you do the same."

We steadied our resolve and steeled our nerve and then left the washroom. Graham looked around and moved two-dozen meters up the platform but then stopped. I could see why he did so. The curious man in black was nowhere in sight. I circled the station looking for him, hoping he would latch himself to me again, but I had no luck. When I returned, I moved over to Graham and asked if he had caught sight of the fellow in my absence. He answered in the negative.

"What do we do now?" he asked.

I shrugged my shoulders. "Perhaps I was mistaken about being followed." Although I was sure that I had marked the tail correctly. "I suppose we should continue to Fintry, perhaps Holmes has already returned."

Outside the station, Graham hailed an enclosed four-wheeler. As we climbed into the coach, Hamish commanded the driver to take us to Fintry Castle. Just as the cab was pulling away, the door on the far side flung open and the mysterious man in black leaped in, closing the door behind him.

"I say, pray explain yourself, sir!" I exclaimed.

"Dr. Watson, you surprise me," he stated in a gravely voice. "You are very irritable this morning. Were you in such a hurry to leave Dunoon that you neglected breakfast? Could you not even grab a bite in Glasgow, before the train departed?"

Graham and I were both aghast. Had this queer chap been shadowing us for the last two days?

"Listen here, what is it you want?" Graham finally ejected in a menacing tone.

"Only to return to Fintry and help you solve your little problem."

His voice began the sentence in the same gravely tenor, but by the time he had reached the word "little," it had changed, and seemed more familiar. A moment later, the hat peeled off, and the gray hair with it. His other hand removed the nose and mustache in one motion and quickly returned to pull off the spectacles.

"Mr. Holmes!" Graham barked in astonishment.

Holmes laughed. "I thought I had better reveal myself before the Duke tossed me from the carriage without the benefit of a stoppage."

Despite the number of times I had seen Holmes adopt a disguise, he could still fool me at will. I have stated before that had my friend chosen the stage for a profession he would have done the thespian trade a grand service.

"Would you care to explain?" I asked, my good humor quickly returning.

"Oh, Watson, it is trifling really. I needed some information from a jewel expert in Edinburgh. He is the foremost authority in the trafficking of diamonds, which as you might guess makes him a criminal by profession. It would not do to call on him as my regular person. The sight of me would have caused him to flee, thinking I meant to place him under arrest. So, I adopted this guise and had I not been late for the train, I would have shed it before I boarded. Unfortunately, I shared a compartment with two ladies, and thus could not transform on the passage to Dundee without a needless barrage of questions. Therefore, I decided to return to the castle before I shed this identity. I fancied a lark by following you and climbing into your cab.

"By the way, Watson, the cigarette case maneuver was excellent! However, never feign to tie your shoe when it is already tied to begin with. It gives you away immediately. Rather, pretend you have a pebble inside, it is a harder deception to detect."

"Your telegram stated that you had acquired another piece of the puzzle," I said, directing our focus back on the case.

"Indeed." He smiled.

Graham and I waited expectantly for some moments before Holmes spoke.

"Watson, you know that I must reveal things in my own way, in my own time. I do indeed have another piece, but I have yet to fit it into place."

I read the disappointment on Graham's face as we sped back to the scene of his uncle's mysterious death.

The sky had clouded over in one of those leaden canopies so common in the British Isles. By the time we had reached the castle, a hazy drizzle had begun to fall. All three of us admitted to hunger pangs and took ourselves to the dining room. Liam promised a speedy return with cold duck left over from the previous night.

"Ah, they have returned the tapestries," I stated, admiring the wall coverings.

While we waited for our meal, Hamish and I surveyed the woven artwork. Holmes did not show the slightest interest, and sat at the table cleaning his pipe.

"I recall some of these," Graham said, gazing at the depictions, "but I left Scotland many years ago, so I cannot claim to be expert in them all."

"This one," said I, pointing to the first in the row, "appears to be a rendition of the conversion of Saint Paul. I am no biblical scholar, but the artwork bore a striking resemblance to the famous painting by Jean Fouquet."

"Aye. Right you are. I believe it is Flemish in origin. This one was commissioned by a Scot," he said, as he indicated the next in line. "It shows the coronation of Robert the Bruce."

"What of this? It looks like a landscape of this very castle and its surroundings," I said, peering at the next tapestry.

"Aye. It is newer than the previous two. If memory serves, it was woven in the early eighteenth century."

"These are some odd markings at the bottom here," I pointed to a dozen short, separate vertical and horizontal black lines across the foot of the cloth.

"Some sort of design, I suppose," Graham mused.

There were three more tapestries. One was a battle scene, another a collage of biblical events, and the last, a design featuring the crest of the Grahams and heraldry of the Duke of Montrose.

Liam returned with our meal, so Hamish and I discussed the remaining scenes from our seats at the table. Holmes's appetite was strong, but he remained quietly lost in his own thoughts.

"Excuse me, Liam?" Holmes roused as the butler deposited a bowl of fruit on the table.

"Aye, can I be of service, sir?" Liam asked, stepping over to Holmes.

"I see you have lemons, limes, and oranges here." He picked up a lime and rolled it between his fingers. "How long have you had citrus fruits at the castle?"

"Pardon, sir?"

"Forgive me. Pray tell, have you been able to fortify your pantry with these items just recently, or for many weeks?"

"I should say many weeks, perhaps two months. Mary begins stocking them as soon as they come to market, despite the cost. She says they ward off the scurvy."

"Indeed, eh, doctor?" Holmes's gray eyes twinkled in my direction.

"Surely, though not everyone can afford such luxuries," I returned.

"Thank you, my good man," Holmes said, dismissing the butler.

Rather than peel the lime he held, Holmes sliced it in half and then carved the fruit from inside the peel. Despite the tartness of the treat, his lips wore a curious smile.

That night, we assumed our customary station in the library. As usual, Holmes reclined on the settee. Although this time he was studying a medical journal he had pulled from one of the shelves. Graham and I engaged in a game of chess.

"If you need assistance translating any of those medical terms, pray do not hesitate to ask," I called over my shoulder, half in jest.

"We all need things translated now and again, aye, Watson?" Graham joined in, pointing a jab in my direction.

I laughed. "Indeed, I would never have understood that secret message had you not translated it from the Gaelic."

Holmes shot bolt upright upon the couch. "What? What was that you said?" he exclaimed.

"I...I merely said that had Graham not translated the message from Gaelic..."

"Of course! I have been a complete fool!" he cut me off. "The original, do you still have the original?" he impatiently asked our host.

"Aye, I do. It is here in the desk. He withdrew the message he had first found.

Holmes grabbed the document. He rubbed the paper between his fingers and then scanned it across and up and down.

"I did not know you could read Gaelic, Holmes," I said, leaving my seat at the chess board.

"I cannot," he replied dismissively, though still peering intently at the message.

"The translation, where is it?" He brusquely extended a hand toward Graham.

"Here ye are, Mr. Holmes." Graham handed over his transcription, shooting a puzzled and intrigued look in my direction.

Holmes moved around behind Hamish's ornate oak desk and took a seat. He placed both sheets upon the blotter and rubbed his hands in delight.

"Now, gentlemen, if you will extend me the use of this room for the extent of the evening, I would be much surprised if I did not produce some conclusive result by morning."

Of course, Graham and I acquiesced. We carried our chessboard to another room of the castle and lit a fire to ward off the chill that the rain had brought.

Chess is a game that requires supreme concentration, and I must admit, I was terribly handicapped by my mind's predisposition to wander back to Holmes in the library. Fortunately, we remained evenly matched, given that Hamish's own eyes frequently drifted from the board and down the hallway to the closed oaken doors behind which my friend was employing his unique talents.

Chapter 8

It was past midnight when Graham and I retired, but yellow light still peeked beneath the doors of the library as we climbed the stairs. The next morning, bright sunlight streamed through my bedroom window. I performed my morning duties with some haste and Hamish and I emerged simultaneously from our rooms. As we descended the landing, the library door opened and Holmes appeared in the hallway.

"Heavens, Holmes, did you sleep at all?" I asked.

"Watson, you know that my constitution works conversely to that of most people. Mental stimulation invigorates me. I am most weary on those occasions when my faculties are unemployed. But I read that displeasure upon your face, doctor. Before you lecture me upon the physical benefits of sleep, yes, I did catch a few winks upon the settee."

Although the sun was shining, the rain that had fallen the previous day had not evaporated, so the lingering dampness necessitated us to breakfast in the dining room rather than upon the terrace.

"So then, Holmes, any luck?" I asked.

"Progress, Watson. Not luck. I have it fairly untangled; there is but one final piece."

Our coffee had just been refilled, when the sun had risen sufficiently to throw its beams through the stained glass windows that adorned the high wall behind us. The light streamed through and projected the images across the room onto the wall facing us.

The sight struck me. "It is beautiful, Hamish," I said pointing to the images. "It reminds me of a magic lantern."

Holmes, not known for his admiration of aesthetic beauty, gazed at the images for a long moment, tapping his fingertips together. A smile burst across his face and he leapt from his seat, and paced the room.

"Gentlemen, I have an important duty I must ask of you."

"Certainly, Mr. Holmes, what is it?" Graham tossed his napkin on the table and stood, sensing the gravity in Holmes's voice.

"You will do me a great service if you would travel to the Dundee Post Office. There I am expecting an important telegram. I do not know when this message will arrive, but I want you on hand so that the moment it does, you can bring it here."

"We will leave at once, Holmes," I chimed in.

"Do not be alarmed if it does not come for some time. If you feel hungry or parched, feel free to seek refreshment nearby, only tell a clerk where you will be so that he may summon you."

Hamish and I stepped toward the door, but Holmes interrupted our egress.

"Watson, if you do seek a bit of refreshment, I suggest you try a new cocktail I sampled in Edinburgh—a Rob Roy."

"A Rob Roy?" I asked, puzzled.

"Indeed. Some months back, De Koven's operetta of the same name debuted on Broadway and some barkeep at the Waldorf Hotel commemorated the event by inventing the cocktail."

"Alright, Holmes, I shall give it a taste," I replied, a bit perplexed by the odd endorsement.

"And one more thing, gentlemen."

"Yes, Holmes?"

"Should no telegram arrive by eight o'clock this evening, return to Fintry."

Graham and I followed Holmes's directions and sped to the Post Office. No message was waiting, so we took up station in the lobby, informing a young clerk to notify us if the wire arrived. Several hours we sat, passing the time in pleasant discussion.

A bit of excitement ensued when a white haired old gentlemen standing in the queue fell upon the floor in convulsions. I quickly determined that the poor fellow was suffering from an apoplectic fit. Although I did not have my medical bag with me, I will say that I may have been instrumental in saving the man's life. You see, he had nearly swallowed his tongue, and I was able to remove the organ from his airway before he suffocated. I was fortunate that the codger did not retain his own teeth or I might have lost a finger in the process. He was taken to the hospital and I later heard that he recovered completely, save a slight drooping of one eye.

Hamish and I dined across the square, leaving word as Holmes instructed. However, no message was forwarded to the pub. By eight o'clock, we had given up hope of any telegram and as per Holmes's instructions, made the ride back to Fintry Castle.

To our surprise, Holmes was not in. Liam stated that he did not know where Holmes had gone. In fact, he had not even known that he had left. A horse and dogcart were missing, so the assumption was that Holmes had driven off.

There was other news though. Holmes was not the only one missing from the castle. Kyata, the maid, had also vanished.

"What do ye mean?" Graham asked in consternation.

"She is nowhere to be found, sir. Her things are missing as well," Liam replied.

"Have ye asked the other girls?"

"Aye, sir. They say they know nothing. They say she did not speak very much to them as is and that they have no idea where she went, or why," Liam replied.

"Do ye believe them?" Graham shot back.

"Aye, sir, I do. She was a tight-lipped one, that. She did not socialize, and I fear she was quite unhappy here at Fintry."

"But to give no notice? To not even speak with me about any troubles?" Graham was not so much angry as hurt. He considered himself a fair man, and was sure that he could have unburdened the girl of any unhappiness had he been given the opportunity.

Evening passed into night and Holmes had not returned. Hamish and I traded chess for backgammon, and were just about to retire when Holmes strode into the room.

"Holmes, wherever have you been?" I asked.

"Edinburgh. I am uncharacteristically tired this evening so I plan on washing up and retiring. If you gentlemen will meet in the dining room for breakfast at a quarter to eight tomorrow morning, I think I shall be able to clear up the whole affair."

The abruptness of Holmes's entry and statement left Graham and I momentarily speechless.

"But what is it, Holmes? If you have solved it, surely you won't make us wait until morning!" I finally stammered out.

"Ah, Watson, you of all people, who have warned me to get adequate rest," he quipped. "I am afraid that it must wait until morning. There is no alternative. It would be physically impossible to bring the problem to a solution tonight."

"We do have news, Holmes," I interjected before he could exit. "One of the maids has gone missing."

He turned back from the door. "The striking lass from South Africa?"

"Aye," Hamish stepped into the conversation. "She and all her possessions are gone."

"We determined that none of the other servants have any information about her disappearance. We did find out that she was unhappy here in Scotland, though," I added, hoping he would approve of our inquiries.

"Indeed, so far from home. Well, I shouldn't worry about it." He waved his hand cavalierly and turned back toward the door.

"And Holmes," I halted him again.

He stopped without turning back to us.

"No telegram arrived."

He sighed heavily. "I suspected as much. Thank you for wasting your day in Dundee. Until tomorrow morning then, gentlemen. Goodnight." He finally made his escape and after a brief discussion about the peculiarity of the exchange with Holmes, Hamish and I finished our game and went to bed.

I must admit that, despite all of my adventures with Holmes, and my familiarity with his penchant for waiting until he had the pieces in place before revealing himself, I had a difficult time sleeping. It is true that this problem did not possess some of the harrowing dangers to life and limb that other cases had involved, but it was to me, one of the most puzzling. I could often postulate a scenario that could explain the events, even if my speculation proved incorrect. Yet, in this case, I simply had no ideas. How and why had the Duke met his end? What was the significance of the message Graham had discovered? Did the missing maid factor into this puzzle? If so, how?

I lay awake more than an hour trying to sift the problem into a logical conclusion. Sleep mercifully overtook me in the early hours of the morning.

At twenty to eight, Graham gently knocked on my door. I woke with a start. It took me a moment to collect my senses.

"Graham, is that you? Pray come in while I shave and dress."

"Is Holmes awake?" I asked, pulling on my trousers.

"Aye, he just went downstairs. He was whistling," Graham chuckled.

"That is a good sign," I laughed.

"Ah, did you rest well, Watson?" Holmes asked, meeting us at the foot of the steps. "You look a bit peaked around the eyes."

"I am fine, thank you, Holmes. Are you finally ready to favor us with some answers?"

"Ha, Watson, direct as always! I admit when I first rose, I had feared that I would have to wait another day, but the clouds have cleared nicely. Pray come into the dining room," he said, leading the way.

Inside the dining room, Holmes had draped a curtain over the center window, the one that had appeared out of place, given its odd design of shapes rather than a pictographic scene like the others.

"Do you notice anything different about that wall?" he asked, pointing toward the one opposite the windows.

"I see something odd about the other," I quipped about the curtain.

Holmes laughed. "Oh, Watson, forget the obvious for the moment."

"Aye, ye exchanged two of the tapestries," Graham stated.

"Excellent observation."

"May I ask why?" I followed up, when Holmes did not offer any explanation.

"Because in 1712, *this* tapestry hung in *this* place," he replied, pointing to the landscape of Fintry Castle and its lands.

"Holmes, do you mean to say that you know the exact position where each of these tapestries hung nearly one-hundred and eighty years ago?"

"Hardly, Watson. No, only this one." He abruptly turned and jumped onto one of the dining room chairs and then onto the table itself. At this height his head was above the level of the windows, and he peered outside. "Give it another few minutes and you will see how I know. Ah, here is Liam with some coffee and biscuits."

We sat and ate, but Holmes was the only one at ease. Graham and I continued to glance at the curtained window as the sun began to crest the unveiled sills.

Finally I stated, "I don't understand Holmes, what is it that…"

He said not a word as he chewed his biscuit, but drew his watch from his waistcoat and consulted the dial. He stood and walked over to the curtain and gave it a strong tug.

The fabric fell away, but I perceived nothing different about the window, save the glare streaming through it. I looked to Holmes, who merely pointed across the room.

"My Heavens!" I exclaimed.

The sun shone through the stained glass, projecting its image directly onto the landscape tapestry. The odd shapes of the window perfectly overlapped the figures on the cloth. Several dark rectangles and squares overlaid the castle, its tower, and walls. Curved half ovals and half circles corresponded with hills and knolls. Thin blue and green panes followed the path of Gelly Burn. Even the cemetery was depicted, by small gray and black squares and rectangles. Most astounding however, was the image that appeared along the bottom of the hanging. The odd hodgepodge of vertical and horizontal lines which Hamish had suggested to be merely a design, dovetailed with the shadows cast by the odd array of perpendicular and flat divers along the bottom of the window. Separately, they were nothing; together they spelled "GAVIN" in block letters. One last feature must be mentioned, as it is perhaps the most significant. A series of leaden dividers cast a black shadow that led from Fintry Castle across Gelly Burn, to the largest square in the cemetery.

"My God," I burst out, "it is a map!"

"A map?" Graham stated, dumbstruck. "Aye! Aye, I see it! It is indeed a map! What is it for, though?" he turned to Holmes.

"Why don't we find out? Surely you recognize that largest square where the path ends. What does it represent?" Holmes asked.

"It's the mausoleum!" Hamish immediately concluded.

"Would you gentlemen think it a worthy endeavor to trek over, then?"

"Indeed!" we said, almost in unison.

The three of us walked at a quick clip. Holmes led the way, and I think it reasonable to say that had either Graham or I been in the lead, we would have fairly run.

We hopped our way across the stones resting in Gelly Burn, and snaked through the ancient monuments until we reached the crypt. Hamish unlocked the gate. The circumstances and atmosphere were much changed from my last visit and I was glad of it. Whether the bright sunshine or the excitement of the moment, I did not feel the least apprehension about entering the tomb.

The sunlight adequately illuminated the vault, so there was no need to light the torches. Excitedly, Graham and I scanned the walls in search of our quarry.

"Ah, here!" Hamish exclaimed.

"Gavin Graham, born 1502, died 1557," I read, dragging my fingers across the raised letters.

"Oh no, we haven't brought a pry bar!" Graham exclaimed in dismay.

Holmes chuckled and reached into his coat. "Here you are," he said, producing the very item.

Holmes beamed quietly as Hamish and I went to work on the stone covering. It had been sealed many years and was fairly frozen in place. Finally, the two of us were able to muster sufficient leverage to crack the seal. We slid back the stone and peered into the dark interior.

The musty, malodorous smell of stagnation and ancient death wafted from the sepulcher. The eyeless sockets of Graham's ancestor peered up at us.

"There is something here!" Hamish hissed, reaching his hand into the stone cavern, past its inhabitant. Slowly he withdrew his arm, careful not to disturb the bones lying upon the slab.

He stepped back into better light and held up an old leather bag cinched with rotting rawhide. Graham tried to delicately untie the knot, but it crumbled in his fingers. He took hold of the lip with both hands and drew apart the top of the pouch. He plunged one hand inside and pulled it out into the sunlight.

In his palm were half a dozen silver coins. The heft of the bag showed that the bag was far from empty. The dates embossed on the silver were from the early 1700s.

Wide-eyed, we both looked to Holmes.

He chuckled and clapped his hands together.

"What does it mean Holmes, and how does it fit together?" I asked.

"I suggest we re-seal Mr. Gavin Graham and head back to the castle. The explanation will be lengthy and I would rather deliver my sermon in a more comfortable setting."

Chapter 9

"Watson, do you remember the little problem I related to you about my old university friend, Reginald Musgrave?"

"Of course. The Musgrave butler decoded the bizarre incantation muttered by the Musgraves upon coming of age. It led not only to the butler's demise, but the unearthing of the crown of Charles I," I related, for Hamish's benefit. "Is this case similar? Is Liam implicated in this foul business?" I excitedly added.

"Oh, hardly that!" Holmes laughed. "It does bear resemblance however in the fact that in both cases a historical object was recovered."

"So it is more than just treasure then?" I asked, glancing at the bag upon the desk.

"I should say so. It clears one man and condemns another, though nearly two centuries too late."

"But how does it relate to the death of the Duke of Montrose?" I asked.

"It doesn't."

"What?" Hamish gasped.

"Holmes, please, this evasion has gone on long enough."

"All right, Watson," Holmes smiled as he lit his pipe. "You see, this case is unique in many respects. Not the least of which is the blundering way I stumbled through it. I do hope you will address my errors should you chose to memorialize this problem. I take pride in the advances made in detection due to your accounts of my methods, but much can also be learned from my mistakes.

"My first and most egregious error was assuming that the bizarre and singular death of the Duke was related to the mystifying message found by Mr. Graham. Each was sufficiently exceptional that I assumed they were connected."

"They were not linked?" Hamish questioned, as he could not get over the point.

"No, Mr. Graham, they were not. There were two separate and distinct mysteries afoot. The death of the Duke, and the text you found. Which shall I address first? The murder I suppose," Holmes decided.

"Aye, so murder it was?" said Hamish.

"Quite," Holmes spat out, between puffs of smoke. "But neither unprovoked nor unwarranted. Mr. Graham, I am afraid that your uncle was a scoundrel. Now, now, do not take offense; I see the color rising in your face. Let me give you the particulars. While in South Africa, the late Duke developed a lustful attraction to the young Kyata. Her father was of Dutch stock and her mother tribal in origin. The Duke made subtle overtures toward the girl, but quickly realized that she would not return his favor. So, he schemed a way to have her anyway. He asked if she would return to Scotland as a member of his household staff. He promised her not only good wages, but to allow her to take classes at the university in Dundee, at his expense.

"Of course, his true intentions were less philanthropic. Once away from her homeland and unable to communicate effectively with anyone besides the Duke, she was in essence his prisoner. He began to order her to his room late at night, after the other servants had retired. He had his way with this poor young girl almost nightly for the two weeks—until she took matters into her own hands."

"But, Holmes, how did she do that?" I asked.

"Watson, do you recall the demise of Bartholomew Sholto?"

"Certainly," I turned toward Hamish to explain. "We found this fellow dead inside a locked room. It turned out that a pygmy native of the Andaman Islands killed him using a poisoned thorn shot through a blowgun."

"Aye, I read the account," Graham stated, in reference to my record of the case.

"But, Holmes," I turned back to my friend, "we detected no poison in either the autopsy of the Duke or the dead hunting dog. Also, the dart left a clear mark on Sholto's neck and we found not a scratch upon either of these victims."

Holmes pulled an object from his pocket and tossed it to me. I turned it over in my hand, and Graham rose and stepped over to examine it as well. It was half of a lime husk. The interior had been scraped clean of fruit, but a needle-thin quill protruded from the cup-like center.

"Watson, you doubtlessly recall that the Duke's manly apparatus had turned black. It is true that you found no mark upon it, and I do not doubt your thoroughness. However, would it not be possible for that quill to cause a miniscule puncture *inside* the urethral orifice?"

"Indeed, it could!" I exclaimed.

"And if the unfortunate dog dug up this implement, could it not also be possible that the needle scraped the inside of his nose as he probed the thing with his proboscis, in the manner in which all dogs examine items."

"It is certainly possible," I confirmed.

"My dear Watson, it is more than possible. I remind you again that when the impossible is eliminated, whatever remains, however improbable, must be the solution. You did not find any mark on either the Duke's appendage or the dog's snout, yet the blackening of these areas inexplicably indicates that they were the point of entry for the toxin. Therefore, the injection must have occurred to tissue you could not have examined: inside the nose and inside the urethra."

"But, Holmes, we found no trace of poison in either instance," I reminded him.

"That is true. Watson, you know that I have made quite a study of venoms and toxins. Yet, there are those that even I have yet to classify. In Edinburgh, I consulted a professor of toxicology and another expert versed in the cultures of sub-Saharan Africa. The toxicologist did not help a bit. In fact, he was too pompous to admit that there was even the possibility that such a poison existed. But the other professor stated that he had heard tell of a potion concocted by priestesses of the Khwe Bushmen, which leaves no trace save a blackened area where it was injected. As you may have guessed, Kyata's mother was Khwe."

"But Mr. Holmes," Graham interjected, "how did she score such a precise injury inside the urethra?"

"The weapon was intended to injure the member itself, in a poetic gesture. To harm the Duke through the same instrument he had so often used to hurt the girl. The fact that the quill threaded the orifice was incidental."

"So this," I held up the lime peel, "was used by the girl, as a diaphragm?"

"Well, not that one exactly, it is a facsimile constructed by myself. Watson, I am sure that you know through your medical training, that such items, whether called 'diaphragms' or 'cervical caps,' have been employed for centuries as birth control devices."

"It was a dangerous method to employ was it not? I mean she could have easily jabbed herself," Graham inquired.

"Indeed. Yet she considered her own death the second best choice, given the circumstances. Had she attacked the Duke outright, he could have raised an alarm, but this method gave the poor girl a silent means that also provided a sense of justice and little chance of implication. Murdering her tormentor in this manner was the only avenue of escape she saw possible. She decided that, in order to end her ordeal, one of them must die. Her preference would be the Duke, of course. "

"How did ye learn all of this?" Graham asked.

"I pieced most of it together myself, but received confirmation and detail from the girl herself."

"Ye could communicate with her?" Graham queried, surprised.

"Ah, well, Watson, will tell you I have a working ability in German, and Dutch is but a small jump from there, and Afrikaans after all is a poor stepchild of Dutch."

"Where is she now?" I asked.

"She is bound for home. My dear Duke," Holmes addressed Graham, "I must confess a bit of deception on my part. I sent you and Watson after a red herring in collecting that telegram. There was no such cable. I wanted to confront the maid privately, fearful that she would not be forthright if we were not alone. Watson will tell you that I am extremely adept at determining if someone is being truthful. I have made elaborate study of the twenty pantomimes of deceit evident in women and Kyata displayed none of these. Despite my assurance that you were a just man, who would not turn her over to the police, she was beside herself with worry. She even threatened suicide. I therefore took it upon myself to escort her to Edinburgh and see her off on a ship for her homeland.

"I hope that you do not disapprove, but I determined that this poor girl had suffered enough. A formal inquiry by the police would have accomplished no good. At best, they would have corroborated my findings, of which I am certain by the way, and at worst they would have put her up for trial, possibly condemning her for what was in truth an act of self defense."

Herein lies one of the advantages Holmes enjoyed in his role as a professional consulting detective. My companion was often less concerned with the law than he was with justice. On more than one occasion, I witnessed him proscribing what he felt was just by holding back evidence or allowing the regular force to follow faulty leads. He himself has admitted that had he been a member of Scotland Yard, he would have no alternative but to follow the letter of the law under circumstances such as these. He found this fact abhorrent. At times, the law simply did not correspond with justice.

Graham slowly paced the room, his head upon his chest and hands behind his back. We stood in silence, waiting for his judgment.

"Mr. Holmes, I truly believe in our court system. I think it just and fair. However, I have read enough of Watson's writings to know that your findings are meticulous in their accuracy. Also, I completely respect the opinion of Watson, and he is completely devoted to ye, and feels that ye are a man of honor. Therefore, ye have nothing to fear from me. I accept your actions, and the conclusion ye have based them upon. That girl has endured enough hardship."

"I am glad to hear you say so," Holmes replied, affectionately clapping a hand upon Graham's back.

"So, she buried the weapon, and when she found that the dog had died, she disposed of it again," I mused.

"Almost, Watson. She saw the dog head into the thicket, and that was enough for her. Upon entering, she found that old Bruce had dug it up, but did not know that he had been pricked. She took the object and tossed it into Gelly Burn."

"So the Duke's murder had nothing to do with diamonds?" I asked.

"Nothing at all. It was a proper line to explore, though."

"And Duncan Dunnahue's death was mere accident?"

"Yes, Watson, it appears so."

I digested the information for a moment. "What of the silver, Holmes?" I jarred their attention to the other mystery.

"Ah, the £1,000 sterling?" he tapped the bag with the stem of his pipe.

"Is that how much it is?" I asked.

"Well, it is how much it *was*, in 1712. It is probably worth much more now, although its real value is not monetary."

"How do you mean?"

"Watson, this will thrill you, given your romantic passions and penchant for novels," he returned.

I looked at him quizzically.

"Certainly you are up on your Walter Scott, or at the very least the poetry of Wordsworth? I read the confusion on your features, Watson. Surely you recall the advice I gave you before you and Mr. Graham went to Dundee. Did you not try the cocktail I advised?"

"No, I forgot to…" Holmes's trick dawned on me. "Rob Roy? Rob Roy *MacGregor*?" My eyes shifted from Holmes's smile to the bag of coins.

"The very rogue!" he replied. "Or, perhaps a man wrongly accused?"

Of course, I knew the name, and from earlier in life than Sir Walter Scott's novel or Wordsworth's *Rob Roy's Grave*. My own mother evoked the same threat that most Englishwomen used on their misbehaving children: *Rob Roy is going to get you*!

The man was as much demonized in England as he was lionized in Scotland. He had been born to clan MacGregor at the head of Lake Katrine in the Trossachs region of the Highlands in the early 1670s. When he was eighteen, he and his father joined the Jacobites in support of the deposed Stuart King James II.

Rob Roy survived the Jacobite wars both physically and politically, and rose to become a chieftain of stature, and a successful cattleman. In those days, stealing cattle and selling protection against its theft, were both respectable endeavors and Rob Roy's daring and swordsmanship made him revered, feared, and respected.

In 1712, he sought to legitimize his business. His plan was to buy cattle from the Lowlands and sell them for a profit. However, he did not have the required capital. He turned to James Graham, 1st Duke of Montrose for a loan. It was known that the Duke coveted MacGregor lands, but this was a business proposition that promised prosperity for all involved.

That prosperity would never be however, and the result would transform Rob Roy into a legend. He, in fact, became Scotland's equivalent of Robin Hood.

Rob obtained the £1,000 sterling from the Duke. He then sent his agent to purchase the cattle. However, the man disappeared. What became of him and the money has long been debated. Some hold that the man betrayed Rob and fled the British Isles with the loot. Another theory is that Rob pocketed the silver himself. Still others suspect that Montrose either bribed the man to disappear, or had him killed so that he would have a pretext for seizing MacGregor lands.

When Rob did not produce the cattle, Montrose began to confiscate his property. The Duke's men even defiled Rob's wife as they evicted her from his home. Rob Roy fought back and the Duke had him declared an outlaw. For the next ten years, Rob conducted a personal guerrilla war against Montrose and his property.

There are many thrilling accounts of Rob's exploits including raids, attacks, and daring escapes, but what made him the darling of the Highlands was his "Robin Hood" exploits. He would often wait for a peasant Highlander to pay his rent to Montrose's men, making sure that they were marked down as "paid." Then he would waylay the factor upon the road and return the money to the family.

Rob warred with the Duke until 1722 when he was coaxed into surrendering. He was imprisoned, but was pardoned in 1727.

"So, this is the £1,000 sterling Montrose loaned Rob Roy MacGregor?" I asked in disbelief.

"The very same," Holmes replied.

"How did it come to be in the crypt? How did you find its whereabouts?" I asked.

"That brings me to my second blunder in the case. When you sent me a copy of the message Graham found, or more specifically his translation of the message, I assumed that it was an exact facsimile of the paper that had been discovered."

"But how could that make a difference, if you do not read Gaelic?" I asked.

"It matters on two fronts. First, upon seeing the original, I was able to easily date the paper to the early 1700s. That in itself was an important clue. Second, I was certain that the message was encrypted. Watson, you have been party to a number of my cases where codes have been employed. Do you remember the Dancing Men? Or the case of the Gloria Scott? I have yet to encounter a cipher that I could not break. But this code confounded me. I got nowhere, despite my efforts to unravel it. Then I learned the message I puzzled over was not the original, and in a matter of hours, I was able to decrypt it."

"But how? I still don't understand the difference between the two, if the Gaelic does not come into play?" I asked.

"Mr. Graham's translation was impeccable. The difference is in the transcription of the message itself. Here, have a look at the original." He handed me the parchment, and Graham and I peered at it together.

THOIR TULLEADH OR DO DUNCAN GLEIDH E CHATIG MIANNAICH

SABHAIL ANN AN AITE-FALAICH AIR SINN AIGE CUIR AIS

ANN SGRIOBHADH DO FUIRICH FLOR SABHAILTE SINNE TIOMNADH MARBH

UILE AN CINNEADH FUEM FUILING ACH MA MI GNATHAICH

AN GLAINNE DEIDH E BEO AIGE CHATIG BHUR TIOMNADH

FUILING AGUS DEIDH AGAINNE MAIR-BEO TIR TIOMNADH FAIGH TABHARTAS

ANN AODACH SEO BI NA BI CUDROMACH ADH'AITHGHEARR GU-LEOR

SINNE TIOMNADH BUANNAICH AIRGEAD AN FIU E TIOMNADH FAIGH

MOR DEAN AN MACGRIOGHAIR BAS MORAN TIOMNADH E THOIR

THU BALL E MONTROSE AIR TILG OR AGUS TIOTAL

"You see nothing unique?" Holmes asked.

"I must admit I do not."

"Nor do I," Graham chimed in.

"Here, look at the translation. Compare the two." Holmes handed over the copy Graham had penned.

GIVE MORE GOLD TO DUNCAN. KEEP IT NO LONGER. SAVE IN THE HIDDEN. FOR US ITS PUT BACK IN WRITING. TO REMAIN VERY SAFE WE WILL KILL ALL. THE CLAN MUST SUFFER BUT IF I USE THE GLASS THEN IT LIVES. HIS NOT YOURS WILL SUFFER AND THEN OURS SURVIVES. LAND WILL BE GRANTED IN CLOTH, THIS IS WHAT IS IMPORTANT. SOON ENOUGH WE WILL GAIN SILVER, THE WORTH IT WILL BE GREAT. MARK THE MACGRIOGHAIR'S DEATH, MUCH WILL IT BRING YOU. SPOT IT MONTROSE FOR MORE GOLD AND TITLE.

"Hmm, I note that Graham's translation is punctuated."

"Yes, undoubtedly the Duke included markers where he believed the sentences ended, so that it made more sense. Isn't that so Mr. Graham?"

"Aye, 'tis true."

"Do you detect no other differences?" Holmes questioned.

"Is the original a poem? Is it written in verse?" I asked.

"Capital, Watson, you almost have it in your grasp. Why would you ask such a question?" Holmes praised.

"Well, I note that each line has nine words."

"Indeed! When Mr. Graham translated the message, he wrote it out as anyone would, beginning a new line when his pen reached the right-hand margin. The symmetry of the lines is the key. Look here at an exact translation, keeping the words nine to a line." He handed me a transcription written in his own hand.

GIVE MORE GOLD TO DUNCAN. KEEP IT NO LONGER.

SAVE IN THE HIDDEN. FOR US ITS PUT BACK

IN WRITING. TO REMAIN VERY SAFE WE WILL KILL

ALL. THE CLAN MUST SUFFER BUT IF I USE

THE GLASS THEN IT LIVES. HIS NOT YOURS WILL

SUFFER AND THEN OURS SURVIVES. LAND WILL BE GRANTED

IN CLOTH, THIS IS WHAT IS IMPORTANT. SOON ENOUGH

WE WILL GAIN SILVER, THE WORTH IT WILL BE

GREAT. MARK THE MACGRIOGHAIR'S DEATH, MUCH WILL IT BRING

YOU. SPOT IT MONTROSE FOR MORE GOLD AND TITLE.

"I am sorry Holmes, but I still don't see it."

"Oh, Watson, and you were making such progress." He took the page and scribbled on it for a moment. "Try it now."

	4-↓				2-↓			
GIVE	MORE	GOLD	TO	DUNCAN	KEEP	IT	NO	LONGER
SAVE	IN	THE	HIDDEN	FOR	US	ITS	PUT	BACK
IN	WRITING	TO	REMAIN	VERY	SAFE	WE	WILL	KILL
ALL	THE	CLAN	MUST	SUFFER	BUT	IF	I	USE
THE	GLASS	THEN	IT	LIVES	HIS	NOT	YOURS	WILL
SUFFER	AND	THEN	OURS	SURVIVES	LAND	WILL	BE	GRANTED
IN	CLOTH	THIS	IS	WHAT	IS	IMPORTANT	SOON	ENOUGH
WE	WILL	GAIN	SILVER	THE	WORTH	IT	WILL	BE
GREAT	MARK	THE	MACGREGOR'S	DEATH	MUCH	WILL	IT	BRING
YOU	SPOT	IT	MONTROSE	FOR	MORE	GOLD	AND	TITLE
			1-↑				3-↑	

154

I immediately understood Holmes's directions. I was to read up one line and then down another in the order he indicated. The decoded message thus read as follows:

MONTROSE - MACGREGOR'S SILVER IS OURS IT MUST REMAIN HIDDEN TO KEEP US SAFE BUT HIS LAND IS WORTH MUCH MORE AND IT WILL SOON BE YOURS I WILL PUT NO MORE IN WRITING THE GLASS AND CLOTH WILL MARK SPOT

"Good heavens!" Graham exclaimed, reading the message over my shoulder. "So the Duke set up Rob Roy in order to claim his lands!"

"And once you deciphered the message, you knew what it was all about?" I asked.

"Yes. Watson, you are well aware that I do not invest time in novels or poetry, but the legend of Rob Roy is a well known piece of folklore. The only snag was determining what 'glass' and 'cloth' marked the spot. When we breakfasted in the dining hall that sunny morning, the solution presented itself. We were fortunate however that the window had obviously been installed during the summer. Otherwise the images would not have matched up and we would have had to wait until after the solstice to follow the map."

Holmes moved over to Hamish's side. "I am sorry that you have had bad news of two relatives today, Mr. Graham," he said, putting a compassionate hand on the Duke's shoulder.

"Aye, 'tis true, it shames me. Yet it would shame me more if I were a party to the injustice. The girl Kyata will not be pursued, and this story shall be made public."

"What should we do now?" I asked Holmes.

"I think Mrs. Watson would be most grateful if I whisked you back to London, now that this little problem has been solved. I read in this morning's paper about an intriguing forgery and unless I am much mistaken, Lestrade will be calling at Baker Street before the day is out. I am confident that Mr. Graham will judiciously convey the MacGregor information to the proper folk, and no doubt you will publicize it yourself in one of your little memoirs, Watson. Now, if we hurry, we can make the next southbound train before it leaves Tay Bridge Station.

Aftermath of the Tay Bridge Disaster

Tay Bridge Railway Station, Dundee

Fintry (Mains) Castle

A Clyde steamer

The Medium Problem

Chapter 1

Holmes and I agreed to suppress these events due to the emotional duress and virulent reaction should they be made public. However, sufficient time has passed and passions have subsided enough that my friend has now granted permission for publication.

"Disturbed by an item in the paper, Watson?" Holmes remarked, as he reclined upon the carpet cleaning his pistol.

My companion's exemplary deductive powers were hardly necessary to read the disgust upon my face or to decipher the violence with which I turned the pages.

"What's that? Yes, I should say so," I spat out.

"That medium business again, I presume," chuckled Holmes as he sighted down the end of the barrel.

"Holmes, do you realize that Lady Winfield is now a devotee of that charlatan?"

"Ah, if I recount correctly, she is the third noble added to the stable," he smirked.

"I don't see any humor in the situation," I rebuked. "This 'Antoinette' is nothing more than a swindler. Do you know she accepts money for her *services*?"

"And well she should. I take it that Lady Winfield desires that Antoinette put her in contact with her late husband? If she can do so, I see no reason why she shouldn't be compensated."

"Holmes, you know as well as I that this Antoinette is a fraud. She can no more contact the dead than you or I. She is merely deceiving these people during her séances."

"You may soon be in the minority in that opinion," laughed Holmes. "It seems that this Spiritualism craze has taken firm root in London."

"Don't you see? That is what makes the situation so vexing! People are being duped en mass and you merely snigger."

"My dear Watson, when you attend the theater, are you permitted to enter for free?"

"Of course not," I huffed.

"Indeed. You pay admission in hopes of being entertained. If the company did its job, you leave happy, having received what you desired. This is no different. The clients of this swami come to her in desperation and sadness. If she succeeds in making them believe that she has put them in touch with their dearly departed, they leave elated. What is the harm in that?"

"Clearly, Holmes, you see the harm. It is fraud. It is deceit. When I take in a show, the man upon the stage does not claim to be the real Richard III. The audience knows it is a performance. This Antoinette makes no such distinction."

"Ah, well, we shall have to disagree then," Holmes replied, waving the issue away with his hand.

"But, Holmes," I persisted, "couldn't you expose this woman? Surely with your skills of observation, you could determine how she is able to deceive these people."

"To what end, Watson?" Holmes replied, his voice taking on a tone of seriousness for the first time.

"Why, to correct a great injustice of course," I stated, amazed that an explanation should be necessary.

"Watson, you are well aware of the successes I have had in my field," he said without any feigned modesty. "My achievements are the result of observation and logic. My methods hold no sway over those ruled by emotion. Do you know how many cases I have solved where a mother refuses to believe her son committed the crime, despite my presentation of irrefutable proof?"

He stood, tossing his revolver upon the sofa. "Let us say you had unassailable evidence that Jesus did not walk on water. Perhaps you discovered that there was a submerged reef in the Sea of Galilee, upon which Jesus had treaded. Do you truly think Christians would thank you for that information, or do you suppose you would be attacked for your exposé?"

Holmes smiled slightly before continuing. "My dear friend, try telling a Mohammedan that his prophet's dream of the Arch Angel giving him instructions to found Islam was a sham. Or, on second thought don't—he may remove your head with a scimitar."

I am not certain if it was my silence or facial features that betrayed my comprehension of Holmes's argument.

In a softer tone he continued, "Spiritualism has become a religion to many, and although I do not doubt that I could determine how the mediums perform their trickery, it would be a worthless endeavor that would serve no constructive purpose. Spiritualists would be less than impressed with my efforts and I would waste valuable time that would grant many a criminal a reprieve."

My friend was correct about the adherents of Spiritualism. The movement had steadily gained followers since its inception at the hands of the Fox sisters some fifty years prior and, despite the findings of the Seybert Commission in '87, the numbers continued to grow. One would think that, when a scientific panel from the esteemed University of Pennsylvania decreed the mediums to be frauds, the movement would have disintegrated. However, even the renowned chemist and physicist William Crookes remained a steadfast practitioner. And Crookes is hardly the only respected personage to tout the "religion."

Although still aggravated by the situation, I acquiesced to Holmes's reasoning and tried to divert my mind from the subject. I folded the paper and shoved it across the table, exchanging it for a volume of Tennyson. A half an hour had passed before the wall clock chimed, reminding me that I must be off.

"Dr. Watson, what brings you out on this fine day?" The familiar voice of Inspector Dickerson arrested my departure from our doorstep.

"Hello, inspector, I was just about to check on a patient. Is it official business then? Should I stay?"

"Oh, hardly that," he laughed. "I was merely passing by and thought that I would return the notes Mr. Holmes loaned me during that nasty affair over at Charing Cross."

"Alright then, good day inspector." As I started off, I was surprised to find Dickerson had taken hold of my arm.

"Doctor, do you know why I haven't returned these notes earlier? Well I am not proud to admit it, but I mislaid them," the heavyset officer confessed, stroking his reddish sideburns.

"Oh, is that so?" I answered, trying to continue on my journey. However the inspector still gripped my arm, having not completed his explanation.

"Do you know of Commodore Peters?" he asked.

I nodded in affirmation as I transformed from hostage to dedicated listener at the mention of the name. Indeed, I had heard of 'the commodore.' Uriah Peters was an Englishman of unclear origins who claimed to have led a fleet of armed merchant ships in the Black Sea during the Crimean War. This unconfirmed service decades ago, however, is not what had thrust him into the public conscience. He was the protector and agent for the illustrious Antoinette.

Dickerson continued, "Well, that gentleman paid me a visit the other day and invited me to one of Antoinette's séances. He stated that having a member of Scotland Yard at the event would help dissuade skeptics. It was astounding! Astounding! Antoinette's spirit guide, Oliver, rang an electric bell that was housed in a wooden box under the table. He even spoke to us through Antoinette! He said he sensed duress upon me. He said I had lost something. Which of course I had! He told me to look behind the file cabinet in my office. Doctor Watson," he tightened his grasp on my arm, "that is exactly where I found Mr. Holmes's notes! It was so amazing that my wife and I have attended several more séances. They have all been fruitful, too!"

As I sauntered down Baker Street, I shook my head in wonderment. Could Dickerson really be that naïve? Certainly, he possessed one of the dullest minds on the force, but to believe such tripe! It was no secret that he attained his position due to the fact that his uncle was a Member of Parliament. And unlike other inspectors, who only begrudgingly asked Holmes's assistance, Dickerson had no qualms about consulting my friend upon the most trivial matters. I suspect Holmes would have denied him aid more frequently had he not pitied the dimwitted, though good-hearted, inspector. It seemed inconceivable that even he could not see the charade performed upon him, but when I asked him if the notes had disappeared before or after the commodore's visit, and he replied that he had seen them shortly before, but could not find them afterward, this fact elicited no illumination. I suppose Holmes is correct; the devout believe only what they desire.

My mind began to navigate the bits and pieces reported about Antoinette. She was an American, approximately thirty years of age. Although I had never seen a photograph or rendering, sources described her as beautiful. Her hair was said to be flaxen, almost platinum in color, which contrasted greatly with large, extremely dark eyes. Bodily, she was more than adequately proportioned and of greater than average height for a woman. She claims to have been a school teacher at one point before the appearance of her "spirit guide" less than two years ago. This "Oliver" allegedly came to her in a vision as she was reading one evening. Her surname has never been revealed, nor is it certain that "Antoinette" is her true Christian name. When prodded upon the subject, she stated that Oliver forbid her to answer, as since her "awakening" her previous identity ceased to be relevant.

The woman's association with the commodore is equally murky. He had the bearing and manner of a well-bred man. He was reportedly silver haired and mustachioed, tall and thin.

His voice was smooth and his demeanor impeccable. His deportment cast doubt upon the premise that he was a former seaman. How he became associated with the lady, he refused to say, beyond that they had both been travelers "drawn together by fate." When pressed about his background, he offered little, claiming that Oliver had forbid him speaking about the subject. He would neither confirm nor deny the origin of his title of "commodore," but did allude to spending some time in Russia.

By the time I had mulled over these facts, I had traversed the dozen blocks to the home of Mrs. Saunders. The day previous, I had been summoned to the Saunders residence to examine their governess, a Miss Ripley. After her noon meal, the young lady began to feel faint and troubled about the stomach. It seemed likely that she was suffering from a mild food poisoning and that her condition would correct itself once her body had purged the contamination. However, in order to be sure that the aliment was not something more sinister, I assured her that I would call again today.

My ruminations faded as I entered the foyer. The maid showed me up to the young lady's room, where I found her much improved. She was out of bed and busy composing a letter.

"Well, Miss Ripley, I see that the crisis has passed," I stated light heartedly.

"Why, yes, Doctor Watson, I feel tip top," she smiled back.

"Let me just have a look at you then, and you can get right back to your correspondence."

"Certainly," she replied as I removed the stethoscope from my bag. "I am anxious to complete this thank you note to Miss Antoinette."

I was not sure I heard her correctly, so I removed the earpieces of the instrument. "Pardon?"

"After you left, Mrs. Saunders received a package from Antoinette, the medium," she searched my eyes to be certain I recognized the identification. "It contained a note stating that she had a premonition that a member of the household was ill and that the elixir in the package would affect a cure. I am truly indebted to her. I took the medicine last evening, and this morning when I awoke, I was my old self!"

"Where is this 'medicine'?" I asked, trying to suppress my anger.

"I consumed it as directed. However, this is the vial it was in," she replied handing me a small bottle.

"Miss Ripley, do you recall my diagnosis?" I asked, somewhat harshly.

"Certainly, Doctor Watson, you said food poisoning."

"Did I not tell you that it would likely leave you before today?"

"Why, yes, you did, but I was suffering, so I could not wait. Sir, what is the difference? I am cured, is that not the important thing?"

In her eyes, I read the devotion of which Holmes had spoken. This innocent girl failed to comprehend that she *did* wait. During the night, the toxin dissipated and this morning, she felt well again just as I had predicted—and I used no magical powers to reach that conclusion. I saw no reason to reprimand the girl further; she had already decided the issue.

"I am glad you are feeling better. Good day, Miss Ripley."

Upon descending the stairs, I looked about for the maid. "Excuse me, young lady, is Mrs. Saunders in?"

"Yes, sir. Wait in the parlor, I will get her."

I paced the room, my teeth clenched. How dare this charlatan interject her fraud into the medical field! It was one thing to pretend to speak with the dead, but this was going too far. Her parlor games could very well cost someone their life!

By the time the lady of the house entered, I had mastered my emotions.

"Dr. Watson, thank you so much for coming back to check on our Miss Ripley," she said as she entered the parlor.

"As I said that I would," I returned. "Madam, how is it that my instructions were not followed?" When a confused look swept across her face, I furthered, "I did not prescribe any medicine."

"True enough, doctor." She smiled and sat down upon the sofa, folding her hands in her lap. "But neither did you prohibit it. When the messenger arrived from Antoinette, I could hardly refuse! She had clairvoyance enough to know that our governess was ill, why should I then doubt her power to produce a remedy?"

The lady's expression was so solemn; it was obvious that her faith in the medium was complete. At once, I determined that chastising her would be fruitless, yet my blood was boiling.

"May I ask how it is you know Antoinette?" I tried my best to stifle my anger.

"My husband and I have attended two or three of her séances."

"I see." I bid Mrs. Saunders good day and left.

"Watson, whatever can you be up to?" Holmes asked as he entered our rooms.

"What's that? Oh, it's you, Holmes?" I recovered from the intrusion. "I hope you don't mind, but I needed to make use of your chemistry equipment."

"Not at all, Watson, but pray tell what the experiment is. Have you developed a serum for brain fever?" he jested.

"I am trying to ascertain what resided in this bottle," I returned, holding up the tiny container the governess had surrendered.

"Any luck, old man?" my roommate asked, hanging his hat upon the rack.

"No, I am sorry to say. The vial is bone dry and there appears to be no film or residue left on the inner walls."

"Give it here," Holmes commanded, striding over to the chemistry table.

He pulled out his magnifying lens and stepped close to the window to take full advantage of the late afternoon sunshine.

"Useless," he replied, tossing the bottle to me.

"Yes," I sighed heavily.

"All right Watson, no need for melodrama. I can see that you need to unburden yourself. I am all ears," he said, seating himself.

"Ha! What do you suspect that vial contained?" Holmes queried after I had recounted what had happened.

"I believe that it was some benign substance, perhaps sugared water."

"Very likely, Watson. Assuming that your diagnosis was correct and the governess had not contracted some malady requiring actual medication."

"I am certain of that, Holmes."

"So by your reckoning, the young lady would have recovered anyway and the remedy sent by the mystic did nothing to affect a cure."

"Yes, Holmes, that is exactly how I see it."

"Your deductions are possible, Watson, but they need to be shifted from the possible to the probable. How did this Antoinette know that someone was ill in the house? Further, if the vial contained a mere placebo, how was she certain that the young lady's illness was one from which she would recover without true medication?"

"Perhaps the patient told someone my diagnosis, and it was forwarded to the medium."

"Ah, Watson, now we are getting somewhere. You must go back to the house and follow up on that line of deduction," he said pulling an index from the shelf, effectively terminating our conversation.

"Oh. I was hoping that I had piqued your interest enough that you might accompany me."

"It is hardly a case requiring my expertise, Watson. Do let me know how it turns out, though."

"So, you told no one other than Mrs. Saunders about my diagnosis?"

"No," the governess replied, perplexed at my return.

"Thank you," I said, exiting the room. "Oh, and you're still feeling alright?" I asked, almost as an afterthought.

"Yes sir. Perfectly fine."

As I left the house, I tumbled the problem over in my mind. Surely Mrs. Saunders had not informed Antoinette. She said that the medium had clairvoyantly determined that the girl was ill, and her amazement at the arrival of the package was genuine. Could this woman actually possess some metaphysical powers? I wondered almost aloud.

"Good day, sir."

Lost in thought, I brushed past the maid sweeping the walk and almost failed to hear her.

I stopped and retraced my steps. "Excuse me."

"Yes, doctor?" The young lass halted her work.

"Did you happen to see the messenger who brought the package of medicine yesterday?"

"Aye, sir. I was scrubbing the front hallway when he arrived.

"What did he look like? Can you describe him?"

"Certainly, sir. He was a little man; dark skin, dark hair, clean shaven. He had dark eyes. There was also a scar on his cheek below the left eye."

"That is a fairly complete description! How can you be so precise?"

"Well, sir, it is the second time I saw him in as many days. He was at the kitchen door yesterday noon."

"What's that? Why was he there?" I sputtered out, shocked by the revelation.

"I cannot say, sir. I guess he was making a delivery to the cook. She was preparing lunch at the time."

I did not want to spar with the devout Mrs. Saunders, so rather than reenter the house through the front door; I hurried around to the rear, anxious to interview the cook. I found her scrubbing out a large pot and she complied when I asked her to step outside for a moment.

"Yes, doctor, what can I do for you?" the portly lady asked, closing the door behind her.

168

"Did a man approach you yesterday when you were preparing lunch?"

"Yes, sir. He had a sack, and said that he was delivering the tomatoes I had ordered. When I told him I had made no such order, he said that perhaps the lady of the house had. I answered back that that was not possible, as I did all of the grocery purchasing. He became agitated and ordered me to ask Mrs. Saunders. I told him there was no need, but he insisted that he was not about to return to the market to be sent back again because I was in error. Seeing that he would not be denied, I went off to find Madam. When I returned to tell him that she had not placed the order, he accepted the news and left."

"Do you know the man?"

"The delivery man? No, sir. I had never laid eyes on him before."

"Do you use a particular grocer? Where might I find this tomato courier?"

"Oh, I usually order our produce from Giovanni; he has that little shop on Kensey Street. But, like I said, sir, I never saw him before, so I doubt if he works for Giovanni. I suspect he was from a different grocer and mistook our house for the proper one."

"I have one further question. When you left to consult your mistress, was there anyone left in the kitchen?"

"Why, no, sir. Erin, the maid was here when he first arrived, but I think she grew uneasy at our heated exchange, so she had scurried off."

Chapter 2

"I am sure of it, Holmes!"

"It is a reasonable deduction, Watson. This swarthy fellow could indeed have sprinkled some substance on one of the plates of food invoking a temporary ailment."

"What I cannot figure, however, is how he could be sure that he was contaminating the meal of the governess."

"Watson, whatever do you mean?" Holmes stepped to the window and surveyed the overcast sky.

"How did Antoinette know the governess was ill?" I replied.

"She didn't," my friend responded. "I do believe we will get some rain this morning," he added offhandedly.

"Holmes, do you not recall that the medium sent her a remedy." I tried to bring him back to the discussion.

He turned from the window and pulled an umbrella from the rack. "It is your memory that is in question, my dear doctor. The note delivered along with the elixir stated that the lady divined that *someone* in the house was ill."

"Of course! You are correct Holmes!" I erupted, although my companion hardly needed my affirmation. I pursed my lips. "Very clever...he sabotages one of the servings and then Antoinette vaguely states that she has foreseen that someone in the household is sick."

"Perhaps, Watson," smiled Holmes. "Despite your slight oversight regarding the note, you are to be commended in constructing a plausible scenario. There is the paper, Watson," he said, reacting to the rap upon our door. "Perhaps it will contain some further clues to your little investigation. I must tie up a few loose ends in the Munsen affair," he said, donning his hat and sliding past the boy at the door. "Kindly leave the paper upon the table when you are finished," he called over his shoulder. "There may be some items that interest me as well."

Holmes was correct; the paper did hold some pertinent information. The medium was again featured in the paper. Contained therein was a testimonial from Lady Winfield assuring the reader that Antoinette had indeed put her in contact with her departed husband. The séance took place in the house rented by the medium in Chelsea. In attendance were Antoinette, Lady Winfield, her niece Miss Fortham, and the commodore. The article went on to describe the ritual.

The gas jets were cranked off and candles were lit in the low hanging chandelier suspended above the circular table at which they sat. They all joined hands. Antoinette and the commodore sat opposite each other, Lady Winfield to Antoinette's right and Miss Fortham to her left. Thus, each woman could attest that the hands of both the medium and her companion remained secure. Once the séance began, Antoinette asked Oliver to act as the conduit to Lord Winfield in the spirit realm. After several prolonged moments of silence, the medium stated that Oliver required that they extinguish the candles. The group stood, hands still embraced, and together blew out the lights.

Once in complete darkness, Antoinette stated that Oliver had reached Lord Winfield. He would reply to questions by knocking on the table once for "yes" or twice for "no," and thrice for "I don't know." A masculine voice, purporting to be Oliver, emanated from the medium. He began by asking if they were indeed speaking to the spirit of Lord Alfred Winfield. Much to the amazement of Lady Winfield and her niece, a single knock reverberated across the table. Other questions were asked by Lady Winfield, always repeated, and at times rephrased, by Antoinette. Again and again the spirit answered with either single or double raps upon the table. Lady Winfield refused to divulge what questions were specifically asked, as she said conversations between a husband and wife are not for public consumption, but she attested that she was certain that the spirit was that of her spouse.

I folded my paper, chagrined by the account. Holmes may have been correct that this business was none of our affair, but it continued to bother me. Here I was, a physician, a man of science, and I sat idly by while people were walking wide eyed into this hocus pocus. As I sat swirling the whiskey in my glass, the justification for action dawned on me. As a doctor, I was duty bound to administer medical attention to anyone in need, even if they refused it. It is a known fact that a jarring physical or mental trauma invariably impaired one's judgment, and justifies a doctor taking command of the situation, even if the patient is uncooperative. I convinced myself that this was a similar situation. Those seeking an audience with Antoinette were not in possession of their full faculties; they were suffering the psychological and emotional trauma wrought by their loss. Using this rationale, I persuaded myself that my Hippocratic obligation required that I investigate the matter on their behalf.

Dickerson waved me into his office and boomed, "Doctor Watson, what brings you to Scotland Yard? Do sit down. Would you care for a cigarette?" he asked, holding forth a chrome case.

"No, thank you, inspector," I declined, as he lit up his own.

"Well," I began uneasily, "I have been reading a lot about this Antoinette in the papers and I was hoping you could take me along to one of her séances. You know, I lost more than one friend serving the empire and I would like it very much if she should be able to put me in contact with them."

"Indeed, indeed!" He beamed at my suggestion. "That's right, you were an army surgeon. It had slipped my mind! I do not think it will be a problem. My wife and I are supposed to attend another session in the near future. I will see what I can do about taking you along," replied the gregarious policeman.

"So, you are going to attend a séance, eh, Watson?" Holmes smiled between puffs on his pipe.

"What makes you say that?" I bashfully returned, having said nothing of the matter to Holmes.

"Simplicity itself, my dear doctor!" Holmes reclined upon the sofa and draped a leg over the arm. "You have dressed to go out this evening, and from your furtive glances out the window, it is obvious that you are waiting for a pre-appointed carriage to arrive. You have never failed to inform me of your destinations before, yet for the last quarter hour you have been unsure whether to conjure a lie, or confide in me. You have been pining over this medium business for more than a week, and since you know I find the idea of an exposé frivolous, it is the one subject that would cause you hesitation."

In large part relieved that I did not have to deceive my friend, I replied, "Of course, you are correct, Holmes. I am curious if I can deduce how Antoinette performs her tricks."

"Your line of thinking was proper in removing your university ring, in order to detract from the number of clues she can use to tell your fortune, Watson. But I'm afraid that the move is far too little," he laughed. "You are no doubt dealing with a very shrewd customer who will already know more about you than you realize."

"How do you mean?" I asked, eager for any guidance that might help guard me against becoming a dupe myself.

"Ah, I see your carriage has arrived!" he said, glancing into the street. "Here is your clue, Watson: Hiram Silver."

"Hiram Silver?" I repeated the name aloud as I descended our stairs.

"Dr. Watson, I was just about to come up for you! Dickerson exclaimed from the cab. "I do not believe that you have met my wife."

Mrs. Dickerson was as affable and dense as her husband. The corpulent woman clucked loudly at her spouse's amusing stories, but became deadly serious when affirming the clairvoyance of Miss Antoinette.

"I tell you, doctor," she said, gripping my wrist with man-like strength, "she has the gift."

I smiled, trying to mask my skepticism. "The good inspector has told me as much, and I have read several convincing accounts in the paper."

"You'll see! You'll see!" she emphatically patted my hand and joined her husband in nodding their heads in verification.

"Ah, inspector! So good to see you again," said the dapper man, brushing aside the attendant who had answered the door. "And the lovely Mrs. Dickerson, always a pleasure my lady," he bowed obsequiously before kissing the blushing woman's hand.

"And this must be the famous Dr. Watson?" he said, fixing his grey eyes upon me.

"Dr. Watson, may I introduce Commodore Peters," Inspector Dickerson stated in a loud clear voice, as if he were announcing royalty.

"Charmed, sir. Although I think 'famous' is a bit of an overstatement," I replied uncomfortably.

"Oh, I think not," smiled the silver-haired gentleman. "I have enjoyed reading many of the adventures undertaken by yourself and Mr. Holmes, as has all of Britain. Your accounts of his crime solving have done wonders to further your friend's career? No?" he said smoothly.

"Benton, take our guests' hats and coats," he instructed the servant. "Now if you will be so kind as to follow me upstairs, Miss Antoinette awaits."

The commodore led the way up the carpeted staircase and down the dimly lit hall to a heavy oak door. "Excuse me for one moment," our guide said, as he narrowly opened the door and slid through the opening.

It betrayed odd manners to be left standing in an upstairs passage facing a closed door. The inspector grasped my annoyance and quickly tried to explain away the perceived affront.

"You see, doctor, he must make sure that Miss Antoinette is prepared. There is no guarantee that Oliver will cooperate, and the lady must meditate privately for a few minutes before assuring the commodore that others may enter. Oh, another thing, Dr. Watson, directly inside the door is a curtained vestibule. There an ebony box with ivory and topaz trimmings sits upon a pedestal. There will be a slot in the top. As soon as you enter, you must deposit the money. But remember, make no mention of it. The protocol is specific. Merely slip in the bills and then duck through the curtains into the room itself."

"Oh, yes, of course." A sour taste materialized in my mouth at the thought of feeding this charlatan's avarice. "You said, twenty would suffice, correct?"

"Yes, I will give the same amount and that will cover the half hour the medium has set aside for us."

The door opened smoothly. "All is in readiness," the commodore's disembodied voice stated in a velvety whisper.

The inspector and I followed Mrs. Dickerson into the curtained foyer. The inspector's wife slipped through the dark purple curtains to the room beyond, but as instructed, he and I paused before the ornamental cube to deposit our offering. Beyond the drapes, I could hear the medium greeting the lady in a hushed tone. After succeeding in sliding the bills into the slot, I followed the inspector through the veil.

The gas jets were turned low, but the light illuminated the room sufficiently enough for my observations. Across the room, Mrs. Dickerson's ample frame blocked the medium from view, so I quickly surveyed the interior. The windows were shuttered and draped with black bunting. The walls were likewise covered with the same purple material as the vestibule, although unlike the entranceway there were oriental symbols painted upon these in a blood red hue. A simple round table sat in the center of the room, the candle laden chandelier above it. There was no carpet upon the wooden floor, which seemed odd given the other accoutrements adorning the room.

The commodore took up his place beside his mistress and waved us over. As we approached, Mrs. Dickerson stepped aside granting my first visage of Miss Antoinette. Even in this dim light, it was apparent that she possessed exquisite beauty. Her flawless porcelain skin contrasted hypnotically with her large ebony eyes. Her hair was only slightly more golden than her skin, but her tiny lips were as red as rose pedals.

"Miss Antoinette, thank you for granting us another session," the inspector whispered in what appeared to be the required etiquette. "This is Dr. Watson," he added in the same low tone.

Rather than speak, Antoinette smiled and nodded then swept her hand in a circular motion indicating that we should take seats around the table.

I sat to the right of the medium, the inspector to her left. Next to the inspector was his wife, the commodore would be sitting in the empty seat between us when he assumed his chair.

The medium motioned at her companion, who disappeared momentarily and returned with a small wooden container approximately the size of a shoe box, constructed from one inch planks. The commodore brought it over to me.

"You see, Dr. Watson," he whispered. "Inside is an electric bell," he lifted the lid as he spoke. I could plainly observe the bell as well as the battery to which it was wired. The planks were held together by copper strips that crossed widthwise. "Spirits can manifest electrical current. If we are fortunate enough to make contact, they should be able to ring the bell." I nodded in confirmation as the commodore abruptly ducked down and placed the contraption upon the floor under the table.

When the commodore reappeared, he produced a match and ignited five of the candles in the chandelier, although "chandelier" is perhaps an overstatement. The construction was simple and inexpensive. A thick metal cord descended from a circular base on the ceiling, connecting to a heavy iron central scalloped disk. Protruding from the disk were six curved iron rods each holding a candle.

The commodore cast his gaze on Antoinette and, after a moment, she nodded in a solemn fashion. The commodore scurried across the room and extinguished the gas jets completely, leaving the room lit only by the candles. He returned to the table and sat down.

"Control." The medium's sonorous voice sounded like a trumpet blast after my ears had become accustomed to the hushed whispers that had previously filled the room. "That means join hands," the inspector hissed in my ear.

We obeyed Miss Antoinette, whose tone was both melodiously feminine and commanding at the same time. The authoritative tenor contrasted greatly with her beauty as well as with the smile that possessed her lips.

"Now stand, and snuff the candle in front of you," she ordered in a beautiful pitch.

We stood and each blew out our respective candles, leaving the room in complete darkness. The medium's dainty right hand held my left, and I followed her lead and seated myself as she returned to her chair. When we were all back in our seats, I stretched out my left leg to cross in front of Antoinette, and my right to cross in front of the commodore. You see, I believed I had deduced how they had worked their tricks. It was my opinion that either she or her companion knocked on the table by raising their knees. With my legs positioned such, their foot would scrape my leg if they lifted a knee.

I also thought that I had figured out the ringing bell ploy. When the commodore showed me the interior of the box, I deduced that the copper strips acted as conductors and, if pressure were put upon the lid, the strip would touch both the positive and negative leads from the bell, completing the circuit. Thus if a foot were depressed upon the lid, the bell would ring. Again, with my legs extended, I had blocked the path to the box.

I could almost feel the smile upon Antoinette's lips as she said, "Dr. Watson, if you will, please place your left shin up against my right one, and your right in contact with the commodore's left. Inspector, kindly place your shin against my right and your left against you wife's right. Mrs. Dickerson, move your left leg so that it touches the commodore's left shin."

Now, not only were all of our hands entwined, so were our legs. My heart sank. I figured that I could make short work of this charlatan, but she had checkmated my move. Then I rallied. It is likely she felt the movement of my legs as I tried to block hers. This necessitated her attempt to prove she never had any intention to use her legs. I suspected that she would now feint an attempt to reach her spirit, eventually concluding that for some reason he was not responding tonight.

Suddenly a deep ghostly voice broke through my thoughts. "That leg remains stiff, doesn't it, doctor? The effects of the tribesman's bullet have never left you."

Chapter 3

The voice startled me. Although it emanated from my left, the deep manly timbre was so different from Antoinette's dainty light tone I found it hard to believe that it was her hand I still embraced.

"Excuse me?" I asked, regaining my composure.

"Your injury during the Afghan campaign, it still troubles you," returned the baritone.

"Yes, at times." I responded.

"The episode haunts you. A red aura surrounds you whenever you think of it."

This observation was untrue. My days in the campaign were eventful, but I was hardly "haunted."

"Your service in Afghanistan is what brought you here," the spirit boldly stated, as if this were some revelation. I had of course told the inspector this was the reason I sought a séance. Further, it was *not* the real reason I was in attendance. Apparently the spirit could not decipher my true motive to debunk the psychic.

"Oliver," the commodore jumped in, "can you make contact with any of the doctor's fallen comrades?"

Silence followed for a long ten seconds. "I can summon one who fell at Kandahar, but he cannot speak through me. I will channel his answers to the bell."

"The same code?" asked the commodore.

"Yes."

"One for 'yes,' two for 'no,' and three for 'I don't know,'" the commodore informed me.

Another long silence followed, before the ghostly voice stated, "Captain Wilkes is ready."

Captain Jason Wilkes and I had met here in England at our embarkation point and shipped together to India before traveling to Afghanistan. He was also in the medical corps, although his duty was to ensure transportation of personnel and supplies. He was indeed my closest companion at the time. He had avoided enemy fire but unfortunately was bitten by a krait which one night had taken refuge in his boot. The snake's powerful neurotoxin threw my friend into respiratory failure, ending his young life.

"Doctor, would you like to ask the captain a question?" the commodore asked.

I was surprised at the mention of Wilkes, and was unprepared for this prospect. Eventually, I blurted out, "Are you alright?"

"Brinnnng!" The bell under the table chimed a long single ring. The sound was startling, especially given that my legs were still in contact with the shins of both the medium and the commodore.

I had no idea how the bell was rung, but confident that I still had an opportunity to expose the gimmick. Quickly, I suppressed my surprise and scoured my brain for questions with which to trip up this "spirit." It would have been easy if I could have asked queries that did not require a yes or no answer, but I suppose that is why "Oliver" refused to translate verbally.

"Jason, if it is indeed you," I finally stated, "did the snake bite you upon the right foot?"

Silence. Then suddenly two rings of the bell. It was the correct answer! I quickly parried; "Was the ship we sailed upon *The Greenwich*?"

Two rings followed.

"Upon *The Suffolk*?" I asked.

Two rings again.

"Upon *The Essex*?"

One ring. It had indeed been *The Essex*.

"Dr. Watson, I knew you would want to confirm that Oliver had reached your friend, but aren't you convinced?" asked Mrs. Dickerson. "Don't you want to ask him more substantial questions?"

"Indeed, doctor, your time is nearing its end, the Dickersons also have spirits to contact tonight," the commodore reminded.

It was evident that the inspector and his wife were anxious to move on to their own conversations with the dead, and they had of course been polite enough to not only include me, but allow me to take my turn first. Regrettably, I admit that I had become flustered. I tried to regain my composure, and made a few hurried inquiries about other comrades and whether they were with him in the afterlife. I hoped to expose the hoax by naming both men who had died in Afghanistan as well as some who were still quite alive. Yet, the bell answered in the affirmative on several occasions, confirming several who had indeed been killed and, at other times, three rings indicated that the ghost did not know. Thus my latest ploy had been deftly brushed aside.

"The captain has left us," Oliver abruptly announced, coincidentally directly upon the quarter hour mark.

Mrs. Dickerson was eager to continue a previous conversation with her mother, and Oliver readily complied. The bell again rang its answers, but ten minutes into the contact, Oliver announced that the bell was requiring too much of the spirit's energy and she would use the same pattern to knock upon the table instead.

I tensed my legs to reaffirm that neither the medium nor Commodore Peters could use their knee to bang underneath the slab. Yet, to my surprise the knocks came, nonetheless. For another ten minutes, the inspector's mother-in-law communicated with her daughter over trivial matters, the substance of which was subjective and impossible to verify.

As we passed our allotted time, Oliver announced that he no longer had sufficient strength to cross the plane and had to retreat back to the netherworld. A long silence was broken by the sweet, soft voice of Antoinette.

"That is all," she almost whispered.

The medium and the commodore released my hands and I heard the gentleman's chair scrape and his footfalls cross the room. A moment later, the gas jet illuminated the room and I caught a fleeting glimpse of Miss Antoinette as she slowly exited through a door on the far side of the room, holding the frame for support.

The commodore followed my glance. "Please excuse her. The effort necessary to bridge our two worlds is enormous," he stated. "She requires immediate rest."

As the Dickersons said their good-byes to the commodore, I stole peeks at the table, bell box, and about the room, but I could not discern anything telling.

Holmes was already asleep when I returned to Baker Street that night. I wish I could have entered the dream state myself, but I could not purge the séance from my mind. How did they know about Jason Wilkes? If it wasn't truly his spirit, how had he answered all of my questions correctly? To be sure, they were not the most challenging of queries, but still there were no slip-ups. And what of the bell box and knocking? Could the Dickersons have been a party to the fraud? They were in control of the medium and the commodore's other hand and leg. I shook my head vigorously, dismissing the thought as absurd. They were true believers, not accomplices. How, then, could the noises have been made?

Holmes was already at his coffee and newspapers when I emerged from my room the next morning.

"Watson, a restless night, I see?" He laughed, before continuing on with his perusal of the news.

Without responding, I sat myself at the table and slid over a portion of the paper he had already dispensed with. I scanned the headlines trying to focus on the newsprint, but I was unable to concentrate. I had hoped Holmes would broach the subject of the séance, giving me an opportunity to unburden myself, but he said not a word and sat quietly sipping his coffee and digesting the morning news.

"All right, Watson, I can torture you no longer," he eventually smirked, putting down his paper.

It was folly, of course, to think that Holmes had failed to recognize my agitated state. The consummate observer had merely been toying with me.

"Holmes, don't you have a curious bone in your body?" I ejected. "Don't you want to know what happened at the séance?"

He chuckled. "My desire to hear is eclipsed by your longing to tell. My dear Watson, my whole profession is based upon my curiosity! However, you are well aware that my focus is a narrow one. I have no craving to fill valuable space in my brain with material that does not pertain to my rather unique vocation. Yet, I am not as callous as some think. If you are troubled, then I am at your disposal."

Everything Holmes said was true. There was no doubt that he thrived on solving problems; a characteristic indicative of a curious mind. Further, although my companion often appeared indifferent to subjects not pertaining to his field, and his demeanor was abrupt at times, he has always been a loyal friend.

I recounted the events of the previous evening with as much detail as I could recall. During my recitation, Holmes moved from the table to the fireplace mantel and filled his pipe. He strolled the room smoking as I told my tale.

"Holmes, I have been at your side for many adventures and am prideful that I have absorbed some of your techniques in observation and deduction. Yet, I cannot seem to figure how the tricks were done."

"Watson, the power of observation is reduced considerably when the lights are extinguished."

"So you confirm that shrouding the room in darkness is a blind."

"A firm grasp of the obvious, Watson!" he chided me. "Although I have no expertise in specters or goblins, I cannot deduce any reason that would prevent them from working their magic in a well-lit room. In fact, doing so would go a long way in crushing the criticism of skeptics."

"How do you suppose the bell was rung? How did they create the knocking? Both Antoinette and the commodore were fully immobilized."

"Those questions cannot be answered given the data provided," he off-handedly proclaimed between puffs of his pipe.

"So you can offer no suggestions?" The disappointment was evident in my tone.

"Chin up, Watson!" he laughed. "More went on in that room than bangs and bells. If I am not mistaken, you are confused as to how the medium conjured up your old friend Captain Wilkes."

"Indeed! Can you explain it?" I rallied.

"I suspect so. Do you recall the clue I gave you before you left for the séance?"

I pondered. "You told me a name... Hiram... Hiram Silver!"

"Capital, Watson! Your memory is commendable," he said, as he moved across the room to the bookshelves. Holmes dragged his finger along the volumes until he found the object of his quest. He thumbed through the pages before dropping the open book on the table before me.

The volume was one of Holmes's private indexes, personally compiled by my friend in order to facilitate his investigations. I read the paragraph under the entry for "Hiram Silver."

"So, this man is a private detective, like you?" I asked.

"I am offended at the comparison, Watson!" He is a private detective, to be sure, but hardly like me. The man has no conscience. He is indiscriminate in his choice of clients, serving anyone willing to meet his fees."

"I see here that you believed him to be in St. Petersburg," I said, pointing to the entry.

"I did, until your little adventure with the Saunders's maid. The physical description you uncovered fits him perfectly."

"But how does he figure into this?"

"My dear Watson, isn't it obvious? He is in the employ of this commodore. Silver was sent to pull off the little caper at the Saunders household and he used his investigative skills to uncover information about your service in Afghanistan."

I digested the thought. "So you believe that this Hiram Silver investigates a client's background prior to a séance? But how would he know what information would be pertinent? The medium cannot possibly memorize complete biographies of the people sitting around her table."

"Watson, you surprise me," he said examining the stem of his pipe. "In your own case, Antoinette and the commodore knew that your purpose was to contact a fallen comrade, so the scope of material shrunk immediately to your time in Afghanistan, the only place you saw action. It would be no small feat for Silver to obtain your military records, or to visit a veteran's home and ask a few who had served in your unit about your relationships. If you should want to spend your time investigating this point, I have no doubt you would eventually find those with whom Silver discussed your past. Although it may take considerable time to follow the thread. If you trust my opinions, you can dispense with the effort and take it as fact.

"Further Watson, the answer system of 'yes' 'no' and 'I don't know' lends itself to deception. Antoinette is briefed about the demise of your most intimate associate and several others in your unit who died in the campaign. All questions for which she has no data, mysteriously elude the spirit as he responds that he does not know."

I sat silent for a moment. "Granted Holmes, I did tip my hand by telling Dickerson the reason I wanted the séance, but the military is meticulous for keeping records so my case must be the exception. How could Silver unearth such details about other clients who have led more reserved lives?"

"Watson, remember I already explained that these 'clients' are ruled by emotion. They are anxious to tell their stories. There can be no doubt that they seek the medium *wanting* to believe and likely gush forth the desired information in their preliminary conversations when asking for a séance. And," he continued, "even those who are not so forthcoming will have some traumatic event in their past. Such an event would not be difficult to uncover and will undoubtedly be the subject of their inquiry."

I digested Holmes's analysis for a moment. "What would you suggest I do next?" I asked.

"Ha! I recommend that you forget this business and tend to Mr. Ross's headache. If I am not mistaken, that is his son's tread upon the stairs. He always leaps them two at a time when sent to fetch you."

Seconds later, our door echoed with the boy's knock. As Holmes predicted, the lad needed me to attend to one of his father's chronic migraines.

"All right, Willie, I will be right along; run home and tell your father that I will dress and be over presently," I told the boy as I receded into my chambers. "But, Holmes, I would appreciate some further counsel on this matter later."

"As you wish, Watson," he said relighting his pipe, "but no good will come of it."

When I returned later that morning, our rooms were abandoned. Silence hung heavily, the only sound emitted from the slow arc of the clock's pendulum. I had just removed my hat and dropped my bag beside the rack when a soft rap sounded on the door.

"Doctor Watson?"

"Yes, Mrs. Hudson?" I replied to our landlady as I swung the door inward.

"Oh, Dr. Watson, you ran out without breakfast this morning!" she said, pushing past me carrying a tray of victuals.

"Indeed, I did, Mrs. Hudson. Thank you, I am famished!"

Our dutiful hostess placed the tray upon the table and I sat eager to relieve the dishes of their burden.

"Do you know where Mr. Holmes is?" I asked.

"No. You know how he is, doctor. He went tearing out of here like a dervish about an hour ago. Although, at least he waited until he had his morning meal." She cast a condemning expression my way.

It was after ten o'clock that evening and Holmes still had not returned. I settled into a chair by the fire to read, but the sleep that eluded me the night prior grabbed firm hold and I nodded off after a few pages.

I awoke as the door slowly creaked open. A stealthy figure clad in a black cape and wide brimmed hat slid surreptitiously into the room. I was still befogged with slumber, but was alert enough to grab up the poker. My vision had not yet cleared as I tried to creep around the sofa to confront the intruder, but my toe slammed squarely into the leg, and I cried out in pain. The figure spun, and grabbed my upraised hand, preventing the poker from descending upon his skull. We locked in an embrace, his sullen, swarthy face so close to my own that his mustache scratched my cheek.

"Watson! Watson!" the familiar voice called out.

"Holmes?" I asked in disbelief.

"My good fellow, kindly relinquish the poker before you injure a brain you have so often admired." He laughed between clenched teeth.

I immediately relaxed my grip, and turned to crank up the gas jet. The illumination did little to expose my friend's identity. Had it not been for the recognition of his voice, I would have resumed my attack.

Holmes ducked into the washroom and emerged wiping his face with a wet cloth. As the makeup stripped away, his familiar features began to appear.

"I am sorry I startled you, old man!" Holmes laughed, tearing the false mustache away. "An opportunity came my way today that required I apply this disguise."

I sat down, the fog of sleep finally shaken away. "What were you doing?"

"A pickpocket was operating outside of several restaurants downtown, and the management engaged me to apprehend the scoundrel."

"Did you catch him?"

"Her, Watson. It turned out to be a woman. Yes, I nabbed her. When I returned, I could see from the street that the jets were down and that the fire had burned low, so I knew you had fallen asleep. I entered so furtively because I was trying not to disturb you. I assure you; from now on, I will loudly announce my presence so as to avoid a thrashing!"

Chapter 4

Holmes and I were both kept busy the next few days, though following different paths. He was engaged in several investigations of small magnitude, while an outbreak of fever in the neighborhood kept me actively employed. I had little time to ruminate over the medium problem, and no opportunity to receive further counsel from Holmes. By the end of the week, both of our schedules had calmed sufficiently, and I hoped to take up the matter once more. However, sensational events intervened.

"Hallo!" exclaimed Holmes slapping the newspaper with the back of his hand.

"What is it, Holmes?"

"Finally a worthy case, Watson!" he said, handing me the paper.

SAGGARN DIAMOND VANISHES! The headline read.

"Good Heavens, Holmes! Doesn't the Saggarn Diamond belong to Lady Winfield?"

"Indeed. The same fair lady who has become a devotee of your medium, Watson."

"But, what happened?"

"An excellent question, doctor. I have only seen the headline. Kindly read the article aloud so that we may both be illuminated," he said, handing me the paper.

I scanned through to the pertinent part of the piece. "*Last evening, Lady Winfield opened her safe in order to return a pair of pearl earrings. After doing so, she fancied a look at her most prized piece of jewelry, the Saggarn Diamond. She removed the hinged silver box holding the stone, and seated herself by her dressing table. Lady Winfield placed the case upon the table and lit a candle. Upon opening the box, she was startled to discover the diamond was missing. Her exclamation brought the butler, who helped the frantic woman sur-*

vey the other valuable items in her safe. However, all were accounted for. Inspectors Lestrade and Dickerson answered the call. The inspectors found no signs of forced entry into either the safe or the Lady's dwelling."

Holmes rubbed his hands together, salivating over the challenge. He motioned me to continue. *"The inspectors attempted to ascertain the time of the theft by asking Lady Winfield the last time she had seen the diamond. The Lady responded that the previous night, she had entertained guests in her home and she had brought the famed jewel out to show the partygoers. She personally returned the diamond to the vault and thus swears that it was safely under lock and key since that time."*

"Does it state who these guests were?" Holmes asked.

"Yes. In attendance were: Colonel Stephens and his wife, Lord Cheltham, Mrs. Curtis, Stanley Kern, MP, Mr. and Mrs. Yarborough, the actress Candice Boice, Baron and Baroness Von Sickle, Chancellor of the Exchequer Paulson and..." I paused, "Commodore Peters."

I saw a slight smile flit across Holmes's face.

"What of the servants?"

"It states that the servants have been questioned, as well as the few additional staff brought on for the party, but no irregularities have been found. All, including the guests and even Lady Winfield herself, present the same story. *At about nine o'clock, Lady Winfield gladly succumbed to requests to see the jewel and went to retrieve it. She opened the case and passed it from guest to guest. Several even handled the gem, but all attest that it was back in place in the case before Lady Winfield closed the lid to return it to the safe.* The only item of note here, Holmes, is that after she closed the lid, a careless servant bumped her and spilled piping hot tea onto the case. It states that the liquid was scorching and would have seriously scalded the woman's hand had she not been wearing gloves. The servant apologized profusely and used a linen napkin to dry the case."

"Did Lestrade and Dickerson examine the case?" Holmes asked.

"Let us see... Yes, it says the inspectors made a thorough examination of the silver box that held the jewel. It is an ornate container approximately six inches wide, six inches long and three inches in height. The lid is festooned with a carved sun, the rays of which contain slender slits one sixteenth of an inch wide thus allowing air to permeate the enclosure. Purple velvet lines the inside of the case. The detectives noted that this velvet was tacky to the touch, undoubtedly the result of the spilled tea."

I scanned further for any other details. "Nothing more, Holmes. It says that the investigation of course is ongoing."

My friend's enthusiasm was evident. It was clear that he considered this crime to be a problem of some enormity. Holmes thrived upon a challenge and the more difficult the problem, the more excited he became.

"Delicious, Watson!" he said, again rubbing his hands together. "I have no doubt that Lestrade and Dickerson are out of the depth. I anticipate a visit before lunch!"

Holmes pulled a few volumes from the bookcase and casually began organizing some of his files. He was jovial, almost giddy, with expectation.

I took up a seat at the desk and began recording billing entries in my ledger and making out the charge slips for the patients I had seen that week. Some hours passed and Holmes moved nonchalantly from his files to his chemistry set. He bided his time, waiting for the inevitable arrival of the detectives by conducting a series of experiments, the aroma of which indicated some study involving sulfuric acid.

By early afternoon, Holmes began making furtive glances out of the window. Twice, carriages stopped on the street below causing him to part the curtains to ascertain if the deputies of Scotland Yard had arrived. However, both occasions were false alarms.

The wall clock chimed seven times as the pink light of day retreated from our rooms. I lit the jets, having to navigate past Holmes as he paced the floor in agitation. I had become so accustomed to the inevitability of my companion's predictions that I was shocked that Lestrade and Dickerson had not yet arrived to seek his guidance.

My friend's demeanor had slowly shifted with the passage of the day and, by this time, he was clearly disturbed. He had not spoken for hours and I was hesitant to draw attention to the point that was certainly the root of his annoyance. At last, however, I felt it necessary, lest Holmes might wear a trench in the carpet.

"Do you suppose they have solved it themselves?" I asked, pouring two glasses of brandy.

"Impossible!" came the curt reply as he waved off the glass I offered him.

"Holmes, do you know the solution?" I again extended the goblet, which Holmes took and immediately placed on an end table. He walked off to the window and peered up and down Baker Street.

"No, which is why I can claim with certainty that Lestrade and Dickerson have not figured it out," he replied, without any awareness of the arrogance of his words.

That evening, Holmes sat smoking by the fire. In his lap rested a notebook, and in his hand, a pen. He claimed that he was going to add to one of his previous monographs on handwriting analysis. However, the tip of his pen sat dry, never once touching the bottle of ink that rested upon the side table. It did not take an observer of Holmes's acumen to determine that his mind was elsewhere.

I believe it was pride alone that kept him anchored in our rooms. There can be little doubt that he was anxious to track down the inspectors and wrangle the case from them. But Holmes could never bring himself to do such a thing. Although he endeavored to remain humble (as humble as he was capable), there existed a degree of conceit in him. This measure of arrogance had been earned, though. He had become the preeminent consulting detective by exacting success after success, based upon not only his innate gifts, but also upon focused dedication to improving his skills and furthering his craft. Time after time, Scotland Yard would call hat in hand and, without fail, my companion would achieve what they could not.

It was not the first time I had seen Holmes in such a state. He often became miserable when he was without a challenging case; however, this was the only occasion in which I ever perceived him to be anxious, perhaps even confused. There he sat, unable to take possession of something that he considered to be rightly his. Although I trusted he was correct, that the detectives were out of their depth, Holmes could not pierce the veil surrounding this newest mystery—why had they not called upon him?

"Holmes?" I called, stooping to clean up the sheets of the morning paper strewn about the room.

I had retrieved but half of the broadsheets when a gentle knock reverberated through the door.

"Dr. Watson, are you up?"

"Yes, Mrs. Hudson, do come in," I called back.

"I thought I heard you moving about. I brought you your morning coffee."

"Thank you, Mrs. Hudson. Do you know where Mr. Holmes went?"

"No, doctor, but he stormed out a few moments after the boy brought up the paper."

I sat myself at the table, rearranging the newspaper into its proper order. I nearly spat the coffee from my lips when I read the headline.

POLICE TURN TO MEDIUM FOR AID IN SAGGARN DIAMOND CASE

I dove into the story and read between the lines of the sterile account to form an idea of what had transpired. Apparently, Antoinette approached Lady Winfield and declared that she had the power to help recover the diamond. Lady Winfield immediately contacted her fellow disciple, Inspector Dickerson, who agreed to conduct the police investigation in conjunction with the medium. The paper expressed some degree of skepticism, and offered several mild scoffs at the aptitude of Dickerson. However, the writer was quite evenhanded, describing the phenomenal successes of the psychic and the number of respected individuals who vouched for her abilities. It was clear that, although the author of the article was a skeptic by nature, he was unwilling to discount the powers of the celebrated medium—or perhaps disinclined to openly insult the beliefs of Lady Winfield.

The disarray with which Holmes had left the paper had indicated his agitation, but the content within the print solidified the reason. I was not sure where Holmes had gone, or what tack he was taking, but I determined that I should endeavor to be of some assistance. Unlike Holmes, I had met Antoinette before, and I had given no indication that I held any contempt for her. As far as she and the commodore knew, I had fallen for their charade. Perhaps Dickerson would put me in contact with her again, and I could probe her for information.

"Inspector Lestrade!" I called, as the constable brushed past me on the precinct steps.

"Oh, Dr. Watson. Pardon, I didn't even see you. I've been a bit distracted." He replied, after turning back toward me.

"Lestrade, I was surprised by the paper this morning! Are you really turning your investigation over to Miss Antoinette?"

"No," he said through clenched teeth. "I plan on conducting my inquiry according to department procedure. It's that daft Dickerson," he jerked a thumb over his shoulder toward the building behind. "He's got the run of things due to his political connections. But you know me, doctor. I am a man of some abilities and have recorded more than a few successes. I am officially attached to Dickerson in this investigation, but I will not go in for the hocus pocus. I plan to use the tried and true methods that have served the Yard well for these many years!"

"I see. I would venture that Mr. Holmes agrees with you on that count."

"I have no doubt. What perchance does Mr. Holmes think about the case?" he asked eagerly.

I refrained from mentioning Holmes's appraisal of Lestrade's prospects for triumph in the matter. "We have not had much opportunity to discuss the subject; Holmes had left the house before I awoke. However, from what little he said yesterday, I can state that he does think the case to be a complex one."

"Indeed! My feelings exactly. I am glad to hear that Mr. Holmes corroborates my opinions. When I saw him this morning, I had feared that he thought the whole thing a lark."

"You saw Holmes this morning?"

"I only caught sight of him from a distance. He was coming out of a confectionary downtown. I wondered that Mr. Holmes would be so lackadaisical to indulge his sweet tooth when one of the most precious gems in Britain has gone missing! I am relieved that you say he considers the case a serious one."

"I have faith in your abilities, Lestrade. Incidentally, what does Dickerson think?

"Who knows?" he jeered, with a wave of his hand. "When he began to spout his spiritualist nonsense, I turned a deaf ear. Well, I really must be off doctor. Good day."

"Good day, Lestrade, and good luck."

I was glad that Lestrade had not inquired as to why I was at Scotland Yard. Given his contempt for Dickerson, it would have been difficult to explain my errand without exposing my own plans to manipulate the inspector.

"Ah, if it isn't the good Dr. Watson!" Dickerson boomed as I entered his office. "I'm very busy, very busy today! What can I do for you?"

"Well, inspector, I cannot get the séance out of my mind. I believe there may be something to this Spiritualism." I played to his devotion to his new faith.

"I thought so. I thought so. I told Mrs. Dickerson as much, too. I told her that you were an intelligent man who would undoubtedly see the light." Thinking he had made a new convert, his pleasure was transparent.

"Do you think Anoinette can solve this diamond caper?" I baited Dickerson.

"Oh, I have no doubt, Dr. Watson," he stated with conviction. "In fact, I'm on my way to consult her now."

"Would you mind if I accompanied you?" I boldly stated, knowing that I had no real right to be privy to official police matters.

The inspector paused for a moment, mulling over the proposition. He stroked his red side whiskers. "I don't see why not! You have been intimately associated with more than a few Scotland Yard cases and no one on the force has ever doubted your integrity or discretion," he concluded, his enthusiasm for inducting what he perceived as a new devotee of Spiritualism overwhelming his professional judgment.

"Hello, inspector, and I see you have Dr. Watson with you," the commodore greeted us after having been summoned by the doorman.

"Yes, Dr. Watson was greatly impressed with the madam's abilities and asked if he might tag along," Dickerson beamed.

"Of course. Few attend one of her séances without being drawn to return. This way, gentlemen, the lady is in the parlor."

He led us into a comfortably furnished living room where the aforementioned woman was seated in an oversized chair. Sitting nearby was none other than Lady Winfield.

"Oh, hello, inspector," Antoinette said without turning toward us. "And Dr. Watson, it is nice to see you again." Her voice was of the natural melodious feminine timbre that contrasted so greatly with the deeper, gruffer accent emitted when she channeled her spirit guide.

"A recurrent pleasure," I stated, bowing slightly. Her platinum locks and ebony eyes had lost none of their enchantment. I turned toward the noblewoman, "A pleasure to see you again as well, my lady."

"Please, sit down," the commodore said, motioning toward the sofa. We took seats, although Commodore Peters himself stood dutifully behind Antoinette.

"No Inspector Lestrade today?" The faintest hint of a smile flashed across Antoinette's face.

Dickerson spoke up, "No, madam, he is a man of hard habits and is insistent in following his own path. Dr. Watson and I, however, prefer a more direct route to the solution." He smiled broadly in my direction, still pleased that I had come around to his new religion.

"Madam, if I might ask," I ventured forth, "do you think you can identify the thief?

"He has been identified," she stated emotionlessly.

"What?" I spat out.

"I told you, Dr. Watson," Dickerson chuckled. "I knew you would come through, madam. Name the man and we will go and nab him and recover the stone," he confidently proclaimed.

Lady Winfield leaned forward, obviously anxious to learn the scoundrel's identity.

"Name him, I can," Antoinette turned her eyes away from us and out of the window. "But you will never lay your hands on him."

The color drained from Dickerson's face as his chance for glory slipped away. "Why on Earth not?" he stammered.

"Because he is not *on* Earth," she said in a near whisper.

"Has...has he been killed?" Dickerson queried.

"Yes. Long ago," her voice trailed off.

"Do you mean to say that some ghost has taken the diamond?" I asked incredulously.

Antoinette closed her eyes. She sat motionless for half a minute. Suddenly she stated, "Oliver was the one who figured it out. A spirit named Randolph is the culprit. Unfortunately, I know no more than his name. He dematerialized the jewel, transporting it to the spirit realm."

"All is lost then!" Lady Winfield threw her hands up in despair.

Chapter 5

Lady Winfield and Inspector Dickerson were ashen. The Spiritualism disciples were so shaken they were oblivious to the skepticism written across my own face.

"There is hope," Miss Antoinette stated in a solemn tone.

This glimmer roused the two devotees and the color returned to their faces. They leaned forward expectantly, their eager eyes trained upon the medium.

"Oliver may be able to recover the gem," she said soothingly.

"We would be greatly indebted," Lady Winfield wrung her hands in a pleading manner.

"I will have to commune with Oliver. If you will be kind enough to return this evening, I should have an answer for you then." The psychic rose from her seat and exited the room without another word.

"She feels the pull," the commodore stated, his eyes following Antoinette from the room. "Please excuse her abruptness. To be sure, something is afoot in the spirit world."

"Not at all, not at all!" the flustered Dickerson proclaimed.

"Do you think she can recover the stone?" Lady Winfield asked Commodore Peters, the anxiety evident in her voice.

"I don't know, my lady. I have been present when she has conjured up ectoplasm, and have witnessed her bringing forth forms of vapor. However, as far as I know, no medium has ever been able to move a solid object across the dimensional plane." Seeing the distress in Lady Winfield's eyes, he quickly followed up, "However, Miss Antoinette is powerful and Oliver does not make idle boasts. I expect that if it *can* be done, it *will* be done."

"Holmes, I'm glad to see you!" I ejected upon entering our rooms.

Holmes was seated by the window, engaged in writing out some correspondence.

"And I you, Watson," he folded the paper and deposited it in his pocket. "What is the news from Dickerson?"

"Dickerson? How do you know I've seen Inspector Dickerson?"

"Watson, you left the house without your medical bag, which means you were not about practicing your trade. Your obsession with this medium business could only have increased due to the disappearance of the Saggarn Stone, so it is logical that you would call on Dickerson, who is not only your contact to the psychic, but also one of the investigators of the crime. So, what does Dickerson have to say?" He impatiently demanded.

I have seldom found my friend as abrupt or surly. It was obvious that, whatever errands he undertook that afternoon, they did little to diminish the displeasure he felt regarding Scotland Yard's decision to turn to the medium rather than to him.

"Well, Holmes, you are correct as usual," I replied, removing my coat and depositing it on the hook. "I went to the Yard to see if I could pry any information from Dickerson," I took the seat next to him before continuing. "He did not have anything to offer there at headquarters, but fortunately, he agreed to take me with him to see Antoinette."

Holmes flashed a pleased smirk, as this information obviously caught him by surprise. "Do go on, Watson," he stated, his composure returning with lightning speed.

"Lady Winfield was there as well. Miss Antoinette told us that the jewel was indeed stolen..."

"Ah, capital, Watson!" he interrupted, his delight increasing as my story progressed. He stood and began to pace the room as I continued.

"She even named the offender. Someone named 'Randolph'."

"A mysterious fellow no doubt, eh, Watson? Someone the police will have a difficult time arresting?"

"Indeed."

"Perhaps this Randolph has hidden the diamond, but now has skipped off, whereabouts unknown?" Holmes postulated.

"Hardly that, Holmes. She said that he is a spirit."

"Ha!" laughed Holmes. "I should have guessed as much!" he rubbed his hands together. "I suppose she foretold that she will commune with her spirit guide and then lead Dickerson right to the diamond."

"Well, not quite. She stated that the ghost transported the gem to the spirit world."

"What?" Holmes froze in place, and then began his pacing anew. "This is far more serious a matter than I originally thought, Watson."

"Holmes, if the stone were not evaporated to the spirit dimension, how did they make it disappear?" I interrupted, completely perplexed as to how the trick was accomplished. But he made no reply. He continued his pacing, lost in thought.

"You think Antoinette and the commodore are complicit, do you not?" I asked.

"Indeed, Watson," he roused from his solitude, "but I did not think they were thieves." He picked up the poker and nudged the fire back to life.

"How do you mean, Holmes?"

"My suspicion was that they had affected the diamond's disappearance for publicity purposes and that they would lead the doddering Dickerson in recovering it."

"You may still be correct, Holmes."

"How's that, Watson?" He again froze in place.

"Antoinette said that she was going to commune with Oliver and see if she could bring the gem back to this plane."

"Ha! I see! She will either prove my original notion correct and produce the gem, adding to her ever-increasing reputation, or she will claim an inability to do so, and thus actually be culpable in robbery.

"Watson," he continued, "you must prod Dickerson as to the outcome of Antoinette's conference with her spirit guide."

"That won't be necessary, Holmes. She appears to believe that I am converted, and invited me to accompany Dickerson tonight."

"Splendid, Watson! Since it is impossible for me to be there myself, you are as good a substitute as is possible."

I smiled at the compliment. "I will report the event to you as best I can, Holmes."

"I have no doubt, Watson. Remember to pay close attention to detail, however small," he instructed.

"I shall do my best. I cannot help but wonder however, how they made the diamond disappear," I pondered aloud.

"That much, I already know. I am more interested in if they will give it back."

I was dumbfounded. "You know how the stone was taken?" I stammered. "How, Holmes?"

He laughed heartily. "Watson, you know I will certainly tell you, but not before I have the complete story. The entrée and the side dishes must all be put on the table at the same time in order to properly enjoy the meal. When all of this food is cooked, I will lay it before you."

That evening, Dickerson and I drove out to the abode of Miss Antoinette. I was in a pensive mood, trying to work out the machinations of the medium and her protector, but the inspector was almost giddy with anticipation. Certainly, he was a true believer in the Spiritualist religion, but he was likewise completely confident in the abilities of Antoinette. He was absolutely certain that she would be able to retrieve the diamond from the netherworld.

"Think what this will mean to science, doctor! Think of the possibilities! Never mind that," he continued, his mind racing from one track to another, "think about the impact on police work! Criminals will no longer be able to hide. Crimes will no longer be consigned to the 'unsolved' bin!"

I tried to reign in the capricious officer. "Now, inspector, don't get ahead of yourself. She has not even told us she can produce the gem."

"A matter of time, dear Watson. Only a matter of time." He patted my arm in a condescending fashion.

"Even if she is able to bring forth the stone, you don't really believe that means that she will be able to solve all crimes do you?"

"Well, you have me there, doctor. No, I did get away with myself a bit there," he chuckled. "We wouldn't want that anyway, would we? I'd be out of a job! No, but I am sure that she would be able to help the force a great deal, though."

"Don't you suppose that Oliver has been able to get a bead on this chap Randolph because they are both spirits?" I patronized his faith in his new religion. "Do you think he will be able to identify flesh and blood criminals just as easily?"

He was thoughtful for a moment. "You know, you bring up a good question, doctor. I hadn't thought of that."

As our carriage arrived, Dickerson was somewhat sullen, obviously dejected that I had let the wind out of his sails regarding the future of a psychic detective bureau.

"Ah, gentlemen! It is a pleasure to see you." Commodore Peters shook each of our hands vigorously. The upbeat demeanor of our host affected an immediate revival of Dickerson's spirits.

"I take it that Miss Antoinette was able to contact Oliver?" I asked, feigning to share in their jubilation.

"Indeed, and he communicated that he will endeavor to return the stone to this plane!"

"Wonderful!" Dickerson exclaimed.

"However," the commodore shifted to a severe and solemn tone, "there are dangers."

"Dangers?" I asked, suppressing a smirk.

He continued in his grave tenor. "Certainly, sir. Nothing like this has ever been attempted. If Miss Antoinette can breach the two dimensions, it is true she may be able to re-trieve the diamond, but who knows what else may force its way through?"

"Egad! I never thought of that!" Dickerson breathed.

"Worse still," the commodore continued, "there is no guarantee that items from this world won't be pulled across the divide."

"You mean, rather than retrieve the stone, we may lose other objects?"

"Objects… or even people."

"People?" The incredulity present in my voice could hardly have been missed.

"Yes, you see, doctor," Dickerson addressed me with full sincerity, "anyone participating in such a séance might be sucked through to the realm of the dead."

I nodded soberly, even though I could hardly believe the inspector was serious. Had I not been on an investigative mis-sion, I may well have laughed aloud and subjected both to a barrage of ridicule. Yet, I kept my composure and maintained my charade. It was absolutely necessary that they have full confidence in my devotion to this Spiritualism despite the transparency of the farce.

"So, I must ask gentlemen; are you willing to take part in the séance?" He grasped both of our hands for emphasis.

Dickerson looked at me and I nodded in assent. "We are game, sir." He answered for both of us.

"Very well, then. Lady Winfield is already upstairs. Fol-low me," he stated and slowly headed for the staircase.

The commodore led us upstairs to the door of the same room that was the setting for the first séance I had attended. Peters rapped on the wood in quick succession, but did not wait for a reply from within. He pushed the door open and we entered in turn, emerging in the same curtained foyer that walled the doorway off from the rest of the room.

I paused briefly at the offering box and began to remove my billfold. The commodore gently grabbed hold of my wrist. "No need for that, doctor. The madam won't be reading for

you tonight. Lady Winfield has already covered the expenses."
I cannot be certain, but I thought I detected a subtle note of
glee in the commodore's voice.

I followed the inspector through the veil and Peters
trailed me. The room appeared unaltered from my last visit.
The gas jets were low, their light absorbed by the purple wall
coverings and black bunting that covered the shuttered windows. Lady Winfield sat alone at the round table under the
unlit candelabra.

"Oh, commodore," a nervous excitement accented her
voice. "I am glad you have returned. Have you spoken to Antoinette? Are we still going to make the attempt?" In her distracted state, the lady did not even acknowledge the inspector
and me.

"My lady," I stepped forward and made a slight bow, a
gesture awkwardly echoed by Dickerson.

"Oh, hello, doctor, inspector." She recognized us with
her voice, but her eyes were still fixated upon Peters.

"Yes, my lady." He came around the table and patted her
arm reassuringly. "We are going to make the attempt. But
please remember there are no guarantees. What we are about
to try has never even been endeavored."

A relieved look swept over the woman's features. "I am
confident, commodore. Antoinette has put me in contact with
more than one loved one who has passed on. Her powers are
undeniable."

"Yes, madam, her powers are strong, and if it can be
done I doubt any other medium could accomplish it. Still, do
not be dismayed if we fail."

At that moment, the door on the far side of the room
opened and the medium slid inside. She looked as exquisite as
before, her long almost white hair falling down past the porcelain face and onto her shoulders. Her dress was of the same
dark purple that hung from the walls and as she shut the door
behind her, her body faded into the background. The pallid,
though beautiful head seemed to float toward us.

Antoinette stood before us without speaking, torturing the poor noblewoman who looked at her with pleading eyes. Finally, she raised her hand, which was obviously a sign to her partner.

"Take your seats please, gentleman," the commodore stated, following the unspoken command. "Doctor, kindly sit where you did upon your last visit, there, to Miss Antoinette's right. Inspector, you will sit to her left as before, and Lady Winfield can remain where she is." This arrangement placed Dickerson and me in control of the medium's arms and legs with the noblewoman between the inspector and commodore. I would complete the link between Peters and the medium.

Before taking his seat, the commodore disappeared through the far door and returned carrying the bell box. He slid under the table and negotiated our legs to place the apparatus on the floor, apparently centered under the table. He then followed the same ritual as before and lit five candles in the candelabra. Next, he danced over to the gas jets and spun them closed, leaving the room lit only by the flicker of the candles. Finally, he took his seat.

"Control," said Antoinette, emitting her first spoken words of the evening. We joined hands. "Please stand and blow out your candle," she almost whispered. My eyes readjusted to the blackness as we again seated ourselves and she instructed that we touch shins with the individual to either side of us, as we did during the first séance, thus preventing any manipulation under the table.

All was silent. More than two minutes had passed and although my own impatience was growing I could only imagine the anxiety building in Lady Winfield.

Suddenly the medium's voice drifted across the table, "Oliver… Oliver…Oliver…" her sonorous tone almost sang the spirit's name.

Silence again. Another minute passed. "I have made contact," she breathed.

"Oliver, are you with us?" she asked, despite already telling us she had contacted her guide. From beneath the table an affirmation came as the shrill electric bell rang once.

"Oliver is telling me that he will not use the box again tonight. Nor will he take control of my vocal cords. Rather, he will converse with me and I will translate what he says and does."

This was a different tack than my first séance where the ghostly voice of the spirit had taken over the medium's voice box. This time, apparently, she would remain herself and merely communicate Oliver's thoughts to us.

"Oliver, can you retrieve the stone?"

A long moment of silence followed. "He says 'No,' " the medium stated curtly.

I could almost feel Lady Winfield deflate across the table. "Will he not even make an attempt? Can you not get him to try?" she finally gasped.

Antoinette again addressed the spirit. "Oliver, in our earlier communication, you told me that you would at least make the attempt. Why are you now unwilling to do so?" Ten seconds elapsed. "He said that he tried to coax Randolph into relinquishing the jewel, but he will not turn it over."

The commodore chimed in, "Can Oliver forcibly take it from him?"

"Oliver, can you wrest it from Randolph?" the medium echoed the inquiry.

A full minute passed. "He will try."

Lady Winfield sighed in relief.

After another long pause, Antoinette began to speak once more. "He is searching... he has located Randolph..." I could imagine the noblewoman squeezing Dickerson's hand like a vice. "He...he is struggling..." The medium's voice showed signs of angst. "Randolph will not let go. He will not release the diamond." The duress in her inflection was as if she herself were having a tug-o-war with the malevolent entity. Long moments passed. Finally, she sung out, "He has it. Oliver has it."

207

Lady Winfield gasped.

"Now, I must endeavor to tear a rift in the fabric between our two planes." Antoinette began to pull at my hand rhythmically, as if she were swaying back and forth. "Oh no!" she hissed. "Randolph is at his heels. I...don't...know...if...I can open...the portal in time!" her labored voice spat between clenched teeth.

Suddenly, there was a small flash of green from above and then two distinct knocks on the table. I felt Antoinette's grip relax as she slumped away from me and toppled from her chair.

"My God!" Dickerson exclaimed.

"The lights, man," I commanded to the commodore as I leapt from my seat.

Peters immediately lit a match and lighted a candle in the chandelier. Suddenly, he dashed toward the gas sconces in the wall. By the time the jets were lit, I was already on the floor beside the stricken lass administering medical attention.

"Is she all right, doctor?" the shaken inspector asked.

I continued my examination without answering. A moment later, I proclaimed, "Yes. She has merely fainted. Peters, what is in that room beyond?"

"It is her bed chamber," he replied, his voice wavering with fretfulness.

"Let us carry her in there."

As Dickerson and the commodore lifted the girl, I caught a glimpse of Lady Winfield. At first, it had not registered that she had not also jumped to the aid of her beloved medium and now I saw the reason. The Lady sat staring at an object in the center of the table. There, light reflecting off its hundreds of facets, sat the Saggarn Diamond.

Chapter 6

I determined that there was nothing ailing Antoinette that a few hours rest would not cure. Whether her fainting spell was real or contrived, her blood pressure had certainly dropped and she thus required a period of respite.

I had at first suspected that the small flash and collapse of Antoinette had been intentional distractions meant to divert our attention while Peters tossed the jewel upon the table. But Lady Winfield stated that the commodore had not released his grip until after the peculiar knocks upon the surface, and I can personally attest that he did not let go of my hand prior to the raps. Further, he lit the match almost instantly upon Antoinette's spell and the noblewoman stated that she spied the stone immediately. Clearly, Peters could not have deposited the diamond.

The commodore stated with conviction that the flash was the rip in the dimensional wall through which Oliver tossed the diamond. Yet, if the jewel landing on the table had caused the sound, why were there two knocks? My thoughts were so engrossed that, when my carriage arrived back at Baker Street, the driver had to call out to get me to leave the cab. It was with great relief that I looked up to see our rooms still lit.

As I entered, Holmes was sitting by the fire quietly reading. He did not look up until after I had deposited my hat and coat upon the hook. Only then did he close the text upon his forefinger. "So Watson, did our illustrious psychic say she will be able to conjure up the diamond?"

"Not only did she say she could, she did."

"Really?" I sensed the concern in my companion's voice, but it appeared that he had mastered the mercurial passion he had earlier displayed. "Did she have it waiting upon your arrival?"

"No, she asked Dickerson and me to participate in a séance. Lady Winfield was already there. During the ritual, the stone appeared."

Holmes leapt from the chair, carelessly tossing the book aside. He paced the room for a moment hands clasped behind his back. "It is of some comfort that they returned the jewel. I had hoped they would turn it over to you and Dickerson as soon as you arrived."

"Why does it matter, Holmes?"

"If they had given you the diamond immediately, rather than stage the séance, it would have indicated that they have acquired cold feet. Such nervousness would have made it unlikely that they would attempt another caper."

"So you believe that there will be still another theft?" I asked in astonishment.

He was silent for a moment. "What's that, Watson? Oh, well, was it a theft? It is hard to call it such since the object was returned," he smirked. "Yes, I am afraid there will be another incident. Their willingness to perform the pageantry of the séance in order to produce the diamond demonstrates that they are emboldened. I dare say, they are rather enjoying themselves."

He returned to his chair and motioned for me to take the opposite seat. "Tell me what occurred at this séance. Do not leave out any detail."

I related the events with as much precision as possible. Holmes listened attentively and, although it was his habit to interrupt for clarification or elaboration, he waited until I had finished before posing any questions.

He stood and began to circle the room. "You say you are certain that Peters could not have tossed the jewel onto the table?"

"I am quite positive about that point, Holmes."

"Did you query Dickerson to determine if Antoinette may have done it?"

"I did, in a sly manner. I did not want him to suspect I doubted the medium's powers, so I framed my questions around her fainting spell, cloaking my query as a medical one."

"Splendid, Watson! You should not tip your hand yet. We may still need you on the inside, so to speak."

"Alas, Holmes, the inspector swears that the knocks came prior to her fainting, and he did not release her hand even as she fell from the chair."

"That leaves only Dickerson and Lady Winfield."

"I assure you, Holmes, that they are both devout spiritualists. Neither would be party to such fraud."

"No, of course not, Watson," he smiled. "I know our dear inspector and, although somewhat dim, he is neither a liar nor a cheat. Although I am sure Lady Winfield is not duplicitous either, you would judge her shock at the stone's appearance as genuine?"

"Indeed, Holmes. Not only was her amazement evident, so was her rapture afterwards. I have rarely seen such an emotional display from nobility. It was quite evident that she was sincere in her bliss at retrieving her gem as well as the affirmation of the medium's spiritualist powers."

"What of this flash, Watson? Was it bright enough to illuminate any of the surroundings?"

"No, it was quite small, perhaps the size of a shilling. Also, having sat in absolute darkness for more than several minutes, my eyes were accustomed to the gloom and could not adjust quickly enough to the surprise effect, even if it had cast more light."

"I suspected as much. How about the odor? Did you detect a hint of phosphorus?"

"Actually, Holmes, I did. I asked the commodore about the peculiar smell and he explained it away as brimstone leaking through the tear in the dimensional fabric. Dickerson and Lady Winfield were quick to affirm Peters, even though they agree that no one has ever breached the barrier before. I have little respect for their opinions on the matter, and was surprised by the vigor with which they spoke about what had occurred."

Holmes laughed heartily. "Now, do you understand why I was reluctant to get involved? They want to believe, Watson. Whether consciously or not, they grasp at any and all evidence and portray it as fact."

"Yes, Holmes, I see your point. Even the inspector, a man trained to be suspicious, accepts these doings without question," I replied pensively.

"Dickerson is hardly the consummate analyst, Watson," he laughed, "but your point is correct. Can you imagine the degree of devotion felt among others more susceptible to this kind of nonsense?"

I immediately thought about those emotionally vulnerable souls who had lost loved ones. There can be no doubt that their fervor was unbounded once they believed they had been put in touch with their dearly departed. However, it was in defense of these same suffering survivors that I had embarked on this mission in the first place. Holmes was correct that it would be nearly impossible to turn these people away from their new religion, but I still felt passionate about waging the battle, even if it was an uphill one. The medium's success was increasing her fold, making our task more difficult as each day passed. However, there was some solace in the fact that, thus far, we had taken the correct tack in meeting the challenge. Rather that barging ahead as I had originally proposed, our surreptitious and clandestine machinations had a greater chance of success.

"So, Holmes, where do we go from here?" I asked.

"That, my dear Watson, is an excellent question." He returned to his seat and stared into the fire.

"You said that you uncovered how the diamond was taken. Now that I've described the séance, have you determined how it was returned?" I asked, taking the seat across from him.

"No, Watson," he replied without looking away from the hearth. "I lack data. But that is immaterial. The real question is, what good would it do if I did? Could we convince others that they are frauds or would we be marginalized as sour non-believers?"

"Holmes, I agree that this spiritualist craze has snowballed. But most Londoners are rational and skeptical of such chicanery."

"Yes, Watson, but for how long? I fear we are in a race and are falling farther behind."

Holmes sat pensively, his eyes closed. "Watson, you have already given me a complete rendition of this séance room, but pray tell, can you describe where it is located in the house itself?"

"It is upstairs Holmes, on the second floor."

"Yes, you stated as much before, but where is it in relation to the rest of the floor plan? What rooms are next to it, above it, and below it?"

I pondered for a moment. "No doors exist before the séance room. There is one beyond. It is the entrance to the bed chamber that adjoins the séance room. I was in that room administering aid to the medium after the commodore and Dickerson had carried her to her bed. It contains two windows which face the front of the house, a large wardrobe closet and a dresser with a mirror affixed. The room is essentially unremarkable." I endeavored to construct a mental schematic of the house before continuing. "Below the séance chamber...is a room I have never seen. To the right of the entryway is the parlor, but to the left, closed double doors blocked off the room. As far as above the room, from the outside of the house a small window is visible, centered between the pitches of the roof. So I would guess that there is a garret or low attic in that area."

I stared at my friend, trying to ascertain if my description had provided any insight, but his appearance remained unchanged. He sat eyes closed, apparently lost in thought.

The following day, I dressed, prepared to make several professional visits, including one to check on the health of the stricken clairvoyant. Mrs. Hudson had already brought in breakfast, but the meal sat untouched; Holmes was busy at work at the writing desk across the room.

"Have you not eaten, Holmes?" I asked, sitting myself down at the table. The occupied man was so lost in his enterprise that he did not even reply. I was too familiar with my friend's habits to take offense and set about my morning repast.

I was patient in my meal, hoping Holmes would interrupt with some breakthrough. I consulted the paper, which as expected, trumpeted the recovery of the precious gem. Lady Winfield, eager to extol the abilities of her muse and vindicate her devotion to her new religion, ran directly to the papers with the story of her heirloom's miraculous restoration. Dickerson must have been at her heels, because he too was quoted in the article. The writer had handled the topic with an even hand, but I detected less skepticism than in previous stories about Miss Antoinette. I cringed when I found that it was also mentioned that I had been in attendance at the séance. I am sure that had it not been for the necessary haste of producing the story for the morning addition, a reporter would have attempted to interview me regarding the evening's events.

I shuddered to think how I would respond if approached by the columnists. If I spoke my mind and denounced Antoinette as a fraud, it would dissolve my chances of working the problem from the inside. If I praised her, I would be disingenuous and I could not stomach having my alleged views etched in print proclaiming to all that I was in fact a supporter of this nonsense. I supposed that my best defense would be to deny any interview, couching my reluctance upon privacy issues. If a member of the press accosted me, I would do my best to deflect him in such a manner.

Holmes had remained attentive to his writing throughout my meal and I eventually reached a point where I could delay my departure no longer. As I collected my bag and made for the door, Holmes finally broke his silence.

"Watson, will you be going past the post office?"

"I can if you require it."

"Excellent. Would you be so kind as to post this letter?"

"Certainly." I took the envelope and paused for a moment but Holmes gave no further instructions. Instead, he pulled a volume from the shelf and engrossed himself in some other pursuit, resuming his disregard for my presence.

As I left the house, I could not help but read the address upon the missive. It was addressed to a Mr. Ehrich Weiss in New York City. I wondered if this correspondence related to the Antoinette case or if it pertained to one of Holmes's numerous other endeavors.

In hopes that the letter related to the medium problem, I made straight for the post office and was sure to hand deliver the correspondence to the clerk. Although Holmes had not directed that the letter be given any special care, I thought it prudent to remove one link from the chain and entrust it directly to a postal official rather than chance any mishap or carelessness that might befall depositing it into the slot in the iron mail chest.

"May I see Miss Antoinette?" I asked the servant who guardedly opened the door no more than a half meter.

"She is not taking any visitors at present," came the curt reply.

"I am the doctor who attended to her yesterday," I said, raising my bag into view to substantiate my identity. "I told Commodore Peters that I would return today to check her progress."

I glanced over the attendant's shoulder and, at the end of the hall, I saw a man disappear into the kitchen. It was but a fleeting glimpse but I believed him to be the swarthy little private detective Holmes had identified as Hiram Silver.

"Wait here a moment, please." The somber man closed the door, leaving me standing upon the doorstep.

A full five minutes passed before the door opened again. "Dr. Watson!" Peters boomed, shaking my hand briskly. "I am sorry about our man, but we have had to install some layers of security. We have been deluged by people seeking Miss Antoinette's counsel. You would be surprised at some of the rabble who have been showing up at the door!" After he made this revelation, he stood silent, looking askance at me, presumably forgetting the reason for my visit.

"Umm, yes, commodore, I said that I would return today to check on the health of Miss Antoinette," I reminded.

"Of course! Of course! Well, there is no need for that, doctor, she recovered fully and is, in fact, out shopping at this very moment. Your attention yesterday was quite sufficient, I suppose!" he chuckled. "Thank you for coming by, though. I must bid you good day, I do not want to stand here with the door agape. I have several interviews with potential clients today, and it would not do for some fanatic to see me from the street and use the opportunity to buttonhole me. Thank you once more, doctor. I am sure we will be seeing you again." With that, he ushered me from the entranceway and closed the door.

I had learned a few observational habits from Holmes and I noted two interesting facts from the commodore. First, it was peculiar that his mood was so upbeat, given the infirmity that had befallen Antoinette the day before. Was he dismissive of her condition due to the glee brought on by an increased number of potential clients? Also, the reference to the "rabble" marked that he was not interested in using the medium's talents to benevolently aid those most in need. Had this been the case, he would have been screening callers based on the severity of their problem. Discriminating solely upon on social class seemed a telling sign.

I had to attend to several errands unrelated to the theme of this narrative, but before I returned to Baker Street, I paid a visit to Scotland Yard. I had hoped Dickerson would spill some more information to someone he perceived as a fellow devotee of Spiritualism, but the good inspector was not present. I next stopped at Lestrade's office, wondering if the traditional methods employed by that more rational constable had born any fruit he would be willing to share. But alas, here too, I found a vacant cubicle.

Two days later, I was on the street when a boy hawking papers caught my attention with an "extra" edition. I quickly tossed him a coin and began to scan the front page. The news was sensational, to put it mildly. A valuable painting by our own English master William Turner had vanished.

Chapter 7

I quickly absorbed the essentials of the story. The Turner was part of a private collection owned by Sir Bradley Timbor. Sir Bradley is the possessor of more than two dozen renowned paintings, his preference being for the English and Dutch masters. Some of the works decorate his country estate in Surrey, but, during this time of the year, he spends most of his days in London and keeps a small gallery in his city home. It was from this locale that the artwork disappeared. The gallery was in a refurbished basement room, where the subterranean setting maintained the climate at a constant temperature, more suitable to the valuable artwork. The room had no windows, and only one door, to which Sir Bradley possessed the only key.

The disappearance was noted on Friday afternoon. On Thursday, a man from Edison Electric Lighting arrived at the door, explaining that he had to check the wiring and fixtures in the residence. Sir Bradley's home had been one of the few private residences equipped with electric incandescent lighting from England's first commercial supplier at the Holborn Viaduct plant. The danger inherent from the direct current that surged from the station's dynamos made such inspections welcome.

Sir Bradley was at home and spoke with the electrician before retiring to his study and allowing his butler to accompany the man in his inspection. The pair traced a path from room to room where the technician probed and prodded at the fixtures and examined any exposed wiring. When they reached the gallery, the butler summoned Sir Bradley, who unlocked the door and remained while the man made his inspection. After this was accomplished, they all removed themselves and the master of the house relocked the door and deposited the only key back in his pocket. Sir Bradley then returned to his study.

At this juncture, the butler said that the electrician seemed disgruntled and examined his tool belt, stating that he had left his screwdriver in another room. He bent down to tie his boot, and asked the butler if he might go and retrieve it for him. The servant agreed, leaving the electrician in the hallway. He returned with the tool approximately five minutes later to find the man waiting patiently where he had left him. They finished their rounds and the man thanked the butler. Sir Bradley was passing through the foyer and stopped to ask the man whether his house was in safe order. The electrician stated that all was well, and took his leave.

Friday, Sir Bradley entered the gallery to find that the Turner had been removed from the frame. He contacted the police, who sought to verify the identity of the electrician. However, officials from Edison Electric stated that they had not sent an employee to the home. The inspectors thus immediately targeted the man as the primary suspect, but neither they, nor Sir Bradley, could offer any explanation as to how the theft was accomplished. Even if the pseudo-electrician could have gained entry to the locked room in the small amount of time the butler was away, he did not carry a bag, only a tool belt, and the picture was far too large to conceal on his person. Scotland Yard had been put upon the case, though a lead inspector had yet to be assigned.

"Holmes! Holmes, have you heard?" I exclaimed, bursting into our rooms waving the newspaper. "The..."

"Indeed, Watson. Do join us," Holmes said, motioning toward a vacant chair. "Inspector Lestrade and I were just discussing the matter."

Lestrade, who sat across from my friend, merely nodded as an abrupt greeting. The man had never been a gregarious fellow, but it hardly took Holmes's observational techniques to discern from his body language and expression that the inspector was bothered to an unusual degree.

"Hello, inspector," I said, refusing to allow Lestrade's ill manners to affect my own comportment.

"Oh, good day, doctor," he grumbled, redeeming himself somewhat.

"Lestrade here was telling me all about the art theft," Holmes interjected with a fleeting smirk. "But I can see that you have already had the particulars from the paper, eh, Watson?"

Lestrade abruptly stood and began pacing. "Mr. Holmes, you and I have worked together successfully in the past, and I propose we do so once more. Dickerson and his nonsense cannot be allowed to triumph again!"

Holmes turned to me. "It seems Lady Winfield called upon Sir Bradley and convinced him to let her guru help recover his painting."

"So, Sir Bradley insisted that Dickerson be assigned the case then?" I asked.

"As long has he incorporates the medium in the investigation," Holmes replied.

The disgruntled inspector broke in, "I was on the scent of the Saggarn Diamond, Mr. Holmes. I don't have to tell you about my methods, nor remind you of the successful entries in my casebook. I had the investigation well underway when Dickerson's charlatan pulled the rug from under me! Surely you can see that the whole episode was contrived!"

"Are you suggesting that Inspector Dickerson is involved in criminal acts?" I asked.

"What?" The distracted inspector ceased his pacing. "No, doctor. Dickerson is an honest man. But he is gullible, and a dupe. Those qualities have made him an unwitting accomplice in this business, but perhaps even worse than that, he is gaining credibility and stature in the force. Can you imagine how many villains will slip away if Dickerson is suddenly assigned the most serious cases?"

"Back to the matter at hand, Lestrade. The newspaper did not provide a description of the imposter electrician. Do you have one?" Holmes queried.

"Yes," he pulled a notebook from his breast pocket and read over his notes. "He was a small man approximately five foot six in height. Dark hair concealed under a cap. Dark complexion. Brown eyes, almost black. He also had a smudge of plaster upon his cheek below the left eye. He said he had cut himself while shaving. He also wore round spectacles."

Holmes shot a furtive glance in my direction. My jaw dropped for an instant as I realized that the description fit that of Hiram Silver, the private detective we believed to be the agent of Commodore Peters. Certainly, the spectacles were false and the plaster meant to cover his distinctive scar. I recovered my composure just as Lestrade closed his notebook and returned it to his pocket.

"That should be helpful, should it not?" Holmes asked coyly.

"It would indeed Mr. Holmes if I were put on the case!" He said, slapping the top of the sofa. "So how about it? Shall we forge a partnership?"

Lestrade was an able-bodied officer, but his caliber did not even remotely approach that of Holmes. The suggestion that he could provide a parity of assistance was almost laughable. However, there was a hint of desperation in the man's voice that prevented any compassionate individual from enlightening him to the inequity of his proposed alliance.

Holmes closed his eyes and drummed his finger tips together. "I will look into it, inspector. However, our forming a joint venture is out of the question." Lestrade opened his mouth to either protest or defend his abilities, but Holmes continued before he could emit a sound. "You see, Lestrade," Holmes stood and put a reassuring hand upon his shoulder, "my position as a private consulting detective allows me latitude of operations which you do not possess. If we were to investigate this matter in conjunction, either I would be constrained by the rules that apply to you as a member of the constabulary, or if I acted according to my own standards, your career might be put in jeopardy."

The inspector stepped over to the window and peered out on Baker Street, presumably thinking the matter over. We sat in silences for a half a minute before Lestrade came back over to us.

"All right, Mr. Holmes, I would not want to limit you in your investigation." Although the risk to Lestrade's career likely played a role in his decision to acquiesce, the proud officer clung to Holmes's first point as the reason. "However, such an arrangement does not preclude me from bringing you any information I uncover."

"Certainly not, inspector," Holmes stood to see him to the door. "In fact, you have already helped by providing a description of the faux electrician." Lestrade left our rooms only slightly mollified by Holmes's compliment.

Once my friend closed the door I interjected, "Holmes, you know that I can probably wrangle any pertinent information from Dickerson. There was no need to include Lestrade at all." I smirked, exposing the charity my friend had extended toward the inspector's pride.

"Ha! Quite so, Watson. Lestrade is hardly the master sleuth he purports himself to be, but he is one of the more capable men at the Yard nonetheless, and I saw no reason to knock him down." He smiled back. "I share his concerns though, Watson," Holmes's countenance assumed a more serious demeanor. "Parlor games and party tricks are one thing, but this paranormal police work needs to be quashed. Even though Lestrade is primarily motivated by inner-office jealousy, what he said is true: many wicked rogues will escape justice if too many people buy into the legitimacy of the Dickerson/Antoinette tandem."

"Should I go and pry what I can from Dickerson?" I asked.

"A grand idea," Holmes returned, lighting his pipe. "Also, see if he will give you a tour of the crime scene. It would be of great benefit if you could provide me with a detailed description of the gallery."

"You know, Holmes, I doubt that Dickerson would put up much of a protest if you accompanied me. Surely, it would be better if you could personally view the room and ply the inspector with questions."

He took a long draw on his pipe. "There can be no doubt of that, Watson," he replied without any feigned modesty. "However, we must avoid pushing too hard for an immediate advantage which may lose us the prize in the end. It is akin to a long distance race. If the runner begins at a sprint, he will surely outdistance his opponents early on, but his stamina will collapse and he will not emerge victorious. I fear that, if I were to take an observable hand in the matter, it would cause the medium and her consort to smell impending defeat and abandon the field. To be honest, Watson, I am quite surprised they have allowed you any access at all. Your affiliation with me is known to most literate Britons."

"Yes, but they believe I am converted to Spiritualism," I stated with some degree of pride in my acting abilities.

"Perhaps. It is plausible that your charade has won them over. Or it could be sheer audacity. Watson, I have dismantled the operations of more than a hundred swindlers and have made an adequate study of not only their methods, but their characters as well. You are aware that I not only play the game for gratification, but also to advance the field of detection. In my annals," he pointed the stem of his pipe to the rows of bound volumes on the bookshelves, "I have not only recorded the scientific data pertinent to criminal analysis, but I have also developed profiles for the various illicit professions. For example, a forger is meticulous by nature, patient and studious. A burglar is cagey and suspicious. A swindler is usually arrogant and exudes confidence. These qualities are necessary in winning over his mark. So, although I doubt this duo would be brazen enough to flaunt their wares in my presence, it is likely that they derive some perverse pleasure in doing so at arm's length through my trusty compatriot, Dr. Watson." He tapped out his pipe upon the tray. "Whether they believe you to be a Spiritualist, or merely enjoy making you complicit in

223

their schemes, at present, it is best if you continue to act as my proxy."

I saw no reason to question Holmes's judgment and the confidence he placed in me buoyed my esteem. However, in all of our adventures, this one was unique because of the distance Holmes was forced to keep from the actual case. It was not the first time my friend undertook an investigation without an actual client, but even in those distinctive circumstances, he at least was able to question witnesses, examine evidence, and confront suspects. I marveled at Holmes's self-control. There could be little doubt that he thirsted to be directly engaged. Not only was the genius of his observational skills forced into dormancy, but inactivity drove him to despair under normal circumstances. With a singular case afoot, it must be maddening for him to sit alone at Baker Street while events unfolded. Yet, Holmes's powers were such that he suppressed his natural urge for active involvement as a logical sacrifice to attain the ultimate goal of solving the problem.

"Doctor Watson, so good to see you," Dickerson boomed, shaking my hand briskly. "Is this a social call or are you curious as to how I am tackling this art theft?" the affable inspector said without any smugness attached to the words.

"Inspector, do you think Antoinette will be able to recover the Turner?" I asked, affecting a high degree of concern in my voice.

"Oh, doctor," he laughed carelessly. "Did she not produce the Saggarn Diamond?"

"Yes," I said, swallowing my consternation, "but the culprit in that case was a phantom. This thief was flesh and blood."

"True enough. True enough." He rubbed his chin thoughtfully as if this consideration had not occurred to him. "We shall see. Lady Winfield has insisted it is within Antoinette's powers, and I am off to see her presently, after I make a brief stop at Sir Bradley's."

"Oh, have you not been to the crime scene yet?" I asked innocently.

"Ha!" he laughed and patted me on the shoulder. "Of course, I have! I was on duty when the call came in. But now that I have been named lead inspector, I wanted to stop in and re-examine the gallery. If Miss Antoinette asks me any questions, I want to make sure I have the answers! What are you up to today, doctor? You cannot be on your rounds as you don't have your bag with you."

"You are quite perceptive," I flattered.

He waved away the compliment, "I am sure you are well aware of the necessity of innate deductive skills in an officer of Scotland Yard."

"Well, to tell you the truth, I am unoccupied today."

"Care to join me, then?"

I was overjoyed that the inspector had extended the invitation, I was afraid that I might have to manipulate him into taking me along. "I would be delighted."

"Well, then, Dr. Watson, let me fetch my hat and we are off." He clapped a friendly hand upon my back.

"Hmm," Dickerson emitted as he examined the keyhole of the gallery door through his magnifying lens. "There are numerous marks here, obviously from attempts to insert the key. If the lock was picked, these key scratches are indistinguishable from any caused by the thief's tool."

"May I have a look?"

"Certainly, doctor," Dickerson handed me the glass and turned to speak with the butler.

"May I have the key?"

"Here you are, sir," he replied, turning over the item.

"All done, doctor?" Dickerson asked.

"What? Oh yes. Thank you, inspector," I replied, handing him back his lens.

"I thought Sir Bradley kept the only key," I stated to the butler.

"Indeed, sir. The master had to step out to speak with the insurance adjustors about this unfortunate theft. Since he knew the inspector was en route, he entrusted it to me temporarily."

I digested what the butler had said. "How much was the painting insured for?" I asked.

"I'm sure I don't know, sir."

"A hefty sum, no doubt!" Dickerson chimed in.

Once we had left the butler and stepped into the room, I turned to Dickerson and coyly stated, "Of course I am sure that Sir Bradley is above suspicion, but won't you be looking into the insurance particulars as well as his financial standing?"

"Indeed I will, doctor. But all in good time. I first want to speak with Antoinette. If she can help recover the painting, those other considerations are of only secondary importance."

The room was painted a pale blue and illuminated by overhead electric lighting. Nearly a dozen paintings hung on the walls. Two oils straddled the doorway. Three paintings occupied the wall opposite the door. The wall to the left of the door also held three pieces of art. Three frames hung on the wall to the right, but the second from the door had been removed from the wall and lay upon the floor. The wooden stretch bars had been pulled from the frame and the staples which had held the canvas to the bars littered the floor.

Dickerson made a beeline for the frame and spreader bars and began scrutinizing these with his lens. I was briefly distracted by the beauty of the artwork that was left in the gallery. There were two watercolors, but the rest were oils. Three were portraits, two were still-lifes, and the remainder were landscapes. As the paper had indicated, all of the works were by either English or Dutch artists. The paintings were of various sizes, from a small thirty centimeter oval portrait to a three meter rectangular landscape. It appeared that Sir Bradley had arranged them by size, the smallest just to the right of the door. As one moved in a counter-clockwise manner, the frames grew larger. The frame of the missing Turner was about two meters wide and slightly under that in height. It hung between a slightly smaller portrait of a British admiral by Lemuel Francis Abbot and a still-life by van Aelst, which was somewhat larger than the frame of the stolen painting.

I pulled myself away from appreciating the aesthetics of the art to examining the features of the room. It was clear that there was no other possible egress from the gallery save the only door. I walked heavily upon the floor trying to assess if there were any loose floorboards. However, the wooden floor had apparently been laid directly atop the concrete sub-floor of the basement, so even if a plank were loose (which none were), there could be no recess or passageway underneath. The ceiling and walls were of heavy plaster and thus likewise impenetrable.

"Doctor, come here." Dickerson called. "See here," he picked up a wooden square from the floor. "The canvas was stapled to this," he tapped the spreader bars with his lens. "If you look at these staples," he said, retrieving several from the floor, "the sharp ends are slanted, which indicates that the culprit did not pull each out individually, but rather used pliers, or a similar tool to grab the overlapping edge of canvas and pull it away from the frame, thus causing this angling of these pins."

"Yes," I peered through his glass. "Yes, I see. I suppose that haste would require such an action."

"Indeed. The butler was returning. And I remind you, doctor, that this so-called electrician had a tool belt equipped with pliers." Dickerson made this statement as if it were a revelation of some kind. After another few minutes of scrutinizing the room, the inspector jotted notes onto his pad.

"All right, doctor. I suppose there is nothing left to see here," he stated abruptly. "Let us catch a cab over and discuss the matter with Antoinette," he said, cavalierly shoving his folding notebook into an inside pocket. Apparently, his faith in the medium was so great that he saw no reason to make further examination of the crime scene.

"Dr. Watson and Inspector Dickerson! A pleasant surprise indeed!" Commodore Peters announced, following the doorman to the foyer where we had been left waiting.

"A pleasure returned!" Dickerson replied, shaking the man's hand with vigor. For some reason, the inspector leaned close to the man's ear before adding, "Can she help with the missing Turner?"

"Come in and sit down," he replied in a normal tone, ushering us into the parlor.

After we were seated, Dickerson looked around inquisitively but the commodore headed off his impending question. "She is resting. She had four vigorous sessions last evening. It is hard to keep up nowadays, inspector!"

"But the Turner?" Dickerson queried, the prospect of failure and subsequent blow to his stature caused his voice to waver.

"Indeed," the commodore accepted a cup of tea from a servant. "Tea, gentlemen?" he asked. I accepted a cup, but the nervous inspector declined, impatient for the girl's departure.

After the servant had left, Peters continued. "Yes, the painting…" he took a sip. "This theft is tricky, inspector."

"Can she identify the thief? Can she help recover the painting?"

"She cannot identify the thief."

Dickerson groaned audibly.

"However, it is possible that she may be able to recover the artwork."

"Splendid! Splendid, indeed!" Dickerson spat out.

"Excuse me, commodore," I interjected. "How is that possible? I understand how Miss Antoinette could bring the Saggarn Stone back because it had been taken into the spirit realm," I endeavored as best I could to sound sincere, "but how can she acquire the Turner when it was stolen by a common thief?"

Chapter 8

"So the illustrious swami says she can get the Turner back," Holmes stated with a snort, before taking a gulp of his coffee.

"Yes. The commodore says that since the Saggarn Diamond had been transported from this world to the next and back again, it proves that items can be teleported in such a manner. He stated that Oliver may be able to locate the stolen painting and then Antoinette may be able to open a rift between the two dimensions again, allowing Oliver to pull it through to the spirit world. Then she can open another portal and Oliver can drop it through to this plane, but at the site of Miss Antoinette."

"How wonderful, Watson! Think what this will mean! Once, I lost my keys and could not find them anywhere. If it happens again, I can merely go to a medium and have her teleport them back home." He rubbed his hands together and chuckled mirthfully. "Do go on, Watson. Tell me of your recent adventure."

I related all that had transpired at Sir Bradley's home. Holmes listened intently as I described the layout of the gallery and Dickerson's commentary on the staples.

"From left to right, beginning at the door, the paintings were a depiction of a naval battle by Edward Bird, done in oil, followed by another oil, a portrait by Ferdinand Bol..."

"Watson, kindly spare me the artistic fop. What of the frames?"

"The frames?"

"Yes, describe the frames in the room." I should have known better than to focus on the visual aesthetics of the paintings themselves, given Holmes's distaste for the romantic. He again focused his attention on my recitation, as I described the size and style of the frames that adorned the walls as well as that which had held the missing Turner.

"Holmes, there is something else. When I examined the lock with Dickerson's lens, I observed that there were indeed numerous scratches, obviously from attempts to insert the key over the years just as he had surmised. However, there was one that was both thinner and brighter than the rest."

"Watson, you are coming along nicely. What do you deduct from these observations?"

"Well, the brightness obviously indicates that the scratch is new. The difference in width may mean that a tool other than the key was hastily inserted into the keyhole, scratching the faceplate before it found the opening."

"Splendid. There can be no doubt that Silver opened the door. I had wondered if he had somehow gained access to the house on a prior occasion and made a mold of the lock and had a key made or if he had merely used a lock pick set."

"So you do think the thief was Silver."

"Of course." He took another sip from his cup.

"But how did he get the painting out of the house?"

Holmes smiled. "That, Watson, is another matter." He left his coffee upon the table and strode across the room to his violin case and removed his instrument. He sat languidly in an overstuffed chair and began to tune the strings. "When will she attempt her séance?" he asked offhandedly.

"Tomorrow night or the next, I think."

"Will you be allowed to attend?" he asked between plucks.

"I believe so; Dickerson seems to regard me as a kindred spirit, so to speak." I chuckled at the unintended pun.

"Capital, Watson. You will have a front row seat for the final performance of Miss Antoinette," he said without looking up from his Stradivarius.

"So, you are going to expose her!" I ejected, slapping the table in satisfaction.

"Expose is bit of an overstatement, Watson."

"What do you mean? What are you going to do?" I asked excitedly.

He laughed. "Go to your séance, and leave me to my music, Watson. Within a few days, I should have the last pieces of the puzzle in place. Then, we can make our move." With that, he ended our conversation by stroking out the sonorous, though melancholy notes of a Paganini piece.

"So, you want to be present when she recovers the painting?" laughed Dickerson. "I think I can manage it, doctor. You should begin to chronicle these events, you know! We are witnessing a revolution in law enforcement. Yes, some of the newspapers are extolling Antoinette's exploits and although most are responsible enough journalists not to argue with the facts of her achievements, some still are critical, a few even outright hostile."

I silently scoffed at Dickerson's exaggeration. In fact, the only paper actually devoting praise to "Antoinette's exploits" was William Thomas Stead's *Borderland*. This hardly offered a surprise since it was completely an instrument to promote the publisher's devotion to Spiritualism. While the *Times*, *Globe*, *Pall Mall*, and *Telegraph* all confined their accounts to the most professional of standards, Stead's paper operated as a full blown advocate for all things psychic, gushing with tales of London's premier medium. Perhaps Stead would have disputed my account in these pages had he the clairvoyance not to sail aboard the *Titanic*.

"Think what your endorsement would do for Spiritualism!" He became almost giddy as the thought fermented in his mind.

"Well, I am not sure if..."

He broke in without missing a beat. "There can be no arguing against the abilities of your friend Mr. Holmes, but in all candor, you must admit that your writings have greatly advanced his reputation and furthered awareness of his methods."

"You may have a point." I pretended to agree, banking on Holmes's revelation that the game would soon be up and I would not actually be put on the spot.

"Indeed I have, doctor!" he chortled. "Now, I will be speaking with the commodore this afternoon, and if you call back here just before dinnertime, I will give you the news about whether you may attend the séance."

I returned as instructed, and caught the inspector as he was about to leave for the evening.

"Ah, doctor, I was just heading home. You will be happy to hear that you may join us in the recovery of the painting." Dickerson's overconfident attitude was a tad bothersome.

"Splendid." I shook his hand. "When is Miss Antoinette going to make the attempt?" I could not help but demote the recovery effort from certainty to trial.

"Tomorrow evening, seven o'clock," he replied, oblivious of my jibe.

"Shall I meet you at the commodore's then?"

"No, doctor. Miss Antoinette says that, in order to pull this off, she will have to utilize the energy residue left in the gallery by the painting."

"Pardon?"

"Oh, I'm sorry, doctor," he laughed and clapped an affectionate hand upon my shoulder. "You see, since the Turner resided in the gallery for some time, it left an energy imprint there. Miss Antoinette will use that imprint as a magnet to pull the picture back through the dimensional rift." Dickerson recited this explanation with such certitude that it made it difficult to imagine the reality that his guru had just fed him this poppycock an hour before.

"So then, the séance will be conducted in the gallery?" I asked trying to decipher the message.

"Right. If you will be so kind, please meet me at Sir Bradley's shortly before seven."

This was an intriguing development. There were any number of ways the charlatans could enact their parlor tricks in their own abode, but now they were becoming even bolder by conducting the séance in a setting where shenanigans were less possible. In all probability, this was an attempt to discredit the naysayers who had cast doubt upon the veracity of the rituals held within the confines of Antoinette's household.

The door was answered by a butler who, despite the fact that I was undoubtedly expected, followed stiff protocol by asking for my card. In fairness, it is probable that he had received some abuse from his employer over being duped into retrieving the tool and thus allowing the thief to steal the painting. There are many among the upper crust who find their servants easy targets for venting their frustrations, whether deserved or not.

"This way, sir." He led me into a formal parlor.

"Dr. Watson, so good to see you," Commodore Peters declared. He crossed the room to shake my hand, leaning heavily upon a cane as he limped over.

"Are you alright, commodore?" I asked.

"Oh, a bit of the rheumatism, is all," he smiled.

"Is your knee swollen? Would you like me to take a look?"

"No, doctor. Thank you anyway. It comes and goes. Today is just one of the bad spells. I'll be fine."

Dickerson also came over to greet me, followed by a distinguished, mustachioed gentleman I presumed to be the owner of the house.

"Dr. Watson, this is Sir Bradley Timbor. Sir Bradley, Dr. Watson."

"Pleasure. I've read some of your stories, doctor." There was no hint of emotion in his voice, so it was impossible to determine if this was a compliment or a mere statement of fact. "Not sure about all this," he waved his hand toward Miss Antoinette, seated stoically upon the sofa in all her mysterious beauty. "But Lady Winfield was persistent...and Dickerson here is also convinced. It's worth a go, eh?" he grunted.

"Shall we proceed, then?" Peters asked.

Sir Bradley led the way to the gallery. He unlocked the door to reveal that a rectangular table and chairs had been installed in the room, somewhat off-center, about two meters from the wall where the Turner had hung. The bell box that had been used in previous séances was conspicuously absent, but a small candelabrum sat in the middle of the table.

Antoinette had yet to speak, and made an immediate bee-line toward the seat closest the wall where the missing painting had resided. The commodore slid her chair in behind her.

"We have placed the table close to this wall, because Miss Antoinette will need to siphon the residual energy imprint left where the painting once hung. Sir Bradley, if you will be so kind as to take the seat at this end of the table. Dr. Watson, the chair just to the left of the lady, if you will. That's right, inspector, you sit across from Miss Antoinette and Dr. Watson. I must sit here at the head of the table, to the right of Miss Antoinette."

"What I am trying to do tonight is quite difficult and I will need to be in contact with the commodore to attune and channel all of my energies," her luminous voice broke in. I am sure this satisfied the devoted Dickerson; to me it seemed a curious excuse to explicate why Antoinette's right hand would be "controlled" by the commodore.

Peters lit the candles and then limped over to the electric wall-switch and cut out the incandescent bulb. He closed the door and suddenly the only illumination was from the five candles on the table. All was quiet as the gentle thump of the commodore's cane marked his return across the room. Peters seated himself, and placed his cane across his lap.

The medium closed her eyes.

"Control," she breathed in a voice just above a whisper.

We clasped hands, and crossed legs. Apparently Sir Bradley had been briefed before my arrival because he showed no confusion when the command came.

"Each please blow out your candle," she ordered. A moment later, the wicks were extinguished. The image of the flames lasted a moment upon my retina, and then all was pitch-black.

We sat in silence for a few minutes, the drama building. Finally the medium spoke, "Oliver? Oliver?" Dead silence once more.

"He is here." She gasped. "Oliver, when we communed earlier, you said you would try to locate the painting. Have you been able to do so?" Silence. Then, "Yes. He has found it," she said. Like the previous séance, Oliver did not assume control of her voice, but rather allowed her to echo his responses.

"Where is it?" Sir Bradley broke in; hoping either to have the opportunity to accost the thief or to retrieve the piece himself should the séance fail.

"Shh!" interjected the commodore. "Do not interrupt, you may cause her to lose contact," he whispered from the side of his mouth.

I could nearly hear the chastised nobleman's teeth grating at the rebuke.

Long stillness followed. Had Sir Bradley ruined the operation? Despite my skepticism, my breath was baited in anticipation.

At last she hissed, "He has it."

There was no flash. There was no visible effect whatsoever. The only indication at all was a gentle knock that sounded as if it came from the wall behind Antoinette. Fifteen seconds later, her hand released mine and she fell upon the table, saying "It is done."

Commodore Peters quickly sprang from his chair and lit the candles. I slid from my seat to attend to the exhausted woman as Peters limped his way to the switch and flooded the gallery with light.

"I am all right, doctor," she panted, as I offered her my handkerchief.

Despite his status as a gentleman, Sir Bradley did not concern himself with the ailing woman. "Where is it? It isn't here!" he scolded, banging the empty table.

"Sir Bradley," Peters said as he moved to comfort his partner.

"What?"

Peters leaned over Miss Antoinette, but at the same time pointed his cane to a spot on the floor behind the table.

"My God!" Sir Bradley exclaimed, knocking over his chair to cross the room.

There, upon the floor, lay the raw canvas of the missing Turner.

Chapter 9

"No bells or rapping this time, Watson?" Holmes asked mischievously as he poured us each a brandy.

"None save the one subtle knock, just as I described."

"I suppose Dickerson was overjoyed?" He handed me a glass.

"To say the least. He is reveling in the corroboration of his religion and the fringe benefit it is bringing to his career." I replied in disgust.

"Holmes, I began this game alone and, although you dissuaded me, I pressed on hoping to expose these charlatans. Instead, my continued involvement in their enterprises has only lent credence to their abilities! I was willing to pretend for the sake of the ultimate goal, but enough is enough."

"Are you so sure Antoinette does not have otherworldly powers? How did she materialize the painting, then?"

"Come now, Holmes," I began to weary of his playfulness. "Will you make good on your promise to expose them?"

"I never declared that I would expose them, Watson."

"What? You agreed with Lestrade that this nonsense is growing dangerous, and you told me that the Turner business would be her last escapade."

"And so it shall," he laughed. "Don't worry Watson; her career has come to an end. Give me another day or so and we will run the endgame."

"Care to join me, Watson?" Holmes asked, depositing an envelope in his coat pocket and a small bag in another.

"Certainly, Holmes. I am unoccupied at present. Where are you headed?"

"To Chelsea, to see your medium."

Three days had passed since the night of the gallery séance and I had done my utmost to remain patient. This was a difficult proposition since Holmes had not spoken of the subject again until this moment. Often over those grueling days I wanted to confront him over the issue, but I laboriously maintained my decorum, allowing Holmes to follow whatever machinations necessary without any interference or interruption.

"Indeed! Let me get my coat!"

"And Watson, kindly bring along your revolver," he added nonchalantly as he himself retrieved one of his favorite weapons, a stiff walking stick.

"What is the plan, Holmes?"

"I have something in mind to be sure, Watson, but I may have to shift tactics mid-stream, so it would be senseless to say too much now. Suffice it to say, follow my lead and hopefully, together we will put an end to this claptrap before the hour is up."

As our hansom sped through London, I pondered the decision to arm ourselves. Although I had longed to confront Antoinette and Commodore Peters, my experience with them gave no indication of violence. My companion often withheld knowledge when working a case, and I wondered what privileged information he held that prompted such a precaution. I was about to broach the subject when we arrived at the residence.

Holmes paid the driver and gave a soft whistle. Immediately, two street urchins he often referred to as "the Baker Street Irregulars" materialized from an alley.

"They are still inside then?" he asked.

"Yes, sir, Mr. Holmes. No one has come to the house yet today, no visitors that is, except that fella with the scar left for a bit, but he came back about ten minutes ago."

"Very good. Here you are, lads." He tossed them each a coin.

"Should we wait, Mr. Holmes, in case you need help?" the other boy asked.

"No, that won't be necessary, Malcolm."

"Watson, you call at the door. Since you are well-known to the house, I doubt the staff would refuse you entry even if you are with an unfamiliar friend."

I rang the bell and, as Holmes predicted, the butler showed us in to the foyer. A moment later, Commodore Peters emerged from the parlor, a wide grin on his face as he saw me, but his expression quickly morphed to one of uncertainty when he spied my friend.

"Dr. Watson—and this must be Mr. Holmes?" he returned to his gregarious nature, but curiously heightened the tone of his voice as he said the name of my companion. I noticed Holmes's head tilt slightly as if he were straining to hear something in the next room.

"A pleasure to finally meet you, commodore," Holmes said, extending his hand.

"The pleasure is all mine," he returned, with a degree of contrived sincerity.

Holmes thought for a second then said, "Perhaps, sir, perhaps. I am after all here to do you a favor."

"A favor? Now I am intrigued." He replied cordially. "Please, let us step into the parlor," he said, leading the way.

Miss Antoinette was seated upon the settee, reading a magazine. Her clothes were less formal than in our past encounters and her body language and manner far less mysterious than before. She showed no sign of surprise at our entry, evidently alerted by the commodore's loud announcement of Holmes's presence. She peered over her magazine, a hint of suspicion in her eyes. Holmes made the audacious gesture of closing the doors after we entered the room.

"Miss Antoinette, Dr. Watson has come again, this time with the famed Mr. Sherlock Holmes," Peters announced. The medium merely nodded a greeting.

"Charmed," Holmes replied to her gesture.

"So, Mr. Holmes, what is this favor you wish to do for us?" Peters left us standing and seated himself on the edge of the large desk.

Before answering, Holmes took hold of a wooden ladder-backed chair and jammed it under the door knob of the closet. A moment later, the knob turned frantically and a banging could be heard from inside. Holmes took my arm and gently pulled me from in front of the door. He took up a position near the closet, but to the side of the door frame.

"Hiram," he said, tapping the door with his cane. "Hiram, stop that commotion." The ruckus ceased. "Do you still carry that .32? I suppose you do. Well, do not fire at the lock or through the door. We are not in range and if you shoot, I shall have to allow Dr. Watson to fire back in self-defense. I assure you that, although only part of the army's medical staff, his marksmanship is sufficient to hit a man confined in a closet not two feet away."

Silence followed. "That's the idea, Hiram. You shall be released presently if you behave yourself," Holmes continued.

Both Antoinette and the commodore wore fright stricken expressions. It was a full ten seconds before Peters stammered out, "Mr. Holmes, what is the meaning of this?"

"Mr. Peters," he laughed, "I should ask you the same question. "Watson and I come here to do you a good turn and you surreptitiously secret away an armed man in the closet? Hardly good manners, sir." Holmes chided.

The commodore regained some of his composure, his features assuming a sour countenance. "What is this favor, you are going to do us?" he asked dourly, without any of the verve and sociable demeanor he had possessed only moments before.

"Why, Mr. Peters, I am giving you the opportunity to pack up shop and leave England without exposing you as frauds."

Just then the butler knocked on the door. "Sir? Is everything alright? I heard some banging."

"Yes, Benton, everything is fine." Peters put on a rosy voice.

"Oh, Benton, could you bring us some tea?" Holmes yelled through the door.

240

"Very good, sir," the butler replied when the commodore had not countermanded the order.

"Bring it to a good boil, would you? I do like my tea especially hot," Holmes called after him.

"Frauds, Mr. Holmes? Surely you jest. A tenth of the population of this city are lining up for séances with Miss Antoinette. You would have a difficult time convincing them that we are not legitimate practitioners of Spiritualism."

"I am afraid that those séances would not be very convincing if I published this in the paper." He pulled the envelope from his pocket and removed the correspondence within. He thumbed through the pages before laying a hand-drawn diagram upon the desk.

The commodore looked at it without lifting it from the surface. I crept from my position near the closet and examined the document. On it was etched a drawing of a chandelier, much like the one in the séance room above. However, the fixture was cross sectioned to reveal that the cord that held the chandelier to the ceiling was hollow and contained a strong wire affixed to the heavy cylindrical base at the bottom of the candelabra. Pulled tight, the base remained part of the fixture. If slack were let out quickly, the weighty piece would drop and bang on the table.

"So that is how the knocking was done!" I gasped.

"And here is your bell box, Watson." Holmes pointed to the second drawing upon the sheet. You see, the bottom of the box is comprised of two boards, but they are not flush. They are separated by a few centimeters. This gap is aligned with a similar one between the floorboards, and a stiff wire can be inserted up through the floor and into the box. It makes contact with the poles and the bell rings."

Neither Peters nor Antoinette commented. Each merely fixed a hard stare at my friend.

"Watson, I have already explained how they used our closeted friend over there to unearth information about their clients. He also operated these devices. All together, the scheme made for a nice little business."

"But how did you get these drawings?" I asked, pointing to the diagrams.

"You may remember, Watson, that I was waiting for a letter from the States. This is what I was waiting on. This diagram is but part of a longer tome discussing all of the various tricks these two might employ. Do you recognize the name, Peters?" Holmes turned the envelope so that the return address showed.

"Ehrich Weiss?" I read, as the commodore and Antoinette shot each other a frightened look.

A knock sounded on the door. "Come in," the commodore somberly announced.

We all remained silent as the butler rested the tray upon a side table and quickly exited, casting furtive glances as he withdrew.

"But what of the crimes? The Saggarn Stone? The Turner theft?" I asked.

"Should you reveal the secrets or should I?" Holmes asked Peters.

The commodore returned a cold stare. "You have speculated on many other things, I would be interested to hear what you have concocted in these matters as well."

"Concocted! Ha! Stoic to the end, eh, Peters? Well, I must claim credit for deducing how you handled both the diamond and painting capers, but it was not I, but Mr. Weiss who enlightened me to the séance trickery.

"Well, if you insist," Holmes continued. "Watson, let us first take the stolen painting. You and I have already determined that Hiram Silver gained access to Sir Bradley's household under the electrician guise and that he purposely left the tool so as to rid himself of the butler for a few minutes. In that time, he picked the lock and entered the gallery. The real conundrum is: how did he make off with the portrait? It was far too large to conceal on his person. The second mystery is: how did our psychic here bring it back? The answer to the first problem is found in the second. How do you figure it, Watson?"

242

"The painting never left the gallery!" I burst forth.

"Excellent, Watson. Certainly you remember that, after you gave me a full account of the séance, I specifically asked you to describe the frames that hung on the walls. Silver had quickly taken the picture from the frame and removed it from the stretching boards. He then pulled the bottom of the frame of the larger painting next to where the Turner had been away from the wall and placed the canvass behind the other painting." Holmes picked up the diagram from the desk and walked over to a framed piece of artwork that hung on the parlor wall. He gently grasped the lower frame and pulled it toward him a few inches. He then slid the diagram up behind the picture and let go the frame. As the picture fell back against the wall, it held the diagram behind it, completely obscured from view.

"You now see why the séance had to be conducted in the gallery, eh, Watson? You stated that, at the ritual, the table had been moved close to the wall 'so that the medium could channel energy' or some such hogwash, and for the same reason, she had to stay in contact with Mr. Peters here. In actuality, the reasons were so that she and Peters could release their grip and he could use his cane—it was a convenient little leg injury wasn't it Watson?—to lift the bottom of the frame and allow the canvas to drop to the floor." Holmes leaned over with his own walking stick and nudged the picture away from the wall, the diagram fluttering to the ground.

"It is all so simple!" I ejected in amazement.

"It is the simplicity that makes it a success, Watson. When people believe a theft has occurred, they view the event through that lens. A theft would require the painting to be taken from the scene, and that is the assumption that everyone, including Scotland Yard, followed. Since the Saggarn Diamond had been returned, I suspected the Turner would also. Therefore I was open to the probability that the picture had not actually been stolen at all."

Through all this, the medium and her consort kept their silence. When Holmes finished, Peters said, "Possible, but hardly definitive Mr. Holmes. I am not sure how many would believe you."

"Mr. Peters, you have not studied my methods enough. What is possible is not of importance here. It is what is *impossible*. When the impossible is eliminated, for instance that the imposter electrician removed the painting from the gallery, what remains however improbable is the truth.

"Well, perhaps I will do a better job convincing you with the Saggarn Diamond. Watson, what do you make of this?" Holmes reached into his pocket and produced a large gemstone.

"Why, it…it is the Saggarn Stone. How did you get it?" I asked in amazement.

"At a confectionary. You see…Oops! Dear me!" he blurted as he dropped the stone into the cup of tea on the table. He dipped his spoon in and swirled it about for several seconds. "I can't seem to get it, Watson. Kindly fish it out, will you?"

I took the saucer from him and scooped the spoon into the tea. I tried again. Despite all of my efforts, I could not find the diamond, despite its large size.

"Holmes, it is gone!" I gasped.

"Not gone, Watson. Dissolved. Taste the tea."

I sipped from the cup and found the tea appallingly sweet.

"Watson, I paid a visit to a reputable candy shop and had the confectioner make the 'diamond' for me. It is a rather simple procedure, actually. Add a large quantity of sugar to boiled water to form a super saturated solution. Suspend a string into the solution and as the sugar solidifies, it forms a crystal upon the end of the string. All that was required was to grind and polish the candy until it took on the size and cut of the Saggarn Diamond. Had you examined it with scrutiny, you would have no doubt seen the difference. However, if one is expecting the Saggarn Stone, that is precisely what one sees."

"Another example of seeing versus observing, Holmes?"

"Indeed, Watson. The night of Lady Winfield's party, she showed off the gem, as was her custom. The newspaper account stated that several of the guests, including our commodore here, handled the stone. Undoubtedly he positioned himself to be the last guest to touch it. He used a common slight of hand technique to switch the real gem with a facsimile of rock candy. Of course, no one, including Lady Winfield, considered taking a jeweler's loupe to the diamond before she put it back in the safe. Do you recall that a servant, or should I say Hiram Silver posing as a servant, spilled piping hot tea upon the gem's case after it had been closed? Remember, the silver case had slits in it. That 'accident' was actually an intentional act to dissolve the 'diamond.' Mind you, the tea was extraordinarily hot, and the blend of sugar used was a very solvable one in order to effect the trick."

"Let me guess. During the séance to recover the stone, it was placed here," I picked up the diagram from the floor and pointed to a small recess in the upper side of the cylinder of the chandelier. When the cylinder was lowered and banged on the table, the real stone tumbled off onto the table."

"Bravo, Watson! That is exactly what the writer of that diagram concluded as well. And the green flash, merely a small firework shot from the thin space between the ceiling and the chandelier cord."

"My dear, will you leave us please," Peters said to the woman upon the settee. She still had not uttered a word. Perhaps it was because she continued to comport an air of mystery, or it could have been that she was the total subordinate to Peters. Either way, she silently left the room without a glance at either Holmes or me as she passed.

"Mr. Holmes, even if you believe everything you just said, you admit that no crime has been committed since neither item was stolen. Therefore, I do not see how any of this concerns a criminal investigator like yourself."

"I did not say that no crime has occurred, Peters. Yet, I also know your true motives. Your goal was not to attain wealth through theft, but to create publicity that would bring you more wealthy marks for séances. Fraud is a crime. You have been bilking people out of their money. That *is* a crime."

Peters thought for a moment. "You must know that if you come forward with all you have said here today, you will do yourself as much harm as you do us. Spiritualists believe in the lady's powers and if you cast aspersions upon her, many will consider you merely a skeptic who is trying to repudiate their religion. It will do no good for your reputation."

"I am not so sure of that. If I were to make a statement you may still receive calls from the fervent and fanatical, but I am confident that most people would respect my opinions. No, I think your concern for my reputation is a bit overplayed. My reputation is established as a righter of wrongs and champion of justice. I have not weighed in publicly on this, or any other issue that is not related directly to crime. No, I think if I air my opinions it will do you considerably more harm that it does me."

The commodore walked across the room and peered out of the window. "So back to your 'favor.' If Antoinette and I leave, you will not make your assertions public?"

"That is what I propose. Keep what proceeds you have garnered in your little game and quietly leave England. Consider your enterprise a success and retire the personas of Commodore Peters and Miss Antoinette."

Peters turned from the window and crossed the room. Without a word, he extended his hand to Holmes. The pact was consummated.

I followed Holmes to the door, and as we were passing the closet, he gave it a rap with his cane. "And take Mr. Silver with you when you go," he added.

"I must say, Holmes as impressed as I am with your abilities in solving the problem, I am disappointed that you let them escape justice and without remunerating those they swindled," I said after we were back in Baker Street.

"Watson, I really had no choice. Much of my game was a bluff. What I told you earlier was true, the devout cannot be swayed. If I tried to have those already under Antoinette's influence take money back from her, it would cause chaos. They would never believe she was a swindler, nor would I likely be able to coerce her to admit it to them. The best I could do would be to cause major doubt and bad publicity, which might hopefully hurt their future earnings and damage their standing."

"Holmes, who is this Ehrich Weiss?"

"He is an American of Hungarian descent whom I met a few years ago. He is a magician by trade and I recalled that he and his wife used to perform medium feats in their stage act. He confided that, when he did spiritualist bits, people truly believed that he was putting them in communication with their deceased loved ones. The guilt of duping these people was too much for him, so he abandoned that part of his act. He finds the practice so reprehensible he is even considering exposing mediums as part of his act. Recently, he has been concentrating on illusions and is beginning to make a splash as an escape artist. He is planning to bring his act to London soon and asked if I might make an introduction to Inspector Melville. You remember him—that business with capturing the anarchist at Victoria Station?"

"Melville...yes. Why would he want an introduction to him?"

"A Chicago policeman has been acting as his agent in the States and suggested Melville represent him here. It helps with the authenticity of his show to have a policeman involved."

"Ehrich Weiss? That name does not ring a bell," I muttered, curious that I had not heard of such a performer.

"Watson, perhaps you know him by his stage name—Houdini."

The medium and her consort vanished, and Dickerson was beside himself with anguish. He vowed to apply his investigative talents to finding what became of them, but needless to say, he never uncovered their whereabouts. Lestrade, however was jubilant and despite the coy manner in which Holmes replied to his queries, insisted he knew Holmes was responsible for the flight of Miss Antoinette.

Curiously though, a good number of years later, a medium fitting Antoinette's description and an elderly companion conspicuously similar to the commodore began holding séances in a prominent American city. Before long, they were discredited by Harry Houdini who, by that time, was not only world-famous, but on a crusade to expose false mediums.

A Victorian Era Séance

Afterword

In the Holmes stories I have written, I have always tried to replicate Doyle's style as much as possible. I am a tremendous fan of the original canon; the one disappointment I have is that there are only sixty stories. It is for this reason that I have written my pastiches to fit into the world and stories created by Doyle. I would like to think that Doyle could have himself written either *The Circle of Blood,* or *The Highland Intrigue.* However, I must admit that *The Medium Problem* is not a story Doyle would have crafted, despite the mimicry of his style.

After the death of his son in World War I, Doyle himself became a devout follower of Spiritualism. His second wife claimed to be a medium, and he participated in séances, automatic writing, and was even duped into endorsing fraudulent photos of fairies. Harry Houdini befriended Doyle in the early 1920s and the two had many conversations and exchanged much correspondence over the supernatural. Houdini said that he did not necessarily disbelieve, but he could not stomach fraudulent mediums exploiting the grief of others. Eventually, the friendship of the two men ended over the issue as Houdini began a crusade to expose fraudulent mediums.

I have always found it fascinating that Houdini, an illusionist who built a career mesmerizing audiences with his trickery, would become a champion of debunking the paranormal, while Doyle, the creator of the world's greatest logician and uber-analyst, would become the most noted spokesperson for Spiritualism.

Suffice it to say, Doyle would never have had Holmes discrediting mediums. However, if the character of Holmes, as created by Doyle, is considered in an organic sense, as a living breathing personage, I am confident that he would act in the manner described in *The Medium Problem.*

BLACK COAT PRESS

M. Allain & P. Souvestre. *The Daughter of Fantômas*
Anicet-Bourgeois. *Rocambole*
Guy d'Armen. *Doc Ardan: The City of Gold and Lepers*
Aloysius Bertrand. *Gaspard de la Nuit*
A. Bisson & G. Livet. *Nick Carter vs. Fantômas*
Félix Bodin. *The Novel of the Future*
Lucien Dabril. *Rocambole*
V. Darlay & H. de Gorsse. *Lupin vs. Holmes: The Stage Play*
C.I. Defontenay. *Star (Psi Cassiopeia)*
Charles Derennes: *The People of the Pole*
Alexandre Dumas. *The Return of Lord Ruthven*
J.-C. Dunyach. *The Night Orchid: Conan Doyle in Toulouse*
Paul Féval: *Anne of the Isles*
Paul Féval. *The Blackcoats: The Companions of the Treasure*
Paul Féval. *The Blackcoats: The Invisible Weapon*
Paul Féval. *The Blackcoats: The Parisian Jungle*
Paul Féval. *The Blackcoats: 'Salem Street*
Paul Féval. *Captain Phantom*
Paul Féval. *Gentlemen of the Night*
Paul Féval. *John Devil*
Paul Féval. *Knightshade*
Paul Féval. *Revenants*
Paul Féval. *Vampire City*
Paul Féval. *The Vampire Countess*
Paul Féval. *The Wandering Jew's Daughter*
Paul Féval, *fils. Felifax, the Tiger-Man*
Arnould Galopin. *Doctor Omega*
V. Hugo, Foucher & Meurice. *The Hunchback of Notre-Dame*
O. Joncquel & Theo Varlet. *The Martian Epic*
Jean de La Hire. *The Nyctalope on Mars*
Jean de La Hire. *The Nyctalope vs. Lucifer*
Maurice Leblanc. *Lupin vs. Holmes: The Hollow Needle*
Maurice Leblanc. *Lupin vs. Holmes: The Blonde Phantom*
Gustave Le Rouge. *The Vampires of Mars*